THE
REVOLUTION

Book 2 in THE RENASCENCE SERIES

James W Powell

ISBN-13: 978-0-9987366-4-8

ISBN-10: 0-9987366-4-3

Wandering Stream

Literary and Publishing

Cover art by Jeremy Zohn

Calligraphy by Ann Powell

Contact us at jimpowell@wandering stream.org

Dedicated to Ann

My wife and best friend, I'm so glad I chose
you. You saw Papa's design and believed.
That made all the difference.

INTRODUCTION

We have yet to see, hear or understand all the revelation and potential experience of The Kingdom of God on earth. Whatever is yet untransformed in our humanity creates a glass ceiling over the operation of Father God's spiritual realities intended for this life. First Corinthians chapter two verse nine says, *"Things never discovered or heard of before, things beyond our ability to imagine—these are the many things God has in store for all his lovers."*

Conceptually, The Renasance Series seeks to break that glass ceiling with fictive representation. Our Heavenly Father is enormously creative, and glimpses in Ezekiel and Revelation reveal his handywork and vast power. Romans one tells us he openly flaunts his creative results for everyone to clearly see. Jesus says in John chapter fourteen, *"I tell you this timeless truth: The person who follows me in faith, believing in me, will do the same mighty miracles I do—even greater miracles than these because I go to the Father! For I will do whatever you ask me to do when you ask me in my name. And that is how the Son will show what the Father is really like and bring glory to him. Ask me anything in my name, and I will do it for you!"* With those words, we've been empowered with his creativity, too!

Ironically, hammering on a glass ceiling looks dangerous if all that one sees is the glass ceiling. It would appear that the traditional walls and coverings that make us feel safe are about to vanish in a ruinous pile. The truth is, a larger picture is about to be revealed in a revolutionary cacophony.

In The Renasance Series, extraordinary is daily fare;

supernatural is normal. God is in every life working things out for their good and giving the characters Kingdom purpose. And he simply loves showing up to be an active player in special events and the training processes of life.

The Ruction was the disruptive entry of the Kingdom on Roee and Dodee's comfortable world. The Revolution is the mess created when the world around them is turned upside down with Father God's purposes.

Welcome to The Revolution; the second book in the series. It isn't necessary to read The Ruction (book one) first to pull on the full depth of the story; some backstory is included. But after you have enjoyed The Revolution, The Ruction will be waiting for you.

TABLE OF CONTENTS

PROLOGUE

Dodee stood at the window with arms crossed, observing the creamy landscape of old snow. Warm days followed with freezing nights iced the surface with crackly sparkles that the radiant sun crafted into a crisp blanket of a million diamonds. Offsetting the chill from the glass, fire in the stone hearth at the cabin's end fed her warmth.

Small movements from her growing baby bump drew a smile and a hum. With both hands she reached through the veil of skin to her hidden daughter and imagined the day when her arms would be cradling the first-fruits of her womb.

"Rachel . . . do you understand what it's like to wait for you? The years have been long for me, you know. But my winter is almost over and you'll bring a dazzling season of beauty and snuggles."

Humming a little, she mused. "You'll love being here, Rachel. Your papa can hardly wait to see your face and make you laugh. You'll enjoy his sense of humor as much as I do. And he likes to play, too." Dodee laughed. "And just think of all the brothers and sisters that will follow you. And all the goats you'll have to talk to and play with." She chuckled then sighed, "How much longer baby girl?"

When Dodee sighed, Roee[a] got up from the trunk he and Shamus were packing for the trip to town. He put his arms around Dodee from behind and caressed her tummy. She leaned into his neck.

"My beautiful little Rachel," he said with a tender chuckle. "To have you with us is the fulfillment of a hope we've had since our wedding day. Oh, we knew you would come . . . we just didn't know it would take so long. But in the pages of Papa God's book, your days were written even from the foundations of the earth. I know your destiny, little lamb. It will be amazing. You'll be the golden lily of this valley and reveal Papa's heart to the nations. There will be signs in the heavens because of you. And before you're even born, you will experience his presence."

Roee knelt and gently turned Dodee. He kissed the baby and snuggled into Dodee.

"And more than anything, we will share times of worship, and enjoy the seasons of life running and playing and tickling and learning. Oh, what a treasure you are."

"Amen and amen," Dodee said. *That's Papa's prophetic voice I hear* she thought. She turned back to the window as Roee got up and held her from the side. "Roee, this snow is like our atonement. It covers all the flaws and failings, and makes everything look perfect and new. Nature gives us so many pictures of Papa God's kindness. And it's his kindness that keeps us turning back to look at him.

"You know, it's been almost a year since we left Grindlay Village. When you left that day to search for a runaway goat and found this valley, were there any clues that we would end up here?"

"None, my beloved," he responded.

"It's been an unimaginable one leap-at-a-time journey by faith, hasn't it? — Then, Papa filled this place with so much of his presence that it even transformed twelve years of the barrenness of my womb into a little girl . . . I can still hear his voice telling me I would be holding her in my arms — even before I was pregnant . . . Just like Sarah. And now look at me Roee, I'm covered in Papa's snow. My hope is beautiful and I no longer feel the years of waiting. It's like they never existed."

She turned her attention back to the white world outside.

"It's so quiet, yet I hear a voice talking . . . Listen Roee. What do you hear?"

Roee quietly responded. "I hear the drip of snow melt running off the roof . . . spring is coming."

"You're such a good outdoorsman, Roee. I know you hear more than that. But really . . . that's what I wanted you to hear, that it's warming up. Tell me again why we have to go to town so early. I have lots of time before I deliver—and I really want to stay here."

"The spring snows pile up deeper than the winter ones. We could get snowed in when it's time for Rachel to show up. We're at three thousand feet, Dodee. The weather is unpredictable and you know how hard we worked to keep the road to town open. We're not prepared to be stuck here if Rachael has a troubled delivery. It's too much to risk."

"Then let's get ready!" she rejoined crisply.

Roee let go and turned her until he could look in her eyes.

"I thought we decided we'd find a midwife you were comfortable with and spend the time with Maria and Rigo[b] in Little Faith before the baby comes."

"They're great friends, Roee," exhaled Dodee. "But you don't know what it's like to be pregnant. It's hard to be consistent. Yesterday, I wanted to be with Maria because her and Rigo have been waiting for a child as long as we have. But today I just . . . I don't want to go. It would be a great day to sit around and talk about daffodils. And it would be a great month to watch them grow. I don't want to talk about going to town.

"Shamus, why don't goats eat daffodils? They eat everything else."

Shamus blinked like he was just yanked from a distant planet and looked at Dodee. Roee went back to his preparations for the trip.

"What? . . . Sorry, I wasn't paying attention."

Dodee gave him a *where were you?* kind of look and smiled. "You think I'm crazy to want to stay. So does Roee."

"I wasn't thinking that at all! I was thinking about the love I see in you guys. And I was wondering if that kind of love was going to find me someday. Until a minute ago, marriage was a foreign language that I could never hope to learn. So, I was praying . . .

"For a wife?" Dodee guessed.

"Yeah, well, kind of . . . You know—when the time's right . . . When God thinks I'm ready."

"When you've learned the language?" Dodee probed.

"Yeah. Roee keeps saying I'm a finished work in Christ." Shamus chuckled. "But, I think I would rather not to be so scary . . . perhaps more finished."

"Just don't learn anything from the goats," said Roee wagging his head playfully. "When it comes to romance, they're a long, long way from finished."

Dodee rolled her eyes and sighed. "The daffodils, Shamus. Why don't the goats eat the daffodils in that Thousand-Acre Wood out there? I'm sure Eeyore would have eaten them. Why not goats?"

"How should I know? Ask Tanny, our *illustrious* historian. The story about why they're here in the valley has got to be a mystery. I'll bet it's got something to do with some old settlers that dropped them off the Conestoga wagon on their way through. And it's mixed in with why generations of goats have lived in this valley without a shepherd until you guys showed up. And why Wonder Valley is now full of angels and supernatural happenings." Shamus raised his arms in a *why?* expression. "Who can explain Wonder Valley?"

"Well, I might just ask him about that," responded Dodee, "when I go out to say goodbye."

Roee groaned in reaction.

"What?" responded Dodee.

"Tanny's stories are measured in hours, not minutes. He loves telling stories, and everybody loves hearing them. We need to be thinking about leaving."

"You're exaggerating," rejoined Dodee.

"Yeah," interrupted Shamus. "I hope to get those stories written down while you guys are gone. There's people that would love to hear them. Especially people like me, Finnegan and Megan. They're stories of promise and hope. Finny and Megan may be animals, but their rescue is like what happens to people that get stuck in a bad life and need an exit."

"That's so true, Shamus," responded Roee.

"So, what else are you going to do while we're gone?" asked Dodee.

Shamus smiled slyly and said, "Have kids."

Dodee guffawed at the irony. Roee chuckled knowingly and shook his head. It was a well timed one-liner with double meanings.

Shamus continued, "When I get back from taking you guys to town, I'll be haying the flock until this snow is gone. But there's a muckle of goat babies waiting for their mothers to bring them into the light."

"Muckle?" queried Roee with a side glance.

"Yeah," responded Shamus sheepishly. "I'm teaching Tanny new words for his stories. It comes from my Celtic roots. 'Many a little makes a mickle and many a mickle makes a muckle.' What do you think?"

"Enlightening," responded Roee with a raised eyebrow.

"But you know, Shamus," Dodee said with concern, "goats don't need human help in the wild. They're used to being on their own. In fact, they're more relaxed when humans aren't around."

"But Tanny, Willie and Sully have talked about losing as much as half the newborns to bad weather. I want to prevent that."

"All you need to do is pray, Shamus," Roee responded. "All those tragic losses happened before Papa filled this valley with his Spirit. There's so much life here that we get harvests from our garden even in the winter. We get more nutrition out of squash plants than other people get from ten bottles of supplements. Papa can handle baby goats. Trust him. He will show you what you need to do and when you need to do it."

His last words caught Dodee's attention and set aside its implication.

"My guess," he continued, "is you'll be worn out playing with those little fuzzers."

Shamus sighed peacefully. "Thanks Roee, I needed to hear that. Like you've said a dozen times, 'If you focus on the problem, the problem is what you'll have.' I think I got captured by the past again."

Dodee smiled. She loved their spiritual father and son banter. Shamus had been a brothel owner that went by the name of James. He trafficked human misery. Roee stumbled onto him during a supernatural experience in Lawless where Shamus was living. Later, some men of the town talked about building a cabin for Roee and Dodee. Shamus came to help. Jesus showed up

. . . and Shamus didn't go back.

"Well," she said, "while you two load up, I'm going to say goodbye to the gang and ask Tanny a question or two about daffodils."

The guys went back to the task at hand. She sat down to put on a snow boot, bent into another chair for help and got a reaction from Rachel. "Sorry Rachel." Pulling on the second boot she asked, "Any sign of our mountain lion, Nara? You know, it seems like it's been too quiet around here. And he wouldn't leave us alone just because it's cold."

Roee answered, "All I've seen is fox tracks. After his last humiliation, he'll need a new scheme. He's more likely hunting the warmer elevations."

"He's an opportunist," declared Shamus gruffly. "I used to be one and know a hundred guys like him. He'll be after us again when he sees he can come out on top." Shamus pointed to the wall. "That's why I practice using your rifle and keep it cleaned and loaded."

Dodee appreciated his protective spirit. She smiled, put on her coat then went into the sunshine.

The path in the snow from the cabin to the pasture had been carved by shovel and tamped by hoof and boot. Beyond the immediate area of the cabin, meandering goats created trails without purpose. The entire pasture crisscrossed with assorted tracks leading from the shed where the hay was kept to rustic shelters Roee built the previous spring.

Dodee headed for the hay shed and said under her breath, "You know, if I feed the gang now, it will save Shamus time later and we can get on the road." A couple goats understood her objective and bolted for the shed. It started a stampede of the other goats that caught the movement. Dodee chuckled at their unity. What one does, they all do. It's the way Papa God created them.

One bale of hay feeds everybody adequately. Normal goats consume voraciously until everything is gone. Unlike ordinary goats, this flock had the experience of being taken to heaven. They returned with a special mission and a different nature. They talk like humans and act just a little more civilized than they were. They also possess gifts of healing and miracles.

Maria; not to be confused with the human Maria; nuzzled Dodee's hand to have her ears rubbed. It was because Maria got lost that Dodee and Roee now live in Wonder Valley. Maria and her sister Carrie, belonged to them when they lived in Grindlay Village at the foot of the western slope.

During a violent encounter with Nara, Carrie was killed, Scampy barely escaped and Finnegan was taken captive. Hours later, Dodee prayed for Carrie's resurrection. Carrie shared her experience in heaven and things she learned. As Dodee mused, she recounted what is now different because of Maria and Carrie.

Later, when the flock was taken to the third heaven, Carrie was permitted to stay. Dodee doesn't understand why and still misses her. But it's best to let God be God.

As the hay was disappeared, the flock wandered off. Dodee called Tanny and headed for the daffodils. "Hey Tanny, what do you know about these daffodils?"

As they walked toward the large patch of them at the dogleg of the long pasture, Dodee let Tanny search his memory for the proper story.

"There is a story that has been passed down for a long time. Both my father and grandfather have told me about them. These flowers other names. They're also called narcissus and it is said they have magical powers."

"Like a medicine?" Dodee rejoined.

"I don't know medicine, Mama Shepherd. But I understand that according to the legend, it made people act strangely. Whatever their purpose, they have been growing here for generations. The humans who brought the flowers also brought our ancestors. Some of them escaped before the humans gave up their adventure and left the valley."

Dodee waited for more. None came.

"That's it? That's the shortest story I've ever heard you tell."

"It's not an interesting story," Tanny replied. "Histories are different than stories; there is little to be learned from this one. There are no names of goats that I know. Without faces and names and a good reason to tell the story, it has no life and just isn't fun to tell. It is simply knowledge. A good story must have a good reason to be told, or it's not worth telling."

Dodee looked at Tanny, then looked at the new daffodils. "They're poking their green blades though the snow, as if they're lifting their hands in worship . . . These guys are symbols of tenacity. They keep growing and multiplying and remain rooted year after year. And without anyone taking care of them, they have survived drought, snow, freeze, wind, being trampled and not being eaten.

"Why do you not eat them?" she asked.

Tanny shook his head vigorously, letting his ears flap.

"They will be blooming soon. Taste one of the flowers. They taste awful. The leafy part is even worse."

Dodee stooped down and dug past the leaves and through the snow with her fingers until she could separate a clump of bulbs.

"Are you going to eat that?" Tanny asked.

"No, I'm going to start some near the cabin where I can enjoy looking at them from the window."

Dodee stood over the daffodils and thought about their endurance . . . and goats giving birth . . . and things said by Roee in his off-hand conversation in the cabin. She nodded her head slowly, turned and went back to the cabin.

Shutting the door, she announced, "We're not going. Whatever we need to do to be prepared, we're going to do it. I want my baby right here in this cabin."

Endnotes

a   Do-dee and Ro-ee prounounced with long o

b   Pronunced Ree-go

MOUNTAIN CONFLICT

Nara was in a relaxed crouch searching the tree line below for a preferable meal that wasn't scrawny from winter hibernation. Hidden from guarded prey on a rock outcrop, he was hungry, but not for food. He just wanted something . . . but didn't know what he wanted.

Eagles gliding on nearby thermals pulled his gaze away from below toward white peaks in the distance. This serenity was his domain, and its solitude used to give him pleasure.

He remembered roaming these mountains with a friend. They were stalking a lamb at a lower elevation when it happened. His face flinched as he relived the rifle fire. Instinct triggered flight. He never saw her again; and never got to see the unborn cubs she was carrying. He brooded for a while, but eventually quit thinking about her . . . So why was he thinking about her now?

He remembered the wild goat herd. Originally, they were just an occasional part of his food chain. Yet, after she was gone, his thoughts about them turned more toward harm than hunger. He would rather torment their spirit for pleasure than kill them for food. He grew skilled at deception . . . why?

Megan and Finnegan were vulnerable. Megan was Finnegan's mother. According to the story Finny told him, an unusual blue colored hair became his lot after a difficult birth during a storm. A mysterious visitation by a human caused his survival and color change. And the legend that grew from it put Finnegan under pressure to conform to something he wasn't. Nara feigned a friendship, gave a sympathetic ear and then promised them a better life elsewhere.

Megan's desperation to relieve her son's distress blinded her to his scheme. She listened to Nara without question as he played on her emotions and enticed her away from the flock. He abandoned her in a wilderness where she would be found and exploited. Robbing her of family and freedom, he delighted in the idea that she would never see home again.

Months later, Finnegan experienced Megan's fate in a different way after Nara killed one goat and kidnapped Finnegan. Nara reveled that he successfully evaded being followed and cleverly whisked the herd's golden boy into a life of desperate loneliness.

Inflicting pain creates enemies. Willie was one of them. Willie's show of hostility only encouraged Nara; he found it comical that Willie could do little about it.

Recently, a human joined up with the goats. Through trickery their shepherd managed to find, and then rescue, Megan and Finnegan. While attempting to kill both rescuer and rescued, Nara was stopped by the appearance of an unusual creature with an unpleasant attitude. It irked him to be out-maneuvered through a show of force and a sword. He found later that the goat Nara killed was brought back from death. That was annoying.

More humans were coming to the valley and Nara's efforts to just be himself were constantly thwarted. Yet, there was something in the new mood of the valley that tugged at him. He looked at the landscape around him and reflected on how long it had been since he simply enjoyed the beauty of his home.

Opinions argued against why he was now questioning everything. What was once a peaceful sanctum was now gratingly empty and filled with thoughts he had grown to suspect weren't really his. He growled at them.

Rocks dislodged from behind. With a leap he reacted

and landed in a poised crouch. Watching him from a boulder with a bow strung across his back and the feathered ends of arrows gathered above his shoulder was a hunter. His arms were wrapped around his knees and his ankles crossed. His face looked curiously quiet.

The hunter's eyes searched Nara's face. A voice that had been subtle shadow now shrieked warnings about the hunter. *No,* thought Nara, resisting the thought. *He's looking at me on the inside.* It intrigued him that this man could see into him. All the things he had done and the thoughts he had were on display. His gaze unnerved him. Yet the hunter's eyes didn't have the hate like Willie's did. They held something else.

Then Nara recognized him. He had been with those crazy goats and their shepherd.

"You're the shepherd's friend," Nara said bravely.

"He's more than a friend, Nara, he's my son. He's a beautiful person in every way, and I know you would love him."

Nara squinted then sat down. Louder now, the voice screamed a rant about the uselessness of love. He had not heard this before.

"I can get rid of those guys if you want to be free of them," the hunter said.

It dawned on Nara that the voice wasn't his own thoughts. "This *thing* doesn't like you . . . It wants me to kill you."

"So why don't you?" the hunter challenged calmly.

"It's a waste of time," the demons cried accusingly through Nara. "We've seen what you do with the death we've created. You have magic powers."

"I have the power of life, Nara. I rule over death and demons. In time, everything and everybody will bow before me. I am greater than those who are in you. I'm giving you an invitation to replace them with me."

His words agitated him. "What is going on?" Nara asked. "I want to leave . . . get away from you."

"It's fear, Nara."

"I've never known fear."

"And you've never known peace and love before. If you want love instead of fear — and kindness instead of brutality, those demons you let in will have to leave. And they won't leave until you want them to."

Nara considered what this man was saying. His love was real. Nara had to make a choice; this man and his love or the voices. He scanned the mountainous horizon, searching for a decision. He turned to the hunter and said, "I want them to leave."

The hunter stood. "Leave him," he commanded.

Immediately Nara growled, gagged, then choked up twin balls that appeared to be entirely hair, grotesque lips and malicious eyes. The hairballs writhed, rolled around then squirmed to the edge of the rock . . . and disappeared.

"That's it?" Nara yelled. "That's all they are? They're *nothing!*"

"When you don't know the truth, demons are bigger than their reality and their lies quite convincing. You've used that strategy yourself on the ignorant and unsuspecting. Either with fierce intimidation or the gentleness of a cub, haven't *you* played on confusion, misguided dreams or brooding desperation to destroy the lives of others?"

"Yes . . . I suppose I have," Nara confessed slowly. "I was being duped by my own strategy. That was stupid."

"Those guys have a skilled craft. They have used it for a long time and will undoubtedly find other victims. But they have a fiery end they cannot avoid.

"But *your* days of deceiving and being deceived end today, Nara. And now that they're gone," the hunter smiled, "you need something new."

The hunter touched Nara. He screamed the shrill girl-ish cry normal to mountain lions, then bolted out of control off the rock shelf into the dirt and down into the tree line like a rambunctious kitten. Nara laughed as he scampered up trees and down again, leapt over rocks and sprinted across a clearing. He ran and laughed and played joyfully, then charged headlong back to the hunter, who laughed with him as he approached. Nara bowled the hunter over and they wrestled playfully until Nara was exhausted and panting heavily.

"Wow! . . . I haven't felt like that since I was a cub."

"You're a new creature. The old lion is gone."

"I'm not going to be a mountain lion anymore?"

The hunter laughed. "That would be quite a revolution—but nothing like that. You will always be a lion, but a different *type* of lion from the inside out. You will have a life of love and trust and be with me all the time. You will continue to be a large, strong cat. But now you will be at peace — even with the goats. You will be my friend instead of my enemy, a cougar that will grow to love and represent who I am."

"I don't know much about love," Nara responded.

"I will help you, Nara." The hunter gently stroked Nara's back.

Nara reflected on the implications of being a new creature. "Will I still eat?" Nara asked with eyes wide.

"Yup," the hunter said with a smile. "Most of your natural habits won't change, at least not for a long time."

"That could make for some unhappy goats," Nara chuckled.

The hunter laughed then said, "Ahhhh yes, there are a few exceptions. Those animals which I have special purposes for are not yours to eat. I have written an invisible ancient symbol for life on them. It's called a *chai*, and you won't be able to pronounce it like I just did. But, you will be able to see it from this day forward."

Nara watched the hunter take a stone from the ground and use it to scratch the symbol he spoke of on a boulder.

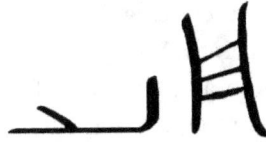

"That is what the symbol looks like and you won't have any problems recognizing it . . . And now for the bad news," the hunter said with a broad smile.

"There will be those who won't want you around. They will question your motives and judge you for what you've done and what you are. Their treatment of you will be used to teach you the ways of love. Through trials you will learn to stand boldly and humbly.

"And from today on, you are no longer a killer. You will be a warrior who gives and fights for life."

Nara was bewildered and wondering what he had gotten himself into. He looked out over the tree tops while considering a thought, then relaxed and sat.

"Not being liked is nothing new," he said with certainty. "I can only think of a few that have. And I guess it's not easy to be friends with someone who's eating your cousins. But if I hang out with your weird goat friends, will I stir up peace or will I stir up war? I don't understand."

"You will stir up both. And it's great that you want to make peace with the goats. There are deep wounds that need healing. It is one of the first things that we will seek to do. But that doesn't mean that our attempts will go well. It will not be easy for everyone to forgive you *and* accept you as a friend. You will have to be patient and prove yourself."

Nara pondered his statement then said, "Yeah, quite a few goats would still be alive if I had not been around . . . It could be awkward. That's a big change."

"Besides that," the hunter said with a chuckle, "the simple and serene life they live would drive you crazy. You couldn't stay long enough to work it all out. You'd be annoyed out of your mind at what little challenge there is for them. What I have in mind is perfectly suited to the way I've created you. And you're the only you that can pull it off perfectly.

"Those weird goats are the second most important group of friends you need. They will be helpful to you in the years ahead. But the first friend you need is me. You and I are going to spend a lot of time together while you learn about me and what will happen when you go where I send you. And spending time with me is not easy. It's not a comfortable life. Many settle for lesser callings.

"But I have done well in choosing you, Nara."

"You *chose* me?" Nara exclaimed. "When?"

"Before the beginnings of creation I knew you would be here at this time and in this place. I have been preparing you for my purposes even while you were wreaking havoc on those I love."

That was weighty. Nara considered what he had done and the dark places he had gone. His mind swam with awe for being wanted when he was so undesirable.

"How could you do that?"

"You were not aware of my nearness to you during those times, and you were certainly ignorant of what I was doing. That is why I can forgive all your wrong choices and your harmful ways . . . everything that is called sin. I will even remove those things from my memory. Your history begins today. The old Nara is dead. Believe in me and accept the new life I offer you."

Nara rose and stood before The Hunter. Stretching out his front paws, he lowered his head in respect.

"I am undeserving and unworthy of your kindness. You hunted me not to take my life, but to give me a new one. You scattered my enemies and extended your hand to me. Although I don't understand, you give me a great honor. I make myself your servant and commit my life to whatever you desire of me."

"Thank you, Nara. I will accept everything you offer freely. But until you become my faithful companion and friend, you will not be ready for the work I have called you to do. You now begin the journey of learning my ways and knowing my heart. I will train you to depend on me and to be in my presence. You will be no servant. You will be my intimate friend and warrior, lovingly attending to matters of my court and my kingdom."

"I can see," Nara said, "why you say it will be hard. I've never depended on anyone but myself, and I have only served myself and those two idiot hairballs. . . I don't know how to do this, but I am willing to learn."

"Think of me as patient and kind, Nara. In time, I will create in you everything you need to be my friend and to represent me well. How long it will take, is up to you."

"Up to me?"

"You have lived a long time serving yourself. Serving me well will grow from deep affection and a commitment to my desires. Letting go of your life to live for me takes trust. Trust that I am good Nara. You will find that I always take care of you."

Nara sat again and considered what he said. "I have another question."

The hunter looked at Nara humorously, knowing the question and answer before Nara asked.

"Do I have to look ridiculously foolish like those goats do when they're singing about you? All that prancing and stuff . . . I don't know if I can do that."

The hunter laughed freely while Nara chuckled stiffly.

"In time, you will gladly give up your refined sophistication for a ridiculously foolish opportunity to express your love for me. No, you have the freedom to be yourself because I am just crazy in love with who you are. And now . . . it is time for us to leave this place and go visit our goat buddies. During our walk, I will teach you some basics."

"Before we go," Nara began, "please tell me your name."

As he ruffled Nara's ears he replied, "It's Yeshua. Some people call me Jesus and others use both. Call me by whatever is in your heart to call me."

Nara stretched out with a leap and appeared to float off the rock ledge. He hit the dirt slope below without breaking stride and loped down the mountain side. At peace with himself and comfortable in his own fur, his only thought was that Jesus would be slow. He put distance between them while enjoying the cool morning air and the updraft brushing his face. Forgetting his hunger, he ignored the scurry of a startled rabbit and continued his easy stride to the lower elevation.

Rounding a giant boulder, he veered left sharply, looking for a familiar break in the forest ahead. As he approached the opening, a man's face suddenly appeared from behind a tree on the right and the man roared.

Nara screamed then slid through the pine needles and loose

granite to an unsteady stop.

Recognizing Jesus, he yelled "Don't do that!"

Jesus slapped his thigh wildly and hooted, "You should've seen the look on your face! What a picture."

A peeved growl quivered from Nara's throat. He peered at Jesus like an intolerant old man scowls at an obnoxious child over the top of his reading glasses.

"Rule number one," quipped Jesus. "Expect the unexpected."

"How did you get here so fast?" queried Nara talking fast from the adrenaline rush. "You couldn't possibly have outrun me."

"That is true, Nara. But I can be anywhere at any time. I'm not subject to human limitations. I can do anything I need to do, supernaturally. And so will you."

"What is supernatural?" asked Nara, still wound up about being laughed at. "What does *that* mean?"

"Look around you. What do you see?"

"I see everything that's here." Nara said dryly, resisting a sarcastic response.

"Great answer," responded Jesus. "What you see in *everything* is all that is natural — But watch this."

Jesus stood over Nara's back and behind his neck. He covered Nara's eyes with his hands. Then he removed them with a flourish. Nara yelled, "Don't do that!"

Standing before him was the large human-like creature that had intervened between him and Roee the shepherd, Finnegan, and Megan when they were returning to the goats' valley after the shepherd managed to find the two and win their freedom. This time, the angel was smiling instead of scowling, and his sword was safely in his sash.

Nara stated to the angel, "You're in a much better mood today." Then other figures scattered around the landscape distracted his attention. He looked about and marveled at the variety of what appeared to be men, beasts, and assorted creatures he had never seen before.

"Who are *they*?"

"These beings are not natural to this world," responded Jesus. "So they would be *super*—natural. They exist, but not in the visible world you touch, see, hear, or smell. Expect them to be around whether you see them or not. Expect the unexpected. They are invisible resources and friends. But also know that you have invisible enemies.

"There are other spiritual strengths and weapons that will come from this supernatural world. . . I will explain those as they are given to you."

"Is all your instruction going this scary? I think you're trying to kill me."

"I'm trying to teach you—What's rule number one?"

"Expect the unexpected," replied Nara.

"That's right. And in some way, I am trying to kill your reactions to the unexpected so you can stay calm and respond. So far I have taught you well. You won't forget it."

"Will my natural reflexes survive this training?" queried Nara.

"Maybe," responded Jesus with a chuckle. "You might need those."

Then Jesus stepped in front of him, knelt and took Nara's face in his hands.

"While you're training, you to learn to do and say only what I tell you. That is rule number two.

"In time, you will know and love me well and you will come to possess my heart. When that time comes you will no longer need to hear about rules. My instructions will be in your heart and you will hear my voice keenly even when you can't see me. You will be a full partner with me in all that I do."

As he finished, he stroked Nara behind the ears, then grabbed him around the neck with a bear hug and started to laugh.

Nara growled in the way humans say "Hmmmmmm."

"I'm not sure," said Nara, "what to do with this kind of attention, Jesus. I've never had this touchy, huggy stuff."

Jesus fluffed the top of his head, smiled, and then stood.

"You will come to appreciate it. I know this about you. You said it yourself, you don't know much about love. Nor do you know much about affection. But, love and affection will find a home in you."

IN THE VALLEY

Nara bounded with long and easy strides through the forest, enjoying the stretch and flex of a good run. Directly ahead, a pair of familiar oak trees formed a natural archway to the valley where he had lived another life. He leapt high and triumphant between them, leaving the shaded forest and landing in brilliant sunlight.

His sudden appearance startled some playing squirrels. They screamed and froze in panic; each little leg a coiled spring waiting for release. Nara saw the ancient sign of life on them and offered the most pleasant "Good afternoon" he could muster. The tension snapped, and the squirrels shot for safety in nearby trees. At first annoyed, he considered the moment then chuckled loudly after hearing them yell, "Don't do that!" and "You scared me!" he responded, "I know how you feel . . . My apologies."

They chattered something Nara couldn't understand and then laughed. He attempted to engage them with, "What are your names?" He drew cautious stares and timid silence for his effort.

Jesus walked up laughing, "Their response will improve with time as they learn to trust you." The squirrels scurried down from the trees pointing noses first at Nara and then Jesus while chattering with excitement. The five walked to the southern promontory and looked down at the valley. The outcrop was called Vision Rock by Roee after he received several visions there. It was his favorite space to watch the mornings break and pray in the sunrises.

Most of the goats grazed tranquilly throughout the one third-mile of meadow that was more than a hundred yards wide; a few lay chewing their cud. The log cabin inhabited the west end of the pasturage. Pine and oak groves surrounded the meadow's edges. The cabin was the first sign of modern man's presence shortly after Mama and Papa Shepherd's arrival. An out-building and small modular house had been added since Nara's last visit.

With mountains on the north and south sides of its length and a stream flowing through it, the mile-long by quarter-mile wide valley made a perfect refuge. Sunshine had unrestricted access to the meadow occupying the middle portion of the valley with a dog-leg turn to the south, ending with a shaded pond. The stream flowed in then out of the pond, keeping the drinking hole fresh and cold. A large patch of yellow daffodils spread out at the inside turn of the dog-leg.

Natural springs dotted the region with one that fed the stream flowing through the valley from east to west and brooked down to Grindlay Village at the foot of the western range. To the east lay an ancient lava flow creating an exit to the two towns of Lawless and Little Faith. With all the mysteries of the past and the miracles of the present, the large glen was named Wonder Valley.

"I will stay up here," said Jesus, "while you go down and talk to everybody about all that's in your heart. Tell them about your encounter with me. And tell them how you feel about what you did to them in the past.

"You won't be able to see me, Nara. But your helper, Holy Spirit, will be with you."

"This would be a lot easier," said Nara calmly, "if you were there. They would believe it all if you explained things to them."

"I am aware of that, Nara. Let me help you understand the bigger picture. More will be accomplished in you . . . and in them . . . if I remain unseen. It's true that they would more readily accept approval of you if I were there. But it's of greater importance that they see what's in your heart, and have the freedom to decide what their responses will be. It's equally important that you hear and understand their hearts, and have the freedom to determine what your response will be. That is how you build friendships under difficult circumstances." Jesus chuckled, rubbed his ears and said, "The Love be with you."

Nara went to an adjacent edge and jumped to where a well-worn trail began. His walk through the forest toward the meadow was brisk until he approached the clearing. He stopped and looked around, sighed for courage then walked out of the tree shadows and into the light.

Goats scattered, sounding alarm when he appeared. Several ran for anywhere safe, others for the buildings. Two bucks charged Nara in earnest.

Nara waited without moving. He could easily dodge aggressive goat horns if it came to that. But as the bucks approached, they slowed. And the three faced each other.

"Hello Finnegan," Nara said, and then turned to the other buck. "I remember your face . . ."

"It's Scampy. And I don't care what brings you back here. You're not welcome."

"I understand how you feel, Scampy. . . But my first concern is with Finnegan. My life has changed and I have much to make amends for."

Scampy and Finnegan exchanged glances. "I just expect another scheme, Nara," Scampy responded.

A quick sigh and Nara pressed on. "Finnegan, I had an encounter with The Hunter whose name is Jesus. He found me when I had doubts and questions. He freed me of the things that made me do the cruel things I did to you and your mother. And I am very sorry for the pain I caused you and this flock. I come seeking forgiveness."

"I don't believe you, Nara" Scampy said.

"What you're saying is too good to be true," Finnegan added. "But, there's something about your face . . . it's changed. And your voice is different, too. You sound . . . truly sorry in some way.

"If I hadn't been so selfish, neither my mother nor I would have fallen prey to your scheme. I would have faced my calling. And my mother wouldn't have spent all that time in exile while I presumed her dead. And Carrie would not have died trying to save me from you.

"I have caused pain, too . . . and I've been forgiven for it. Can I withhold forgiveness when I've been given so much?"

Finnegan looked at Scampy, whose face wagged slowly.

He turned back to Nara and said, "If you are really changed, I will forgive you with all my heart. But if you are false toward us again . . . I honestly don't know what to say to that. That's an if that I hope I won't have to face."

"You are kind and generous, Finnegan," Nara said with an involuntary bow of his head that reflected relief. "I don't think I understand how hard this is for you. Perhaps I will in time." Nara paused not knowing what else he could say. But other business beckoned.

"I would like to talk with your mother. And with the others that I have wronged . . . if that can be allowed."

Willie heard about Nara's return as it was told to Roee and Shamus by Rosie, one of the nannies who had been nearby when Nara walked into the pasture.

"I'll get the rifle," responded Shamus, and went inside.

"Papa Shepherd," Willie barked harshly. "This can't be tolerated, no good can come of it!"

"Don't be too quick, Willie. Remember the conversation we had about Nara?"

Willie looked back at Roee and recalled their conversation which followed the night when Nara killed several goats in a crazed blood lust. Willie had Nara cornered and would have killed him. But Roee stopped the fight. "There are better ways to defeat Nara," Papa Shepherd said at the time. Willie relented and let Nara go. But Willie stayed angry until their conversation the following day.

"Why Papa Shepherd? We could have been rid of Nara for good if you let me finish him off. Help me understand why that wasn't a good idea. It goes against everything in my guts."

"Willie, I thought you might be troubled by that. And before I respond, I want you to know what a beautiful heart you have, courageous and selfless. You were ready to give your life for all of us if that was to be the result of your tangle with Nara."

"Willie, we are the victors on this planet. It doesn't look like Super Goat against the lions. It looks like humble Willie who knows who he is and where his power comes from against an enemy who will flee when resisted."

After that, Papa Shepherd said things that made him laugh and change his perspective.

"What kind of person are you?

"I'm a goat. You know that."

"Yup, I am aware of that. But what kind of goat?"

"A long haired, long horned, stinky at times kind of goat," Willie had said with a smile.

"And what is your purpose in life?"

"To eat the good things Papa has created. Rest and enjoy eating it over again in peace when I chew my cud."

"What else?"

"Bringing more goats into this world? That's a lot of fun."

"And all that makes you an ordinary goat, doesn't it?"

"Yeah, I think that's pretty ordinary."

"But you're not ordinary, Willie. What is different about you?"

"What is different about me is that which is different about all of the goats in this valley. Papa God has made us a unique breed that talks with people and has an especially nice shepherd and we can raise other goats from the dead. And when we die, we will be in heaven. He said he has never done that before. So I guess that makes us Super Goats after all, doesn't it?"

Papa Shepherd laughed.

"You got me there. That was brilliant, Willie."

"Yeah, I know. That happens a lot lately. So do we all get special hoof coverings or something? Maybe some nice boots like you wear."

"That's funny," Roee chuckled. "It means you're extraordinary, Willie. It also means you have a message about Papa's goodness that you can share with others."

"Will they become goats?"

"Uhhhhhh, nope. But they become special creations like all y'all are. They will have a shepherd, be with Papa in heaven and be able to heal the sick, raise people from the dead and do a lot of special stuff that Jesus said we can do because he already did it."

"So what does that have to do with Nara?" asked Willie.

"Papa didn't introduce you to heaven so you can get a glimpse of it, then sit here blissfully eating and chewing cud for the rest of your life and killing mountain lions on safari. He took you to heaven so you could see him and see what it's like. Then bring that message back here to share with those who have never experienced it.

"Nara unknowingly hates that culture. It doesn't serve his purposes. In his selfishness, he mistakenly works to stop the good life Papa wants to export from this valley. Outside of this place, there are a thousand others like Nara doing the same thing."

Willie looked down at the grass, then pulled several bites off the top to chew on while considering Roee's words. Minutes passed and he thought he got the point.

"If there are a thousand like Nara spitting their death culture, then my killing Nara would mean I'm just like him. And when I run into someone like him, my response would be a mind of death toward those people instead of a heart of life. Not exactly the love Papa showed us."

"Nope . . . not exactly."

"So what I thought was your concern for Nara, was actually your concern for my heart?"

"That's a large part of it. But there's more."

Willie's eyes grew large as he considered an astonishing thought invading his mind.

"Are you trying to tell me . . . that Nara could become one of us?"

Willie remembered his shock at the possibility that Nara could change. When Shamus stepped out of the cabin with a rifle in hand, he left Papa Shepherd's question unanswered and stated instead, "Let's go see if this lion has changed his fur."

Willie took the lead of the goats and humans, looking back to see that Shamus' rifle was ready for use as they arrived. He was satisfied with what he saw.

Scampy turned to the mob and shouted, "Everything is okay. He comes in peace. Don't shoot!"

"He's not to be trusted," bellowed Willie in response. "Get away from him!" The atmosphere grew tense.

Finnegan stood between Nara and Willie.

"Why are you protecting him, Finny!" shrieked Willie. "Step aside and let Shamus shoot him."

Papa Shepherd responded, "Willie, there won't be any shots fired. We need a better understanding of this situation. I'm not going to back you on this."

Nara moved from behind Finnegan.

"Hello Roee, I came to declare to all who will hear me that I am no longer your enemy. I am now your servant on behalf of The Hunter, the one known as Jesus."

Willie listened impatiently as Nara told the story of his encounter with Jesus. He talked of a sincere desire to be forgiven by everyone he had wronged. Willie stewed about the impact Nara's supposed change would create in the valley from the least of the chipmunk to the biggest of brawly bears. By evening, the forest chatter chain would have the news to every critter.

He watched as others leaned toward a willingness to forgive. Some had lost relatives who would never return. Megan had suffered horribly from Nara's treachery. The emotional cost was considerable to her and to Finnegan. Although reluctant, she forgave, but Finnegan's zeal to do the right thing was apparent. Willie remembered forgiving Finny for the thoughtless stuff he did . . . But — Nara's not family he thought.

Willie was getting agitated. Roee had prepared him for this

possibility, but its reality stood in front of him. Nara had to pay for his crimes against the flock . . . with his life. He wanted justice. But forgiveness was being thrown at him, meaning there would be no punishment. On top of that, the conversation was setting the stage for Nara to be an accepted member in the life of the community. I can't let that happen he argued within.

The pain of losing other goats who were no longer with the flock because of Nara's reign of terror chewed on him. As a leader, he was responsible for their well-being. He felt the weight of their loss; it happened on his watch. He couldn't believe that Nara's heart was so changed that he was no longer a liar and a killer.

The moment came. He was the last one of all who needed to respond.

"He's a deceiver and he'll never change. I can't do this," he bellowed and walked away.

He wandered and paced the eastern end of the valley alone while he wrestled with the heat of his heart. Was forgiveness his only option? He went to Papa Shepherd for help. As he approached the dogleg of the meadow, Willie saw the shepherds' cabin. Nara and Papa Shepherd appeared to be locked in an intense conversation in front of it. He compulsively sprinted to the rescue, presuming trouble.

Papa Shepherd must have heard Willie bearing down on them, because he turned to get between him and Nara.

"Stop Willie!" yelled Papa Shepherd with arms flailing. "This is not what it looks like."

Willie was focused to intervene and ignored the shepherd's words and movements. He corrected to go around him. Nara deftly side-stepped his attack. Out of control, Willie turned and set himself for another assault.

Papa Shepherd grabbed Willie's horns and wrestled him to the ground. Infuriated, Willie shrieked, "Let me go! He killed my family. He can't get away with that."

"Stop fighting me Willie!" Papa Shepherd shouted while Willie jerked and squirmed on his side.

"I won't. Let . . . me . . . go."

"Not till you calm down."

"I understand your pain, Willie." A compassionate voice spoke at his back. Mama Shepherd stroked his fur while Papa Shepherd gripped him tightly.

"All the years," she continued, "of loss to the flock under your watch and the feelings of helplessness to do anything about it have been hurtful. Even the death of your father, Willie, you told me how hard that was for you as a young kid . . . I'm so sorry you had to go through that Willie."

As she stroked Willie's neck, he began to relax. She removed one of Papa Shepherd's hands from Willie's horn and knelt to encircle his neck with her arms. The endearment quieted his rage. She understood there was a hurting heart below the surface creating a storm. And Mama Shepherd supernaturally knew what the turbulence was about. Wave after wave of loss needed resolution.

As his fury subsided, Willie warmed to the shepherdess and Roee's restraint was no longer needed. Mama Shepherd continued to pray quietly in a language Willie did not understand in his mind, but could feel in his spirit.

"How did you know?" Willie asked after a few moments.

"There's no magic in it, Willie," Mama Shepherd responded. "Papa God knows and he revealed it to me."

"I feel like I had a rock taken out of my hoof."

Dodee smiled and stroked him behind the ears. "Yeah, I can picture that," she responded.

Willie slowly stood considering what to do next.

"Even with all that, I'm not sure I can do the right thing. I still don't believe he's different. I don't believe his story. But I'm willing to think about it.

"Sometimes, I wish I were human. I would have all the answers. I'm just a goat, stuck with a goat's heart in this goat body. And I don't always know what to do with what I feel."

"Willie," said Nara, "I think I am beginning to see the harm I have done."

Willie looked at him without expression and said, "Yeah, I believe you think you do."

Without saying more, he turned and walked toward the watering hole, leaving the rest of the flock to sort out their own hearts. Willie felt the weight of confusion. Hope for a better day seemed far away.

While Willie went off to think, Sully, another leader of the goat herd, seized the moment to quietly explain how he saw things. Sully understood Willie's connection with the love of law and justice, while Sully embraced the law of love and freedom. Their values were polar opposites.

"I cannot speak for the feelings of the entire flock, Nara," Sully began. "But I trust Finnegan and Scampy's confidence of your sincerity. Finnegan says you have changed. He knows better than anyone here, what you were like before this. . . I truly hope this change doesn't mean you have simply become smarter and more deadly. We're just goats, so I think we should trust our two shepherds on this.

"What thoughts do you have to help us, Papa Shepherd?"

Roee sighed before speaking.

"Nara and I were having a discussion about why he came here. We can't make up for the loss of life or torment he created. Reconciling that seems impossible to consider. The fact that he came seeking forgiveness puts a burden on us for making this come out right while Nara simply receives the benefit.

"I didn't like that. . . But there's no other way than to whole-heartedly forgive Nara and moving on.

"Dodee, please feel free to share what's on your heart."

"Papa has it all spelled out in his word, Roee. There's nothing hard about this. It just doesn't feel good to do the right thing. But as you know, this isn't about crime and punishment; this is about love, grace, and restoration.

"Maybe Shamus could enlighten us about Nara's perspective. What's it like to come out of the darkness like that?"

Shamus had been quietly observing, but kept the rifle ready. He pulled the bolt action back, walked over to Roee and handed it to him. Then he stood in front of Nara.

"Nara, I stole so much life from other people during my years of insanity. I used people for my own gain, forced them into a life that no human should have to live. Grievously, for a few, death was their only escape. And because of me, they will never know the love I'm experiencing today. In the awful darkness of all that, Jesus found me—just like he found you. He forgave me and gave me a new life of hope, love, and peace. And I'm learning to forgive myself."

Shamus kneeled to look Nara in the eye.

"If I can be forgiven, then so can you."

Roee saw a tear slip from Nara's eye.

"You're right Dodee," said Roee. "Love and restoration is the next step for any of us who want to move forward. . . Nara, I forgive you."

A chorus of voices expressed agreement in varying degrees of enthusiasm.

"In time Nara," said Dodee, "I think our hearts will catch up with our mouths. I hope you understand."

"I am a mountain lion, Dodee. Sentiment has never been part of my world, yet I am touched by this now. I accept your forgiveness as my starting place for whatever restoration plans Jesus has for us. I don't understand yet what my response should be to make your gestures honored. But with all this being done I must leave. I have much to learn. . . . Then, perhaps, I shall return."

"Nara, you will be welcomed here," said Dodee.

"And I agree," added Roee. "Go with our blessing. And return when you will."

"Thank you," said Nara. . . "And with that, I will be off."

He turned and sauntered toward Vision Rock. By the time he hit the trailhead at forest edge, he was bounding sideways like a kitten at play. He was free.

Within minutes, he was at the top of the ledge looking over the valley. Roee glimpsed a man's head standing behind Nara before they turned away from the edge.

Roee faced Dodee and said, "I need to take a walk." Dodee smiled as he headed toward the water hole.

Roee caught up with Willie near the manzanita grove. As Roee got close, Willie stated, "I guess we won't have to be so careful around this grove anymore. So many awful things have happened here. Is it possible they won't happen again?"

"Realistically speaking, Willie," responded the shepherd in a fatherly manner. "Nara isn't the only puma in the world. There may be another one someday."

"Maybe Nara will protect us from that one." Willie said sarcastically.

"Papa is our protector, Willie. You know that."

Willie thought quietly. He was trying to believe what he heard. "Why would Papa make a murderous mountain lion a part of his family? It's a crazy idea."

"For the same reason he would adopt a flock of peaceful, lovable goats, Willie. The most important reason being that he loves and cares for everyone everywhere. That alone is reason enough.

"But it doesn't stop there. His plans to make us his representatives includes teaching us to forgive unconditionally and use his power through love. Who he chooses to use is not our concern. All the motivation you and I need is to love Papa, love ourselves and love the ones he loves."

"I can love other goats, Roee. And I'm getting better with people. But loving a mountain lion? That causes me so much grief my head hurts. I don't know if I can do it."

"I hear you, Willie, and I understand what you're saying. There's a huge gap between justice and mercy. We find judgment and punishment easier ideas to embrace than forgiveness and restoration. We're in constant tension over it."

"I don't know if I understand either one of those ideas, Roee. I'm just a goat."

"You're a goat with a big heart, Willie, a heart that Papa loves. If you ask him to help you, he will."

"You can't help me?" asked Willie.

"I can point you toward him. He's the only one who fixes hearts."

"What Mama Shepherd did fixed me."

"That was Holy Spirit working through Mama Shepherd to

help restore your peace. In the process he healed you of the pain in your heart. What you face now is still a choice only you can make. You either forgive Nara from your heart for what he's done or choose not to and live with the consequences. It's something God is very clear about. Nobody can do that for you."

"The problem is I don't feel like forgiving him."

"You don't have to feel like it, Willie. Be willing to forgive him. Your feelings will catch up with you."

"I think you're forgetting how stubborn old goats can be, Papa Shepherd."

Roee reached over to rub the back of Willie's head.

"Some old goats are stubborn," said Roee with a warm smile. "I'm confident you're not one of them and that you're going to get through this."

There was a comfortable silence between them.

"I'm going to head back now and see how the others are doing."

"Is Nara still here?"

"No, he's gone."

"How can I forgive him if he's not here?"

"Just tell Papa. And you can tell Nara when he returns."

Willie reacted indignantly, "He's coming back?"

Roee looked in Willie's eyes. "Yes Willie. We aren't going through this, then force him to stay away; that's hypocrisy."

"You not only want me to forgive him," Willie responded with displeasure, "you want me to treat him like one of the flock?"

"We need to love everyone that God loves, Willie. And honor them as best we can. That's the nature of unconditional love."

"But he's a killer and a deceiver. I can't . . .

"He was, Willie." Roee interrupted, getting irritated. "He was a killer and deceiver. . . He is no longer what he was. We've already talked about this.

"And goats aren't the only flock Papa has. Goats are a part of a much bigger flock that includes lions."

Willie's face reflected his unsettled emotions. He looked at Papa Shepherd first with anger, then frustration, then perplexity.

"I'm not cut out for this restoration stuff. I'm tired . . . I need a nap."

Roee watched Willie walk away. "He's yours, Papa," Roee prayed. "I know you'll bring him through."

Rachel Arrives

Daffodils were budding before oak leaves completely filled in their trees. Breezes visiting the valley made the air feel cold in the shade and carried the fresh pollen off the pines. Spring had awakened and stretched its stiff arms after winter's beauty sleep. Nature's blossoms sent an invitation to come and regard its marvels. Seeds that had fallen to the earth and died resurrected to take root and live. This season of life offered challenges that only hard work and good preparation would solve and bring a rich harvest.

Spring was when Kings of old went off to war with hope of successfully defending their realms or be conquered. The aggressors sought to enrich and expand power. New covenants were created and old ones put to rest. Change was the theme of spring.

Among creatures great and small, it is also a time for giving birth. Dodee's body sent a message to Rachel that it was occasion for her debut. Not knowing a language didn't keep her spirit from anticipating the love and wealth of life she was moving toward. The voices she heard until now were continuous blessings during her floating baptism. Worship songs awakened her prophetic ears before they were fully developed. Light moved on the other side of a thin veil to prepare her as a seer. She knew the exhilaration of Daddy's voice and her Mama's prayers swam with her.

Before Rachel's journey began, all her years were written on pages in a heavenly book. Those pages created her; formed her and held her and spoke destiny to her spirit. She knew the voice of those pages as well.

Rachel felt pressure against her and heard her Mama's voice squeal, then laugh.

Dodee laughed. The first labor pain was a welcome one; a sign she would be holding Rachel shortly. She was in the pasture, chatting with her friend Maria. Maria the goat was along as well with her twin kids. At two weeks old they sprung about like four-footed pogo sticks, adding entertainment and laughter to their stroll together.

After the first throe of labor subsided, Dodee took Maria's arm and said, "Papa's faithfulness is always certain, Maria. Every promise he makes, he keeps. I know this won't be easy for you, but I'm so pleased you're here with me."

"It may not be so easy," Maria responded with her South American accent, "but I am happy for you. You have also known empty womb. And you will understand me because of it, and because we love each other. . . . Perhaps we should call for the midwife, yes?"

Dodee sighed with joy. "Yes, Maria. I am ready to see my little girl."

Roee and Shamus were in the garden for a daily workout of spring preparation that made way for a supernatural abundance to follow. They planted a variety of squash started from seeds provided by Jesus' own hand last year. Their nutritional value was so unique that there was no need to eat meat, or even crave it. But as it is with having great blessing, it was great work to nurture it and keep it healthy.

The high pitched bah of a baby goat looking for its mama's milk caused Roee to look up from his task. The mama returned her cry and the kid darted across the front of the fence energetically. He followed the kid's antics until he spotted Dodee and Maria walking toward them. Maria waved excitedly as Dodee waddled. He chuckled with the realization that it was time for delivery.

When Dodee insisted on having the baby at home, he prepared accordingly and brought in everything the midwife listed to have on hand. It turned out that his fears of a heavy spring snowfall trapping them without help were unfounded. Dodee was right. If Papa God could cultivate a century of unfarmed daffodils, raise generations of feral goats without human help and change the heart of a mountain lion, he could safely bring a baby to birth. The idea that she had more confidence than he did amused him. *I'm so glad she chose me,* he thought.

"You can do what you want Shamus, but I'm going to have a baby." With those words he laughed and walked to the gate, leaned the hoe against the fence, then trotted toward the women. After a brief chat, he went to the cabin to call the midwife while the ladies walked among the goat mothers to share the good news. Their symphony of advice and laughter played sweetly.

Roee returned with the satellite phone to his ear. He waded through the flock and handed it off to Dodee and then waited while she made her report to the midwife. Shamus arrived to get updated.

"Nikki will be here in a few hours," Dodee announced. "She said to stay normally active unless my water breaks . . . So Maria, let's go get everything laid out and ready for Nikki . . . Guys, there's plenty of time. You can go back to work. I'll let you know if I need anything."

Nikki arrived safely by early afternoon. Rachel arrived without complication by early evening. A blessing of song and prayer followed, then mother and baby rested. Afterward, Roee prepared a simple dinner to celebrate Rachel's birthday. Maria and Nikki cleaned up. Shamus kept the fire going and drank in the privilege of being included as family.

Nikki remained overnight as a precaution and to enjoy the mountain air. After a thorough baby and mother inspection in the morning, she declared all was well. "I wish every delivery was this routine, Dodee. You had an easy time of it. Call me each morning and evening for the next two days so I can monitor how you're doing . . . And with that, I'll be on my way."

Rachel's arrival provoked unexpected reflections.

In Roee and Dodee, Rachel was a hope fulfilled. Twelve years they waited for a child. At the right time and in the right place, their long-standing desire was now a reality. Their joy was richly full as they realized the new season their lives were entering. Until now, their children had been spiritual ones as they discipled those Papa entrusted to their care. They all eventually grew out of constant need for them and leaned on a life plugged into Jesus. Natural children would give them another perspective.

For Maria, Rachel was a test of her love. She was delighted for her friend, Dodee. But her and Rigo had been waiting even longer for a child. From the ache of her heart she offered a sacrifice of praise and thanksgiving. "Jesus, I refuse to give up hope and be sad. I choose to thank you for and believe for that which is still unseen. I choose faith because you are good and truly love us and will not withhold anything good from us. Even now, I believe your glorious presence in this valley works amazing wonders and will for us also. It has for Dodee and Roee. So, it certainly can for Rigo and me. I know you haven't forgotten us and that everything is made beautiful in its time. Thank you for hearing my heart, Jesus."

Maria had committed to staying with Dodee until she had her baby and was strong enough to be left alone. Rigo would return for her soon and she foresaw an opportunity to have pleasure with him in the rich presence of God's Spirit that filled this valley. Peace and joy rose up within and replaced all the sadness of deferred hope that was trying to overtake her. Grateful tears flowed down her cheeks.

As she sat and gazed through the living room window of the house that was built for other purposes of restoration and recovery, she had the awareness that she represented a prophetic release of new life. The conception of her child in this house would be a significant statement of Papa God's purposes for many. "We are just a small part of a much bigger plan than we can imagine," she said to herself.

Shamus was leaning on a shovel in the garden. He had been turning dirt over to blend in goat manure when he had a thought that stopped him. Papa was going to restore his family. He was trying to figure out the implications of it; marriage, children, grandchildren, legacy; ideas that were far off. But he knew it included extended family that was still alive. Father? Mother? Uncles? Aunts? Cousins? How extended does it go? He vaguely remembered even having anyone besides his father and mother. "Why is that important?" he asked aloud. "I have a brand new mom and dad right here. I don't understand."

He thought of Mary and her response to the angel. "Be it unto me according to your word."

"Yes Lord, I agree with you. Not just for my sake, but theirs also. Be it unto all of us according to your word. Restore the generational destiny and calling of my whole family, in Jesus name."

THE ABYSS

Even after a week to work things out, Willie rationalized grounds to reject Nara's claims of change. A history of deception and death proved Nara was evil and there needed to be a just punishment for those actions. With everyone else so quick to forgive, it was obvious that he alone was left clear-headed enough to carry out the justice Nara rightly deserved.

In thoughtfulness for the feelings of his flock, any plan had to be out of sight and scrutiny of the rest. As he saw it, Nara would simply have to disappear. He would offer subtle opinions to form notions in others about what happened to him. Notional story would eventually become history and his world would have peace. In time Nara would be forgotten.

His next step was to come up with a good reason to be gone. The idea of feigning some sickness came to mind. He would pretend confusion and restlessness then simply go away for a time. Upon his return, he would explain his delirium and they would understand that he couldn't help being away. He laughed to himself considering how easy it was to visualize things so clearly.

* * * * * * * * *

Roee's topic of discussion with Dodee at the breakfast table started with the work agenda for the day. Dodee had other concerns.

"Roee," said Dodee forcefully, "you *have* to take a stronger stance with Willie about forgiving Nara. He can't go on like this!

Roee responded calmly. "I've explained to him the importance of forgiving. I can compel him to do what's right, but I can't make the decision for him. It's his journey. If he does it without conviction, it won't last. His heart won't change unless he makes that choice on his own."

"Then try spending more time with him. He's a goat! He doesn't have the emotional constitution humans do. Do you know he keeps going off by himself? That's not healthy goat behavior. You've got to intervene!"

Work boots stomped up the wooden steps and onto the porch. Dodee finished expressing her concerns with a look that said *you're not getting it.* She stood to clear the table and said, "I'm *really* upset with the way you're handling this."

Shamus knocked and entered without waiting for a response. His face revealed concern. "Roee, Willie didn't come in last night. Nobody's seen him since yesterday morning."

The shepherds looked at each other. Roee winced, "We might be too late for intervention."

"Well, get going and look for him." Dodee said irritated. "And I'll get Rachel ready to come join you."

He had been resisting Dodee's post partum roller coaster. Now, he knew she was right. As the door shut behind them, Roee redirected his thoughts about Willie to include Shamus. "What do you think, Shamus? Do we need to talk to the goats to find out where he was last seen?"

"Scampy said that Willy was up before the others yesterday and headed for the water hole. Nobody saw him after that."

Roee thought briefly then responded, "Then let's just head out there and see if we can find his tracks. That might not be possible with all the activity that goes on there . . . But, we have to try."

Roee spent an hour with Shamus thoroughly searching the perimeter of the water hole and explaining what to look for. The results were not encouraging. Roee told Shamus what to look for and they spent a while in growing a perimeter search without result.

"Let's head toward town and the falls. You take the right side of the road and I'll take the left."

Under the canopy of the trees, the ground was soft enough to yield to weight.

"I think I got something here, Roee."

Roee joined him. "Those might be an old deer, or they might be goat. Could be both."

Roee squinted up the road. "There's more over there."

A few paces further, one set went into the forest opposite the falls. "That's the deer," Roee said. "This is Willie."

At the water fall the tracks went up into the rocks. Climbing the short rise, they spread out.

"This leaf and pine needle stuff makes it a bit hard to track." Shamus noted.

"You catch on quick, Shamus. If we had been here sooner, there would be indentions in it. But it's bounced back. Let's spread out and try to find something cleaner. If he started running, he could have broken this cover to expose the ground. Look for that . . . and goat droppings."

The two lost time and the forest grew shadows.

"This is **not** looking good, Shamus."

Roee and Shamus stood without talking, looking into the forest hoping for a sign or some movement. Roee wondered out loud without thinking. "Is it possible that a goat would take his own life?"

Shamus jerked toward Roee with a concerned look. "You think all that moody crap was sadness?"

"No Shamus, the book of James says that a double-minded man, or goat in this case, who cannot make up his mind about how he will respond to wisdom, will become unstable about everything that he is. I think **that** is what happened to Willie. He wrestled with forgiveness, but couldn't get a breakthrough . . . It's difficult to say where his thoughts are now. And the last time we talked he wasn't revealing what he was thinking. He was hiding . . . But, he isn't hiding from Papa. **Nothing** is hidden from him, and Papa isn't showing me anything."

"Shamus, let's pray. Papa knows how to make this work out."

* * * * * * * * * *

Willie had never been far from Wonder Valley. The forest north of home had strange odors and odd sounds. Yet after two days of wandering he was confident his mission would pay off. Thinking of vengeance empowered him with growing intensity to fight Nara at any cost. What food and water he needed wasn't hard to come by. So, he wouldn't grow faint along the way.

Besides, he knew where to go and what to do. It seemed like there were thoughts in the forest that gave him direction. Nature was on his side and encouraged a keener focus.

As another night approached without sight or smell of Nara, Willie bedded down. Although weary, his thoughts of Nara wouldn't rest. He obsessed on what he would do when he caught up with the arrogant beast. *He thinks he's changed,* he thought. *The only change he's going to see is when his life is given account for. He can't do what he did to us and get away with paying for it. You reap what you sow. Isn't that what it's all about? He'll see.*

Sunrise was slow in getting to the ridge at the east. Eventually, there was enough visibility for Willie to be on his way. Even without a quiet night's rest, he covered ground energetically. The curious ability to know where he was going became a determined force within him.

The ridge he walked dropped into a canyon and created a natural gateway to whatever waited on the other side. Now invincible, he stopped, looked and jumped. The canyon was patched with scrub oak and manzanita. It was good enough fare for a hunter like himself and he ate and resumed his mission.

At canyon's end the terrain sloped gently down over broken granite into more forest. He startled a trio of does grazing in the shadows, who popped their heads up to stare. They nosed up for his scent cautiously. Curious but not alarmed, they walked toward Willie to make acquaintance. A fawn stepped out of the shrubbery.

Attack! Kill! The words screamed in his thoughts. He resisted.

This is practice for when you face Nara. He'll be as easy as these deer. Kill them!

Willie's rage exploded when he heard Nara's name. He charged the deer for a random target. The deer scattered, but the traumatized fawn froze. Willie cracked head to head with the baby buck, hurtling it into a boulder. It slid off and settled in a disheveled heap.

Willie stood over the fawn, breathing hard. Then a fog enveloped him. He lowered his head and touched the dead fawn's nose with his own. "What have I done?"

Get over it, his thoughts said. *You're on a mission.*

He wondered if those thoughts were his own. The old Willie would never take an innocent life. *What am I becoming?*

Killing Nara will save the flock years of confusion and pain. It would be a big mistake for the herd to believe that Nara could ever be a friend.

Willie saw the reasoning . . . but it was empty. He gaped

briefly at the fawn then walked away.

An hour further into the forest brought Willie to a rock formation. He walked up to it and felt its protection. Sorrow gripped him and his mouth was dry with guilt. Weary and thirsty he sniffed in hope of smelling water.

"I've been expecting you, and I'll bet you found those idiot hairballs anywhere. I see them on your face. How did you manage to pick *them* up?"

Willie turned to face his enemy. Anger swelled his chest.

Kill him! Destroy him! This is what you're here for. His thoughts were screaming again. Earlier in the morning, Willie would have caved to their goading in blind agreement. He just looked at Nara strangely. Screaming rants kept his mind occupied.

Nara said flatly, "In Jesus name, shut up!"

Willie's thoughts were suddenly quiet. His brain turned off and he shook his head to get it going again.

"What was that?" Willie asked sharply. "What did you just do?"

"I recognized the presence of those squeaky idiots. I used to have them in *my* head."

"What are you talking about?"

"Demons Willie. I was stuck in their lies for years. I let them turn me into that moron I used to be. Funny thing, they don't have any power over you if you don't believe them. I was too far gone to get free on my own, so Jesus did it for me. They went packing in search of another victim . . . How did they manage to find you?"

"I guess they showed up while I was trying to figure out how to kill you. I didn't want to forgive you. I wanted to punish you.

It seemed right that I should be the one to do it." He then added with more force, "And I didn't want you coming back and messing up our community."

Yeah, he's no good! You don't want that scum around. "Be quiet," yelled Willie.

"It doesn't take a lot to get them going again does it?"

"Do I look like an expert?" responded Nara sarcastically . . . "So, are you tired of having those guys around?"

"I deserve them. You have any idea what I've done today? I let this happen. I listened to them thinking they were my own good and noble thoughts. I believed their lies. They convinced me that killing you would be doing everybody a favor. I was so caught up in myself I killed an innocent fawn to practice killing you."

"Willie, I feel your pain. I was sucked into their scheme, too. But, you can be free of those liars by renouncing the agreements you made with them . . . And forgiving me would help a lot. Those are the choices you need to make. I've asked you before and now ask you again. Will you forgive me for all the harm I've done to you?"

Willie hesitated then rejoined, "Yes . . . I choose to forgive you."

There was a whooshing sound like arrows in flight.

"My peace is back!" shouted Willie. "Oh, how I have missed that. Thank you, Papa."

"You're welcome."

Willie turned to see Jesus.

"I knew you would come through this, Willie."

"I lost my mind for a while. I'm sorry."

"You would have lost your life if you had continued in your

stubbornness."

"Why didn't you stop me?" asked Willie.

"When I knew you would respond, I did. I softened your hard heart . . . just long enough for you to see what was at the end of the path you were on. Unforgiveness and bitterness destroys life. If you hadn't seen that, you would have become what Nara was before I called him . . . or dead from carelessness."

"You mean you sent those deer to stop me? You sent the fawn to get my attention?"

"I didn't send them, Willie. But their presence made you aware of what you were headed for. Killing the fawn was your choice regardless of who influenced you to do it. Those creatures didn't force you to kill that fawn. You became the predator that Nara was. You became what you were judging."

"Can we go back and raise that poor baby from the dead like you did with our flock?"

"Not this time Willie. Everything will work out fine the way it is."

"I am so sorry, Jesus," Willie said sadly. "Please, forgive me."

"It's done. I am happy and eager to forgive so you can get on the right path again."

Willie breathed a sigh of remembrance for the fawn and considered what the mama doe must be feeling.

"Mind if I walk with you back to the valley?" Jesus asked. "The shepherds are concerned about you and I would enjoy the chat time."

"I would like that a lot."

Willie turned to Nara and asked, "Are you coming with us?"

"Uhhhhhh no," replied Nara. He looked distracted by other thoughts. "I have some business to take care of. I haven't eaten in a couple of days and need a little something."

Willie wrinkled his face at the thought of what Nara needed to do to survive.

"I guess you will always be a mountain lion, Nara. That will not change. . . And it shouldn't change."

For the first time, Willie looked Nara in the eye and felt they were equals. It would be different between them from now on.

"I'm ready to go when you are, Jesus." Willie said. And they began their journey.

"I'll see you soon, Willie." Nara called when they were a short distance away.

LESSONS LEARNED

Willie's emotions were tangled threads. One thread wanted the comfort of extended time with Jesus while they walked back to the valley. Yet he felt unworthy of his presence because of his wretched failure. He was in the wrong and he deserved punishment for what he had done with the fawn and how he treated Nara.

"That's blame, shame and guilt, Willie." The statement stopped Willie's wandering mind. "My death on the cross paid for your guilt *and* your punishment so you could be restored and have a life of freedom. Plus, when I forgive, I don't remember what your sin. I don't find fault, blame you or punish you for what is covered in forgiveness.

"I put no shame on you, Willie; only restoration. If you carry shame, you're believing a lie. I took the shame on me for your sin when I hung on the cross. If you carry hope, you're completely restored to life."

"But, I *deserve* to be punished for what I did." Willie responded.

"What did you do, Willie?"

"I took an innocent life and I refused to forgive someone who *really* desired to be forgiven."

"Really?" Jesus responded and stopped walking. "I don't remember."

Willie's face contorted, then relaxed. "Then how can I be held accountable for my actions?"

"The accounting isn't about your actions, it's about the condition of your heart. What problem in your heart would have determined different actions? Bring that to me. Let me heal you and show you the truth."

Willie looked at Jesus then said, "I don't know. . . I don't know if I *see* the problem."

"Why was it you couldn't forgive Nara?"

"Because he was so stinking **evil**, he always made me angry. And he deserved to get back what he dished out. He played games with our confusion and took advantage of our desperation. Some even died for trusting him. Justice requires a payback."

"Where did you get that idea, Willie?"

Willie looked in Jesus face. "I don't know. . . Didn't I hear that from Mama Shepherd reading the Bible to us?"

"That's not justice, Willie; that's revenge. You wanted revenge for the pain you felt for being helpless to do anything about it. You wanted to inflict pain for the pain you felt. It's retaliation you passionately wanted to be a part of for the wrongs you felt you suffered. You really wanted Nara to be punished and you were afraid he wouldn't get what you thought he deserved.

"Let's take a look at the bigger picture. Why did Finny look to Nara in the first place?"

Willie thought a moment. "Finny said we were forcing him to be something he wasn't. Sully, Tanny and I talked about that and agreed we could have done things differently. But at the time, we were afraid he would be reckless and mess everything up for the next generation of kids. But we haven't figured out what we *should* have done."

Jesus looked at him with compassion and said, "I know you did it unknowingly. But he ended up doing what your fears were trying to prevent, didn't he?"

"Yeah, that's what it looks like," responded Willie nodding his head.

"Control got different results than if you had trained Finny by giving him the freedom to learn and make mistakes under guidance. It would have been a better atmosphere for him to grow in.

"Finny's was frustrated with the control you guys inflicted on him. Wisdom would have given him training and the experience to grow up understanding right choices. He would have learned much, much more from your example and patience.

"Finny made some wrong choices, and through the hurtful consequences of those choices, I turned his heart back toward me. I forgave him and everything is going in a new direction. The journey all of you went through is what justice is about. Are you still following me?"

"Yes," responded Willie slowly. "I think you're saying we all had a part in the mess that was made."

"That's what I want you to see. You thought Nara was the problem. But the truth is *everyone* had a part in creating the problem. All were blind, and now all are being given new vision. What does that mean to you?"

A light was brightening inside Willie. He stopped walking and looked ahead at the very path where he had been going the other direction with horrific intent just hours before. He thought about what he had done to Finny, what Finny's dissatisfaction had done to Megan, and what the both of them did to cause the flock grief. He thought about how Nara had *opportunity* to do evil only because of what *they* had done to Finny. It formed a circle that came back on itself rather than a platform for making judgments about who was the worst offender.

"Baaaaaah," bawled Willie. It echoed off the rocks and hills around him and returned. Willie felt better. "I think that best describes what I feel about that.

"Jesus, if you had not come we would be stuck in an endless circle of blaming, shaming, and guilting each other. You put an end to that, didn't you?"

"Freedom, Willie. I give you the freedom to become everything I've created you to be and be at peace with an imperfect journey. Explore and discover who you are while I walk along with you to show you the ways of love. I give you freedom to find out what you can do and what you can't do. Do it in love and do it with responsibility, sensitivity and self-control. If you make a mess and offend, clean it up. If you get offended, respond with understanding. Own your mistakes and forgive the mistakes of others.

"Here's the hard part. What freedom I give to you, you must give to others."

Willie smiled. "I suppose that includes Nara, Finny and Megan."

"You're one of the leaders of the flock, Willie, so that includes *everybody* I have put in your care. You must not only give them freedom, but help them discover their identity. It's what fathers do.

"From now on, instead of molding Finny into what you think he should be, look into his life and discern what he was *created* to be. Encourage him and love him and he will respond to you. If you have any questions, I'm here to help. He's as special as the legends say. I was there when he was healed the night of the storm. I'm the one who changed the color of his fur to blue. His calling was written before the foundations of the earth and his life will have an impact on this world. No matter what happens to him, I'm in control of the outcome."

Willie thought a while then said, "Can we just walk? I have a lot to chew on."

"That's fine, Willie."

Willie thought of times when Papa Shepherd would sit up on Vision Rock and sing loudly over the valley. The flock would graze in the meadow and listen. Angels would show up and indescribable wonders would take place. He thought of home and longed to be there.

Jesus hummed while Willie mused. He broke into whistling, ranging from high pitches to low. He warbled and swirled in an odd melody that filled the forest with variations that returned to Willie from every direction. The local birds joined his song with a love language that started as a whimsical pastorale and grew to an improvisational ensemble. The movements changed from simple to complex, tender to vibrant. Billows of mist began to form. Willie anticipated that the notes of the song should start to materialize. It had happened before according to Roee. Although Willie was there when it happened, he had not seen it. Instead, forms flowed together and became a dewy substance that turned to a solid layer on the ground like fallen hail.

Willie stood and watched. Jesus stopped whistling to listen to the bird choir finish what he started. The music faded and the forest was quietly peaceful again.

Jesus smiled and spread his hand toward the stuff on the ground. "Try some. They made it just for you."

"What is it?"

"That's a good name for it," Jesus replied. "What is it?"

Willie walked over and wrapped his lips around a sizable cluster. It melted on his tongue, yet formed a ball for him to chew. The flavor was similar to the lemon that Dodee had given him once. He really liked it and ate until he was content. The remainder melted into the ground moments later.

"Will the cud taste like that?" Willie asked.

Jesus laughed. "You tell me when that moment comes."

They resumed their walk and Jesus renewed their conversation. "Isn't it wonderful to be a part of all this, Willie?"

"Yup," Willie responded.

"Tell me what you're thankful for. What's the first thing that comes to mind?"

"I'm thankful for . . ." Willie drawled. "I'm thankful for a family that loves, and shepherds that gave up their home to bring us that love."

Jesus walked on without response.

"I'm thankful for the beauty and mystery that is Wonder Valley. You've made more of it than anything I could have dreamed about. We have a safe pasture to graze in and fresh, cool water to drink. We have peace with our enemy and a promise of being in your house forever."

As Willie said more, he thought of more. Joy grew inside.

"It's not just the quietness of our lives; it's what we leave behind when we are gone. Our kids have a unique something to pass on and the birthright of being a chosen race of goats. I'm thankful for their sake that you have given us something besides stories of what was. They will have their own journeys and stories to encourage their kids."

Willie stood and sighed to express another thought. "I'm thankful for Nara, Jesus. He helped me see when I was blinded by the darkness in my heart. And thank you for your patient love and forgiveness."

Jesus smiled, "The dwelling places of my Father's house are many, Willie. There are valleys of wonder and valleys of trial. There are mountains of exciting adventure and mountains to overcome and to conquer. Those you call neighbor can be friend or foe. But loving them all is what I have asked of those who love me. It may not be an easy life, but it is abundantly full with things to be grateful for.

"You're doing well, Willie. Never give up.

"And this is where I leave you to complete your journey back. The valley is still a ways ahead and through the arch of the twin oak trees. You won't miss it. My Spirit will not leave you. I am always with you . . . Be blessed as you go . . . And thank you for all that you are. I'm crazy in love with you, Willie."

Willie leaned into Jesus' leg for a pet. It's the closest thing to a hug that he had been able to figure out. He burped up a cud as he pulled away.

He tasted it and said, "As sweet as the original."

Sometime later, Willie passed under the twin oaks and onto a flat rocky area. Willie looked down from the ledge on his home with appreciation. His eyes took in the woods and meadows and rocks and old stumps. At the east end, a small herd of deer grazed near the edge of their habitat. There were twin fawns romping together around their mother. His eyes misted as they scampered over to check out a baby raccoon. It darted into the nearby bushes.

"Perhaps," he said with a mix of regret and hope, "the loss of that fawn has worked to do something good." It was a grieving loss in exchange for his transformation. And in his heart he knew it wasn't Papa's best. The hardness of his heart left no room for another outcome.

"What a strange world I live in."

A perceptible peace enveloped him. He could see people that had not been there minutes earlier. He knew they were angels. The younger kids saw them all the time. This was the first time he had seen them since the flock had been caught up to heaven in what Tanny called in his story version of it, The Ruction. It was good to have this experience. He was right with everything around him.

He spotted Mama Shepherd near the cabin. Two angels watched her nearby. She held her new baby and walked about. He had to talk with her. He dropped off the ledge, leapt to the trail below and headed for the meadow by way of the woods.

His had a moment of appreciation for the surroundings he had grown to take for granted. He walked into a quartet of squirrels romping and laughing with angels chasing them about. The squirrels chattered hellos and the angels stopped from their play to acknowledge Willie's presence. They smiled then continued their antics.

The reality of belonging to a family like this flooded his emotions. He had changed while he was gone. He possessed something he never realized he needed. He was loved and knew he could give love. *If I can change, anyone can change . . . even Nara.*

At the edge of the forest where shade and sunlit brilliance met, he entered the meadow. He squinted then headed for the cabin. He managed a short distance through the meadow before being spotted. Scampy and Finnegan were the first to chime in. "Hey everyone, Willie's back!"

Goats and wildlife ran to welcome their Papa goat home with warm enthusiasm. While he was gone the valley had changed, too. There was a different atmosphere than before. Then it came . . . *he* was seeing through clearer vision. He started to laugh at himself. Others caught his infectious laughter. Kids frolicked and kicked and giggled.

Dodee, with Rachel in her arms, had been walking the baby in the fresh air and praying. She turned to see the excitement and smiled. Tears of joy followed.

Roee and Shamus were working in the fenced garden gathering and watering vegetables. They looked at each other, relieved to see Willie alive. They put down their tools and turned off the hose.

Papa Shepherd and Willie made eye contact. Roee could see that Willie was different. He had come through his dark night of the soul victorious.

Mama Shepherd would have to wait for a more convenient opportunity to have her time alone with Willie. For the remainder of the day, Willie talked about where he had been and what he had done. Reluctantly at first, then as family poured their love on him, the balm of acceptance gave him freedom to be vulnerable and tell the whole story.

By days end, Willie was more than restored. He was ready to take up a very different role as father to a very precious flock of goats. He understood something he had not known before. It is an easy thing to bring babies into the life of the flock. It is another realm altogether to bring life to those babies. Tomorrow would be different.

A NEW DAY

Willie's good-natured interaction with the rambunctious kids got noticed by Sully. For Wille, that was unusual behavior. So, he invited Willie for a walk. They strolled through the dog-legged meadow to the east end of the valley beyond Vision Rock. An area frequented by deer rather than goats, it was out of range of listening ears. Squirrels came out of the forest and frolicked about Willie and Sully in the sunshine.

"You've talked to us a little," Sully began, "about what happened *out there*. But your actions are telling an unspoken story. What's with the new Willie I'm experiencing?

"Sully," Willie slowly said, "Hmmmm. Yes, I'm sorry about what I put myself and everyone else through. But I was sick inside and going through it somehow made me well. But my struggle through unforgiveness got me to *this* side of the problem. I'm not going to mope around feeling guilty and be embarrassed. It was worth having everybody see my ugly heart. The old me came out, and now that guy is gone."

Willie shivered involuntarily at the remembrance of his actions.

"It was worth it to know just how *much* I'm loved by Jesus. He's the greatest shepherd there is. And I had a two day walk alone with him. I'll cherish that forever.

"And it was worth it to know how much I'm loved by all of you. You guys are the greatest family there is. Everyone of you should be treasured for who you are and what Papa God has created you to be. And now, I've committed myself to being an example of that kind of treasure seeker."

Sully waited for Willie to say more. When he didn't, Sully responded.

"I've never heard you talk like this before, Willie."

"Sully, I'm a simple goat. I don't have great words to explain what I went through. The plainness of it is this. I was a mess with unforgiveness. The longer I chose not to forgive, the messier I got."

Willie looked Sully in the face. "You know what's really scary, Sully . . . I was becoming what Nara had been.

"Killing that fawn broke my heart. But it woke me up and everything started looking different. Whatever it was that I believed, wasn't worth holding on to after that. When I caught up with Nara, the fight I wanted to pick with him was broken, too."

Sully reeled from the level of openness Willie was sharing from. "Willie, I never thought of you as being a killer . . . Grumpy and unreasonable, yes . . . But, I guess we all have something ugly under our fur when the right things bring them to the surface. It makes me wonder about myself."

Willie chuckled. "Nara did the strangest thing, Sully. He started talking to my thoughts like they weren't me and he had met them before. He said they were lying to me, and stirring up my hate. He *ordered* them to be silent. When they quit talking, the silence made my head spin. He helped me get rid of them—said he had them before I did.

"When I forgave Nara, I didn't see anything, but I heard them leave like a bird had just left the top of my head. That peace we have with Jesus returned, and then *he* appeared."

"Jesus?" Sully asked.

"Yes."

Sully thought and chewed cud.

"Did you ask Jesus to raise that fawn from the dead?" queried Sully. "That's what *I* would have done."

"I did. But he said no. I think I know why, but I'll keep that opinion to myself. But it's okay that he didn't. I won't *ever* forget killing that fawn. It was a strong, strong lesson. The look in his eyes . . ." Willie's throat tightened.

"I've *never* known you to hold back an opinion, Willie."

Willie sniffed, "I used my opinions to make me feel important, Sully. I don't need that now. Love is important and knowing Jesus and having his Spirit and what he knows and the truth that is in his word."

The conversation moved to quiet reflection; there was no hurry to move on. There was a closer bond between them, and Sully understood that the flock had come into a new day.

Willie watched the squirrels chase and tussle with each other. He remembered how the angels, on the day of his return, had played with the squirrels. Those angels were standing at the edge of the forest keeping watch. He looked around and saw several more. He wondered why they remained since Nara was now a part of their world and no longer a threat.

His eyes were drawn to a movement in the sky. At first, he thought it was an eagle. But as it circled closer from the north, he saw it had a long neck like a goose and its' tail resembled a snake.

"Sully, have you seen anything like that before?"

Sully followed Willie's gaze into the sky.

Slowly drawing out his response, Sully said, "I don't see anything, Willie."

Willie watched as two angels took flight to confront the intruder. The first angel tackled the unsuspecting creature and held it. The second angel stood with spear at the ready.

As far away as they were, Willie heard their voices in a language he did not understand. It was obvious they were not friends as the creature made several attempts to taunt the angels and provoke a skirmish. The angels were quiet and stood their ground. The second angel pointed his spear to the north and gave a command. "L'khu al artzekha!"

The creature said, "Lo!"

The angel reacted. A whistle, a flash of lightning quick movement and several angels from the ground were up and conveying the creature northward and out of sight. The incident was over in seconds.

In short order, the angels returned and resumed their positions as before.

Willie looked on curiously. Sully looked confused.

"Come on Sully, let's go talk to them." Willie started walking. "That was interesting."

"Talk to *who*, Willie?"

Willie approached one of the angels.

"Uhhhhhh sir, what was that thing up there? I've never seen anything like that before."

"Willie, *who* are you talking to? I wanna see them!"

"The angel says it's not his place to make that happen."

"So, what did you see Willie?"

"I can try to describe it later. It's gone now."

Willie looked up at the angel and waited.

"That was just a demon from a city north of here." The angel said. "It was spying for places to defile. This area is protected, so we drove it away. It won't be back."

"There are cities that have those things living in them?"

"Yes." The angel answered simply.

Not exactly a little hairball, Willie thought.

A New Song

The walk to Vision Rock held as much meaning as the waiting for sunrise. *Those who wait for Yahweh's grace,* Roee believed, *will walk through life without giving up*[a]. A thin canopy of clouds on the horizon meant the dawn would be intensely colorful. Papa was already speaking of promise and a multihued story by day's end.

Starting the day in Papa's presence was Roee's highest priority. When he arrived, he sat cross-legged and looked around at the land placed in his care. He was aware that even the dirt was in universal agony and groaning in anticipation of the full revelation of the sons and daughters of God[b]. His spirit longed to experience his full transformation and inheritance.

A royal fan of gold and rose colored hues with splashes of white and blue announced the arrival of the sun. It split the horizon and came out laughing, stretching rays across the cloud bottoms with brilliance. As it rose, the fan narrowed to a pillar of fire that pierced through the cloud layers and flamed high into the blue atmosphere. The sudden change caught his breath and startled his quiet vigil. A psalm flooded his heart like the rising sun.

> The God of gods, the mighty Lord himself, has spoken!
> He shouts out over all the people of the earth,
> In every brilliant sunrise and every brilliant sunset, saying,
> 'Listen to me!'"[c]

The cool dawn pulled light down to the tree tops and embraced the hills beyond. An ancient Celtic hymn kindled within, then set fire as his prayer.

Be Thou my vision O Lord of my heart;
Be all else but naught to me save that Thou art.
Be Thou my best thought in the day and the night,
Both waking and sleeping Thy presence my light.

Be Thou my wisdom be Thou my true word;
Be Thou ever with me and I with Thee, Lord;
Be Thou my great Father and I Thy true son;
Be Thou in me dwelling and I with Thee one.

Papa's presence poured over him like liquid joy. Roee rose to kneeling and continued. He brought his hands to his chest, caressing the Spirit within as the words ran deep.

Be Thou my breastplate, my sword for the fight;
Be Thou my whole armor, be Thou my true might;
Be Thou my soul's shelter, be Thou my strong tower:
O raise Thou me heav'nward, great power of my power.

The shepherd stood for the last stanzas through tears. He lifted his hands in surrender, the timbre and volume of his baritone voice increasing. Previous verses returned in echo from across the valley, adding layers to what was coming.

Riches I need not, nor man's empty praise,
Be Thou mine inheritance, now and always:
Be Thou and Thou only the first in my heart,
O Sov'reign of Heaven, my treasure Thou art.

High King of Heaven, Thou Heaven's bright sun,
O grant me its joys after victory is won.
Great heart of my own heart, whatever befalls,
Still be Thou my Vision, O Ruler of all.[d]

By the end of the song, his forehead received the sun-drenched touch of the finger of God.

"My King, my joy, my eternal hope, may this day be filled with the riches of your Kingdom and the reward of the price you paid for the souls of this world. Please use me to join your love to those whose hearts have been prepared. I commit my spirit to sit in heavenly places and heavenly councils and to eavesdrop in the conversations of the Godhead.

"Please share with your son what is on your heart today, my Lord?" A response came to Roee as a quote from the book of Samuel[e]. *"In the spring, at the time when kings go off to battle, David sent Joab out with the king's men and the whole Israelite army."*

Roee didn't understand. "What are you purposing?" He whispered. "Help me to see the mystery."

A sniffle came from behind him. He turned to see Nara wiping an eye with his paw. Nara was touched by the shepherd's song and wondered what connection Nara had with the scripture he heard. *Is Nara David or Joab?*

Affection connected between him and Nara. He saw Nara changing from gangster to warrior; his restlessness trumped with peace. The difference shown in his face and bearing.

"Come and join me, Nara. Watching the sun chase the shadows away is like a picture of our lives . . . Creation's true colors awaken with the sunrise like our true identity is painted as we see greater revelations of Jesus; we're meant to be like him, you know . . . Squirrels and chipmunks resume their search for the mysterious locations of provision that is guaranteed them. All we have need of is guaranteed because Jesus cares for us; it often comes to us mysteriously . . . Deer and goat drink of the faithful dew that is new every morning on the meadow's grass as we receive of the mercies that are given freely every new day . . . Wild flowers open their faces and speak praises of their creator as we raise our faces to heaven in worship . . . And just as the sun makes everything grow, the light of God's son brings everything in us to life."

Nara sat within reach of Roee's hand. The shepherd smiled and rubbed the big cat behind the ears. Nara let him, but Roee was uncertain how much affection the big cat was ready for. He kept the moment brief.

Nara observed the valley thoughtfully. "I have not yet learned to enjoy the details you see."

"Your eyes are unique, Nara. I wouldn't expect you to have the same appreciation that I have."

Nara nodded. "I do appreciate your singing. I would like to do that. Jesus sang, too. When I tried, it sounded like little girl screams . . . It was annoying."

Roee was slow to respond through his chuckles. "Papa enjoys working wonders. You will have a new song if you keep asking. How much do you want a gift like that? . . . Don't give up, Nara"

Nara glanced wishfully at Roee without answering and changed the subject.

"Jesus The Hunter tells me you are a general in the making and I have been sent to be your servant and to learn from you." He looked into the shepherd's face and continued. "I would be honored to serve with you in the battles ahead."

Roee knelt to talk with Nara face to face. "It appears to me that *you* are the general in training. And given the timing of your appearance today, your first lesson will be to understand that song is a warrior's weapon. Praise and thankfulness prepare a soldier's heart for the unexpected things that happen. But Papa's presence dwells in praise; he fills praise with himself. And you will need his presence to fight his battles."

Nara flashed a squinted glance at him, "Why is thankfulness a big deal?"

"Everything about you is designed by Papa God. As a warrior, you will have to depend on him. Your strengths are gifts from him. Your weaknesses are perfected and defended by him. You are completed and restored through his presence in you. Your destiny has been determined by him. And your unique identity is formed by his hands. Being genuinely thankful leaves room for Papa to give you more."

Nara was swaying his head. "I don't understand."

"It'll take practice and experience to fully grasp how it all connects, Nara."

"How do I get the practice and experience?"

"Papa provides it."

"Then, if that is true, we should pray. I need an experience."

Roee laughed at Nara's simplicity, then put one hand on Nara's chest and the other hand behind his ears.

"Nara I impart to you wisdom for praise and gratefulness in Jesus' name. May you grasp the heights and depths of them quickly. And Papa, I pray you'll give Nara lots of experience to grow by."

Nara's head and chest twitched like being hit with an electric shock.

"Wow," he yelled. "What was that?

Roee laughed again and added, "Papa, thank you for the wonder of a new song and a new voice to sing it."

"Hoa!" Nara shrieked as another jolt sprung him off his feet. "Is this normal?" he whined. "Am I going to live through this?"

Another wave flowed over him and he staggered rubber legged.

"I like this." He slurred. "Woohoo!"

The shepherd propped him against his leg.

"Okay, Nara, let's make a test run on this thing and see how it's humming. I'm going to teach you a very simple song. You'll love it. I'll sing it first, then we'll sing it together."

Roee sang the first verse of Amazing Grace, then sung the same thing a second time. With a nudge of encouragement Nara opened his mouth to try . . . What came out was gravelly and caused Nara to laugh. "Hey, that's an improvement."

Roee laughed with him and ruffled his ears. He made motion with his hands to keep going and restarted the verse.

Nara's voice cleared a bit and the change encouraged him. A few rounds showed improvement. Nara was getting the hang of it; albeit, a bit off pitch.

Roee had an idea. "Let me pray for your ears. Ears are an important part of singing." He prayed again and they started over with more daring; each attempt adding clarity.

"Now Nara, you know that verse well enough to sing it by yourself."

They took off together. Nara and Roee filled the mountain air fearlessly. Roee dropped out to let Nara go on alone.

By verse's end, Nara sung with his eyes closed. In the third round, he created new words. And with the fourth he was not using words at all. He was creatively playing with the melody and exploring his range.

He opened his eyes and looked around the valley. The words and melody changed.

"I can see, I can see all the wonders of your world
I can hear, I can hear all the movement of your heart
I can feel, I can feel all the pleasures of your touch
I can know, I can know all the greatness of your love"

He held the last note for as long as he could and ended with a deep sigh. Roee smiled in wonder as Nara finished in the weight of Papa's presence. Angels gathered to admire Papa's workmanship and add their voices to the new song left stirring the atmosphere.

"He does all things well," they began, adding verses that portrayed the heart of their song. They returned to the beginning and encouraged Papa Shepherd and Nara to join them. Winds of passionate praise swirled through the valley that formed a translucent canopy from their sound. The top of the canopy opened to form a majestic crown of clear gold. A cloud of presence flowed down as a vortex within the crown. With it descended a fragrance that tasted sweet.

A crowd of forest critters gathered in response to the created awe of the music. The goats walked among them joyously singing and assuring the newcomers that the encounter was safe.

As intensity increased, the music took on life. Notes of pearlescent sapphire formed streams. Then the streams came together forming a river that flowed to the center just under the crown. The river flowed upward and created a throne. A rainbow floated down and settled above the back of the throne and around the base. An embossed sign appeared in front of the rainbow that said, "The Throne of David."

The composite creation settled into the meadow and touched the ground. Praise rose in a fresh wave. Roee could no longer stand and dropped to his knees. Joy-filled waves of worship rolled in from every direction. The mountains, the meadows and the trees raised their voices. Roee watched in awe as trees swayed and brought their branches together. The snapping of wood sounded like clapping.

The daffodils began to sway as being blown by wind. Their green leaves stretched to reach the height of nearby goats that were dancing in the field. As they swayed, they flexed up and down to the beat of the song. Yellow faces of daffodils reappeared to stand in the midst of their extended leaves and spun their pedals deftly to form a blanket of green and yellow praise.

White lucent smoke formed at the seat of the throne and rose to fill the crown above it. Once it rose, it spun and grew shoots like luminous ropes that created a path for the music notes of the throne to dance upon. Their dancing made processions over the crowd below until Roee could no longer see the ground from the top of Vision Rock. The dance from David's throne expanded in collected smoke and notes until it covered the crown.

The angelic choir slowly quieted their song and the smoke gradually dissipated to a haze. The crowd in the valley skipped and danced in the afterglow while Roee and Nara looked on in amazement. Heaven had touched earth.

"My government is firmly established and increasing," spoke the voice of Jesus from the cloud. "The battle for the lost souls of Lawless and Little Faith is ready to be waged. My servants with the message of life, love, and power will fill my Kingdom with the fruit of the cross."

Roee lay prostrate in prayer until a noiseless calm saturated him. Unaware of time, when he rose to his knees the world about him was back to normal and Nara sat speechlessly looking around.

* * * * * * * * *

Roee was sharing with Dodee and Shamus the word he received from Jesus and tried to explain what the event looked like from his position above it all. Nara joined them, but found greater fascination with baby Rachel. He nuzzled and rubbed the child on the floor until she giggled several times. With the story told, Dodee left the details for Roee and Shamus to rehash, then grabbed a throw pillow and got on the floor with Rachel and Nara.

"Considering a family Nara?" asked Dodee.

"Mountain lions aren't like humans. The cubs of my tribe are raised by their mothers. Fathers are notorious loners and leave shortly after mating. If they find the cubs, they tend to kill them . . . I never knew my father. And my mother taught me everything I needed to know . . . then left me in the wilderness to survive on my own."

"That would explain a lot. From a human perspective, it's a wonder you survived."

"Doesn't that make us what we are?" responded the cougar. "If you think about it, isn't it Papa who created my surroundings and the way I would be raised?"

"You have a point. Humans where not created for a life of isolation. But I also wonder, might it be the case for you as well? You have the choice to raise your cubs differently."

Nara thought for a moment.

"I don't think I understand what you're saying."

"Picture this, Nara. In the wilderness, mountain lions have *learned* to live like they do. They're lonely, self-sufficient creatures that see other creatures as either a threat to the security of their territory, or as a meal. Traditionally speaking, you were raised in a culture of isolation; that is all you knew. No love, no one to tell you how valuable you are, and no one to share your deepest thoughts with."

"Yeah, that's the life of a mountain lion . . . until you guys showed up. Before that I ate and drank as I pleased and took advantage of the weak and vulnerable. It messed up my world when you came. You all cared for each other and cared about the goats. I hated you for showing me what I didn't have. I despised you for rescuing the goats from my schemes. But inside . . . I wanted what you had. That's when Jesus showed up and took away my hairballs."

Nara smiled and Dodee laughed. Roee and Shamus laughed. They had been listening to the conversation.

"Your what?" Dodee responded.

"Jesus called them demons, and he got rid of them for me. But when they came out they looked like great hairballs with giant lips. It was a shocking surprise that they had any ability to control my life and my thoughts."

Dodee shook her head, not knowing what to say.

"Now that you are with us, you'll get to see a different way of living with others. It's a new normal for you, Nara, and a new opportunity to look at your tribe and think about a future with other pumas such as yourself. You can create a whole new tribe that lives in harmony with people."

"We have some habits that will never change. We eat animals, you know. And we like to hunt."

"This might surprise you, Nara," said Roee. "I eat animals and I like to hunt for wild game. And as you already know, we raise chickens for food, not just for eggs. And until we came here and started talking with them, we used to eat goat."

Nara puffed his chest out, raised his chin snootily and said with an arrogant air, "How disgusting." Laughter filled the room.

Endnotes
a   Isaiah 40:31
b   Romans 8
c   Psalm 50:1
d   Be Thou My Vision. Attributed: Dallan Forgaill (public
domain) Lyric changes by Eden's Bridge.
e   2 Samuel 11:1, NKJV

A Telling History

Five generations earlier the foundation of a diabolical fortress was laid. Its walls were raised by stones of offense and rocks of self-righteousness. Division attracted sleepless watchers to ensure the wall remained as unforgiveness and bitterness mixed together to create the mortar that strengthened it.

An industrious new saloon keeper baited the men with lulling seduction through the allure of her girls. The unwary and foolish found no harm in their gratifications and the hook was set. A spiritual firestorm grew and their indiscretions formed strongholds; marriage covenants collapsed.

Hot resentment and virulent scorn shunned the unfaithful without conciliation. Unkindness became the norm. Those few with a voice for reason; who sought to reconcile with unconditional love; went unheeded as the leaven of malice spawned a social cancer.

The town divided morally, economically and geopolitically. A visiting journalist of the day, seeing a story, branded the place Two Towns because of their factional character. He pointed the finger at a religious community with little faith and a hedonistic community determined to be lawless. The tags took root by repeated use and eventually eclipsed the original name.

The railroad landmarked their division shortly after the tracks was laid years later. Constant rants and gossip across fences and in market places ratified agreement with the powers of darkness.

This early years conversation tells the harsh story.

"Harlan, have you heard about the latest victim of those

deuces across the tracks?"

"You're kidding, Earl, who is it this time?"

"It's Mister McBride. Ricky Grubb seen 'im crossin' the tracks last night. He follered 'im to one of them hookshops and watched 'im go in."

"Well that chucklehead better write his epitaph," stated Harlan. "He's in hot fat now."

"Yup, Harlan, if his wife don't give 'im a thumpin', the church folk gonna make him a prairie oyster."

"Dang Earl, we gotta run those lawless people out of town."

"I dunno, Harlan. It's like trying to get rid of whistle berries without a wind. Unless folk stop wanting to eat at that table, it ain't gonna quit stinkin'. I ain't so sure the problem sits on the other side of the tracks."

"The other side of the tracks," is what was said. "Us and them" is what was meant. Animosity was one of the perpetual watchers. The societal clime of the day set up the wall, but even a post modern morality couldn't bring it down. But God was looking for someone to make a difference. And Earl's redneck wisdom would be a prophetic statement that another generation would hear.

Seeds of change were planted when two brothers, Del and Jake, and their wives Kathy and Anna, realized there had to be a better way. The land itself was proof of a problem. It was seen in the barrenness of the fields on the Lawless side of the tracks, and the constant struggle to thrive on the Little Faith side. They prayed for an awakening.

"Del," Jake said one day. "The people of Lawless see us as religious devils. And the church people of Little Faith see them as a heathen enemy. How in the world are we going to change that?"

"Jake, God's word holds the answer to everything. Let's start there and see where it takes us.

"It says in 2 Corinthians that one man died for everyone. He included everyone in his death so that everyone could also be included in his resurrection life. It's an abundant life far better than anyone could think or imagine.

"Because of that, we don't evaluate people by what they have or how they look or what they do. We look at the inside, and what we see is that *anyone* united with the Messiah gets a fresh start. The old life is gone and a new life is created!

"Look at it! God settled the relationship between us and him by putting our wrongs on the one who never sinned. Then God told us to straighten out our relationships with each other. He put the world square with himself through the Messiah and offered the world a fresh start by the forgiveness and removal of our sins."

"Del," Jake interjected. "You're preaching to the choir. We know this. What's your point?"

"The word says we are Christ's ambassadors. God uses us to appeal for men and women to consider their differences and enter into God's work of making things right between them. Jake, God is now making his appeal to us. What are we going to do about it?"

Del raised his hands to his mouth like a megaphone and said, "Become friends with God, he's already a friend with you."

"You know Del, I think we've been moral sheriffs, not ambassadors of a kingdom. If all we do is site people for their violations and don't show them the terms of peace and reconnection with God, we continue to look like the bad guys oppressing our victims. Jesus never intended it to be that way. Our critical attitude toward them is part of the problem.

"Jesus didn't come to judge people. He came to save them, and we make it hard for them to see God's heart."

The four of them turned to God's face that day.

To answer their prayer, Roee supernaturally appeared in Lawless when he was transported during a conversation with Sully; one of the goats from Wonder Valley. Through that experience Roee befriended Shamus, and showed him what an unconditional friendship looked like. In the context of that unexpected visit, Jake, Anna, Del and Kathy saw a signal from heaven that something could change. Through Roee, their hungry searching for answers was fed with the manna of truth and wisdom.

During a kitchen table discussion Roee shared, "Jesus clearly stated that the antidote for sin was belief in him, not making judgments about sin's actions and punishing those who fail. Jesus came to find and to save the lost, and then redeem them through personal transformation.

"Authentic moral change," Roee taught them, "won't be cultivated in self-modified behavior. Powerful people who have learned to love through the presence of God is what stirs a cultural awakening. Bringing heaven to earth is a reformation that will turn the existing culture upside down. This entire region can be affected and moved in a new direction through the power of lives that have had an encounter with God.

"Have you ever heard the expression, 'We need to see it, to have it?' It's foundational to the idea that an encounter with another reality is essential to open hearts to believe a better way of life is available. That's why Jesus performed miracles and told us to do the same. His miracles prove his compassion is real and that he desires to remove the heavy burdens from lives without hope."

Since their arrival in the community, Rigo and Maria had said repeatedly that "change is found in the law of love, not the love of law." People started believing what they said when Roee showed up as reinforcement. He proved a difference could be made by extending unconditional love to just one of Lawless' toughest citizens.

When love won Shamus over, hard hearts softened to the idea that they were dealing with broken lives in need of relief from their pain, instead of people in love with their sins.

The tipping point in Two Towns was at hand. It needed an intercessory push.

Battle Over Little Faith

"Remember those hairballs you told me about?" Roee asked.

"Uh huh," Nara responded.

"Remember the ugly serpents in your dream you told me about?"

"I don't think I'll forget them."

"My guess is those are some of the guys we're up against today, along with their friends and family if they have such things. As you may remember, they're the critters that keep lies sounding like truth, wounds of the heart hurting and bitterness aggravating."

"You're talking about those hairballs?"

"Yeah."

"Then what do those big guys do?"

"I don't know exactly."

"That's helpful. How do we fight them if we don't understand what they're doing?"

"I don't think we need to understand what they're doing. We need to understand what they are *keeping us* from doing and get about doing it. Their basic mission is to resist anything that looks like authentic love. Joy, peace, compassion, forgiveness, acceptance . . ."

"Like accepting even mountain lions as belonging to the community?" Nara interrupted.

"Mountain lions, goats, and peculiar people who've made wrong choices and have peculiar habits. The list goes on and on.

But, what I'm talking about is not the list. I'm talking about the freedom to love in every situation. It's resistance to that freedom that keeps this community; and even this entire planet; from expressing the love of God in the multitude of different expressions God has created through his people and giving people hope."

"So," Nara concluded. "We are going to have a battle with a bunch of dragons and hairballs and probably some other weird things, and that will make everything different?"

"What Jesus told me is that you will be taken into the second heaven and . . ."

"I'm going alone?" Nara choked. "Shouldn't *you* be leading the battle?"

"Jesus is the Commander-in-Chief." Roee replied. "He is leading the battle. Strategically, he has already won the war. Tactically, you just need to go in and fight the battle as if you already won. And when we're done, we'll have a clean platform to build on."

"What you just said is too big for lion brains. I don't get it."

"You will when it's over."

"I think I'll go sharpen my claws on a tree and think about that."

Roee laughed. "Listen, Nara. You and I are going to pray. Then I'm going into this farmhouse and pray with the rest of the team. What the intercessors do here is vital to what you do there. Whatever the Lord tells you to do, just do it. It's really very simple for everybody involved."

A wave of song swept over Nara and Roee as they prayed. The energy in the song swept away Nara's uncertainties and filled him with confidence. In the emotion of the moment he found it hard to stand still and sprung about as he sang praises.

The urge to run impelled him down the driveway from the farmhouse toward the road. Stretch, grab, pull; it felt good to reach and propel faster like the chase of a hunt.

He heard a familiar voice say, "Come up here!" The invitation parted the farm scene in front of him and he ran up into the spiritual atmosphere over Little Faith. He could see a wall separating Little Faith from Lawless. He was so united with peacefulness of the moment, he simply knew what to do and where to go without being told. The nature of the day's battle would be waged for the Little Faith community. Lawless would be another day.

An ominous cloud caught his attention, and he closed in on it. A bright arc discharged through the cloud, and out of it scattered serpent-like creatures with short legs and wolf-faced beings with biped bodies. A thunder shook the beings and they responded in angry snarls.

The muscles in Nara's chest and legs flexed and relaxed as he overtook the demons. He clawed the first man-wolf, spun it upward to set up his next move. An unseen whoosh removed its head and the body went limp. The unexpected assistance distracted him. He pushed the disruption aside and regained focus. He cast the carcass away, then set off in pursuit of others. The ease and timing he had to catch and dispatch his enemies was obviously from outside help. The Hunter was fighting Nara's battle although he couldn't figure how.

From the moment the confrontation started Nara held an advantage. He knew it was the prayer team at work along with the efforts of other unseen warriors. Even when the enemy shifted strategy to over-power Nara with superior numbers a shift in the atmosphere stalled their counter-offensive in confusion.

Nara realized that the spiritual heavens above Little Faith was nearly clean. He now understood what Roee meant when he said, "You will when it's over."

What was left of the demonic forces was retreating in loud objections beyond the wall into Lawless. His work for the moment was finished. As he rested, he looked toward the dividing wall and the town of Lawless beyond it. It was dark shadowed and dingy. On the wide wall were grotesque and defiant creatures that kept the wall alive. He didn't know how he knew, but he knew each stone was a betrayal, killing or surrender to hopelessness. Although it looked formidable, it would come down.

"Yes, Nara," said a young female voice to the left of him. "With Jesus' help, they will be conquered. By faith, they are already defeated. But they will not give up until they are destroyed"

A she-goat wearing leather armor stood next to him. She was bearing two swords on each side of her body that gave her an appearance as having wings. Her countenance radiated confidence and purpose.

"What is your name?"

"My name is Carrie, and I was sent to help you."

"You anticipated my moves and turns and struck with perfect timing. I am fortunate to have had you at my side. Thank you."

"I volunteered for the assignment, Nara. Jesus honored my persistence and let me come."

Nara studied her face as she spoke. The memory of her connected. "I was not very kind to you at one time. I remember taking your life rather cruelly." He lowered his head humbly and added, "Please, forgive me."

"There is little need to do what is already done. Everything works together for the good of Papa God's eternal purposes. I would not be here to help you unless it happened the way it did. And I am glad to be here. Someday, the others will be here along with you and your family. That will be glorious, won't it?"

Nara's heart skipped. "My family?"

Carrie giggled and said, "Yes you silly lion, you will have a family."

As Carrie and Nara talked, angels gathered from throughout the area. One angel approached to interrupt Nara and Carrie's conversation.

"Well done, warriors . . . But you will have to talk later. It's time for Nara to return.

Carrie skipped over to Nara, touched his nose with hers and disappeared.

"Come with me," The angel said. He turned and moved toward the wall of division between Lawless and Little Faith. As the angelic captain stood in position above and near the wall, the demonic watchers gathered to protest the intrusion. The angel showed no concern.

Nara saw flames in some of the windows and doors. And a vine of thorns grew throughout the town that reached toward everything with light. There was darkness where it grew and dimness where it sought to grow. The sounds of torment were profoundly penetrating.

"What you see and hear, Nara, are the schemes of the enemy and the cries of their captives. You and your praying army will conquer all with the help of the Lord of Hosts. With him, nothing is impossible. When the time is appointed, you will return here and fight this darkness.

"Tell the intercessors we will guard their advance as long as the community continues in love and unity. If they neglect to do so, today's progress will be lost . . . Go in peace and make your report."

When Nara turned about, he was standing in front of Roee in the living room of the farmhouse. Nara shook his head and Roee jerked.

"I've done that before." Roee reacted and then laughed. "It's quite a head shaker, isn't it?"

Nara looked around and said, "It's so different here."

The others in the prayer group sat, surprised by Nara's sudden entry, but with expectant looks on their faces.

"Do you think they're waiting to hear something from me?" Nara asked Roee. "Maybe I should tell you, and you could pass it on."

Roee looked at Nara amused, then understood Nara's reluctance. "Take courage my friend. One must be strong to bring changes to old realities." Roee chuckled and added, "It's time to man up to your new role. Or maybe I should say lion down in your case."

Nara rolled his eyes and said, "Funny. . . I could use some water."

Jake brought a bowl of cool water. Nara drank then gave his report of the actual events and passed on the message the angel had given him.

Jake, the owner of the grocery store in Little Faith, stepped forward after that chuckling, and said with a raised hand, "Am I the only one that feels awkward about this moment?" The elephant left the room, the people laughed then relaxed.

"Good. Because the angel that Nara quoted said something we cannot afford to overlook. Church history records spiritual gains made in one generation that was lost by neglect in successive ones. Just because the messenger is a mountain lion doesn't mean we should take less heed to the message. But I get the warning. Are we in this for the long haul? Can we keep our love on for the rest of our lives and pass the vision on when we're done? Those are sobering thoughts to consider. And I know all of you want to finish well as much as I do.

"From what I understand, we've been given a new day and a clean slate free of the generational baggage that has kept this community divided. Winning this revolution isn't a one-time deal. Occupation of what we've won takes a resolve to move what we have forward and create something beautiful. I think that's called a reformation. And if we keep our eyes on the Lord, he'll show us how to do it.

"Can we say 'Yes, Lord' to that?"

A hearty response followed.

"Nara, I don't know how to be friends with a mountain lion. It's way outside my grasp as a goat herder and as a farmer. But, I think we can figure it out somehow. Can you think of anything we have in common?"

Nara squinted one eye and looked back at Jake curiously. "I like goats."

A RESTING PLACE

They insisted that he take it. No doubt, they meant to be generous. He took the hefty chunk of frozen salmon in his mouth, thanked them with a look and went outside. Nara sat on the veranda pondering why humans made such a fuss about talking and eating. He wondered if humans ever needed to hunt to satisfy hunger or if they experienced pleasure being alone in wide and spacious surroundings.

He could be alone and not be lonely. Solitude was a dear friend. His thoughts wandered without aim because he was drained and longed for a shady mountain spot to stretch out and rest. He sighed.

Nara had heard the baby crying as Dodee moved around the house trying to quiet her. She was nursing her by the time she walked out carrying Rachel and let the screen door close softly.

"It seems," Dodee said, "that Rachel likes being outside as much as you do."

"What I want is to be up there, Mama Shepherd." He pointed to the mountains with his nose. "Give me the fresh air and the mountain life I was created for, and I'll be a happy cat."

"I feel the same way, Nara," Dodee responded. "It's a wonderful blessing to live where I belong."

Mama Shepherd paused then looked at Nara. "You know . . . you don't have to stay here and be human. The first battle is won. The team had a great experience and will be here when Jesus plans the next battle. You have *my* permission if you want to leave. Papa God will put the next thing together when the time comes."

Nara looked at Dodee startled. "Was I trying to fit in?" He paused, chuckled at himself and added, "I was . . . Thank you for pointing that out. Tell Papa Shepherd I am looking forward to seeing him soon."

"Come and visit us, Nara. You're always welcome"

Nara nodded his head while thinking about the direction he would take back to the mountains. He sniffed Rachel's head, rubbed her ear with his cheek, then smiled and bounced down the steps.

Walking briskly toward the fields west of town, Nara encountered different responses from people. Pleasant surprise by some, fear by others, a pointing finger by children and even nervous laughter. Someone addressed him by name. He responded politely and kept going. When the populace was behind him, he set off on an impelling run. Catching a coyote unawares in tall grass, Nara laughed freely and gave it a spirited chase then relented. He considered the notion that the coyote was annoyed for being played with. "He'll get over it." A short rest and Nara headed for the foothills and what was beyond.

By late afternoon Nara was up the front range of the mountains anticipating one of his favorite high places among rocks and ridges. He stopped to fill up on the serenity and sniffed the breeze flowing up the mountain. There was a familiar scent on the wind but couldn't remember what it was.

His eye caught movement just below him, so he quickly crouched and waited. Tawny fur strolled into the open, drawing an involuntary gasp from Nara. He stood as she looked up in surprise. Her beauty matched the scent, and he went to her. She extended her nose to take in the musk of his odor and she smiled. Her lips parted before she rolled on the ground. Her eyes invited a response. He would not resist.

A Frightening Reality

Unsettledness crept in with occasional thoughts about his former life as a pimp living in Lawless. He saw himself back on the streets talking with familiar people about his new life. But something about the idea resisted and caused him to question. Shamus reminded himself that he was done with that life and would never go back. He remembered the danger, the craziness and the lives he ruined. He ended up preoccupied with pushing thoughts of guilt away.

After that, blame showed up to accuse him of injuries he inflicted against people in the sex trade that ended in brokenness and injury. He prayed and read scriptures that insured his forgiveness for everything he had ever done. He was a new creation unlike what he had been. At the end of the day, the assault against him was gone and he slept peacefully.

The next day was a work day in the garden with Roee. The early morning banter was refreshing and laughable in the valley's crisp air. Dialogue morphed into a rhythm of weeding and pruning. Kid goats paced the other side of the fence waiting for fresh snippets. Shamus was near the fence taking a water break and talking with his favorite audience when the goats deserted him for fresh cuttings from Papa Shepherd on the other side of the garden. Roee saw what happened and laughed heartily.

"Betrayal from the hands of a friend are the deepest wounds indeed. Sorry Shamus, they are a fickle lot." Although meant to be harmless, it triggered shame.

Hatch stood in front of him. It wasn't real, but it was as clear as the last time he saw him. Shamus saw his face as it looked when he told Hatch he was leaving the streets for a life with Jesus. Now he knew what that look was. In Hatch's eyes, Shamus had betrayed him.

Shamus had been thinking about Hatch and the others involved with him. Hatch was his former business partner during his days in Lawless. But their relationship started long before they came to town. Their childhood had left the same brutal imprints and together they determined to overcome them. As much as people on the street can be, they were friends. Trust issues kept them from getting really close. But Hatch and Shamus got closer than most.

When Shamus left the streets, their association was fractured. Hatch's world demanded alliances to survive. And Shamus knew when he walked away, he was leaving Hatch vulnerable. But he had to go.

He couldn't remember Hatch's last words, but the wretched look on his face was difficult to forget. It wasn't fear or anger; it was something else. Now Shamus knew that pained look was the face of betrayal. He felt compassion for Hatch, but guilt for his actions kept him from pursuing return and showing authentic kindness.

Shamus talked with Roee about the three-day journey he'd been on. What questions arose had no answers that satisfied Shamus.

Shamus was exhausted and slept deeply. He dreamed he was with Hatch running desperately. A giant anaconda with red eyes and spitting bullets chased them. They ran bare foot slogging through beach sand and making difficult progress. Darkness wrapped around them in a cloud that retched from the snake. Their focus on retreat left little room to anticipate their escape. In the morass, they crashed into a mass of boneless flesh. They bounced off, and landed sitting in front of what looked like a leering eel with drooping lips and carnivorous teeth. The snake arrived to book-end their capture.

Even in the low visibility Shamus could see they were undone. Before they could rethink their possibilities, the hulking eel swallowed them.

Unharmed, they went headlong down the ogre's gullet. Their fall was deep and intense heat increased as they fell. Fire could be seen at the bottom. They bounced into cavernous obsidian and quickly scrambled away from a nearby inferno. As Hatch reached for a boulder to steady himself, the mere touch of it tormented his mind and spirit. Hatch's face exploded with the horror of knowing where he was.

What appeared to be tentacles, came out of the fire, wrapped around Hatch and pulled him toward the fire. Hatch was petrified with terror; his quivering eyes looking back at him with uncontrollable panic. He was too stricken to make noise, but Shamus could read his mouth as he tried to scream, "Help me Shamus! Save me."

Shamus couldn't move. His arms and legs felt enclosed in a wrapper. Out of crushing despair, he yelled, "Nooooooooooooo!"

Shamus woke up, tangled in his sleeping bag. He was not hurt, but certainly not unaffected. "Hell is real," he screamed.

Shamus fell to his knees and agonizing for Hatch's deliverance from an eternity without God. If Hatch were killed by the evil that surrounded him, that fiery chamber would be his lot. The likelihood of it broke his heart.

Shamus groaned deeply for Hatch. He bore the intercession as if the dream was a frightening reality. Hatch was in danger; the dream a prophetic warning. It *wasn't* too late. Shamus peeled off his sleeping bag and stumbled out of the tent. He shivered from the cold morning air and the adrenaline rush.

"Hatch deserves an encounter with Jesus," he declared. "I have to go see him."

He reached back in the tent for a jacket and put it on. In the teal blue of predawn Shamus paced as he considered how to approach Hatch. Running boots pounded closer.

"Shamus, I heard you calling out. You sounded terrified."

"I *was* terrified! . . . I still am"

Roee reached out for him.

"Hell is *real,* Roee . . . I was there . . I felt the heat. I saw the agony."

Goats streamed in from the pasture and questions rolled out. Through tears, Shamus attempted to answer.

"I can't stand the thought of *anyone* going to hell after experiencing that. I wasn't there more than a minute. I would have gone insane if I'd been there any longer.

"Roee, I need to go into Lawless right away."

"I wanna go," rejoined Maria. "I'd like to visit some other humans."

"Yeah, me too," followed Rosie. "I've been wondering what we were going to do with these gifts we've been given."

"I better speak up before the Jeep gets full," declared Scampy. "I want to be part of this!"

"And I want to be in it too," exclaimed Finnegan. "I could use an adventure."

Shamus broke loose from his anguish by their enthusiasm. He looked at Roee for his approval, not knowing how to respond.

"Can I take these guys with me? Hatch might listen to talking goats."

Roee pondered why it would be smarter to *not* let them go

and couldn't come up with a satisfactory reason for not allowing it. Shamus' moving plea about Hatch formed an emotion-filled response.

"I think . . . it might be a good experience for them," stated Roee with a grimaced uncertainty in his face.

"Yeah," rejoined Shamus to reinforce the idea, "it would be great to take you guys with me."

"How are you going to keep us from falling out of the Jeep, Shamus?" asked Finnegan.

Roee turned to Shamus. "Maybe you could pull the back seats out to make room for them and put rope around the roll cage to keep them from falling out. Let's build some safety into this mission."

"Sure, that's easy," responded Shamus.

"And when you get there Shamus, get another person to go along for backup. I'll call ahead and let them know you're coming."

"Good idea, Roee. Maybe they could meet us there."

"I'll call when you're on the road."

It took an hour to remove the seats and secure ropes around the roll cage of the Jeep. The four got inside to see how they fit and jumped out to readjust the heights on the roping.

Gassed up and ready, it was time to make the call. Roee found Jake in his store in Little Faith.

"Save the minutes on your sat phone," Jake concluded after hearing the game plan. "I'll pass the word around."

The adventurers got on their way as they settled in for the bumpy trip out of the valley.

"Whatever the cost, Father," Shamus prayed with urgency. "Make a way to save him. Don't let our courage fail us. "

UNEXPECTED RESPONSE

The goats played off the tightly pulled ropes while the Jeep bucked and swayed over the unimproved trail leading out of the valley. Their play ended when Shamus observed injury being an outcome, and they turned to creating ridiculous songs. With a little collaboration from Shamus, the quartet managed a nice diddee.

We are bouncing off the ropes that help us make our moves
We have everything we need to keep us on our hooves
I'm rolling . . . with every groove I'm rolling
I wanna play, I just can't sway, yes I'm rolling.

Feeling like some kids, we're jumping up and down,
Butting head to head, we're just acting like some clowns
We're bouncing . . . with every rut, we're bouncing.
Off the ropes, we ain't no dopes, yes we're bouncing.

Once they reached pavement, the ride smoothed out and the hiccup beat of the rut and groove song changed considerably. The goats, with Shamus joining, were a picture of considerable enthusiasm.

At the end of another verse, Rosie spoke up, "Hey Shamus, I gotta pee. Can I go in the Jeep?"

"Can you hold on a minute?" Shamus responded nervously. "Thanks for asking."

He spotted a lush patch of meadow ahead as they approached the northern edge of Lawless. He pulled over slowly to keep everyone upright and said, "Stretch your legs and get a bite while you're at it."

The troupe piled out and eagerly indulged in the tall grass.

"Are you going to join us?" asked Scampy mischievously.

"Why don't you go first and let me know how it tastes, Scamp." Shamus responded. "I'm pretty new to this gourmet grass thing."

Rosie shouted back her report, "Tastes like chicken, Shamus."

"Cordon bleu sans doute," Shamus rejoined in red-neck French.

"Huh?" . . . "What?" they reacted.

"It's from the French language and it roughly means 'of the finest quality no doubt.' It's something I learned in school."

"What's a school?" Finnegan asked.

Cupping his chin with his right hand, and his other arm across his body Shamus thought for a moment. He smiled and raised his eye brows. "It's a flock of fish, Finnegan."

Finnegan was busy eating and didn't catch playful hook. He lifted his head and said with his mouth full, "Do fish shpeak the Frensh languashe too?"

"No, they speak Fishlips. It's a system of tail wags and lip puckers. It's very interesting to watch . . . kind of like this." Shamus demonstrated by cupping his hands around his mouth and puckering. He then bent over slightly to wag his behind like a fish. Then he did a little two-step and ended with his arms stretched out to the side. "Give it a try."

"I can do that," said Maria. She then wagged her stubby tail, formed her lips like a horse laugh and said something unintelligible.

"Is that it, Shamus?"

"That's perfect Maria. But, what was that you said?"

"I don't know." She giggled. "I thought you knew. Weren't you in school?"

"I don't speak Fishlips. It's an extinct language. What *I* said was French."

"It stinks?" responded Finnegan. "I can't smell and talk at the same time. They must be amazing people."

"Yes, they sure are." The ad lib had run its course and Shamus' thoughts returned to Hatch. The idea of walking to give him time to pray came to mind, "Let's walk the rest of the way and leave the Jeep here. The exercise will do us good."

The band strolled into Lawless. At the intersection near the train station, they chatted it up with curious passersby. One person referred to Shamus as James, his old street name. That caused questions. Shamus explained how he'd used another name in those days but nobody asked why.

"What's with the dog and pony show, James?" asked a familiar voice with a mocking tone. It was the flavor of the hard-heartedness of the street. Memories flooded in as he turned around.

The next question was deliberately challenging, "What the hell are *you* doing back in this neighborhood?"

"I came to see you, Hatch."

Hatch had a coarse complexion from too many years of not eating well. His dark hair was a curly bush that he ceased trying to control, and he was slightly taller than Shamus with less muscle mass. The combination gave onlookers the impression that he was a weakling and an easy mark. Hatch made up for it by being intense and invincible. Like Shamus, Hatch had grown up with abuse and constant anxiety. He hadn't known a father's love and his mother had been like the girls he kept in his brood; victims who had fallen prey to predators. Parental alcohol and drug use kept daily provision and affection from his personal security. He left home when he had had enough.

He was an expert in the protocols of street life. Shamus' exit as a partner left Hatch's back without eyes. Exposed and vulnerable, fear forced him to act tougher, grow harder and keep people away from the pain.

"What the flip for James? You gave up this turf when you bailed on me. The only reason I can think of that you want to see me is that you want back in. That ain't gonna happen, *homey*. I don't want you here."

"I had a *dream* about you Hatch," Shamus said as he moved a few steps closer. "You're on the mafia's radar and they want you dead. I came to warn you and get you to turn to God before it's too late. God loves you more than you can possibly imagine. And I don't want you to get killed. Please, let me tell you about Jesus and pray with you."

"That's sweet, you had a dream!" Hatch said with mocking. Anger was in his next words. "That was a wonky-sized pizza dream, James. You're talking trash. I know you know what's goin' on here. Somebody is always wanting to kill us. You know that. It's nothing new. Dude . . . it comes with this freaking lifestyle."

"Hatch," Shamus interrupted, "this dream was *real*. I saw us getting pulled into the flames of hell. It was the most horrible thing I've ever experienced. I'm afraid for you. I want to help you."

"Get out of my territory. I've worked hard to protect all this, and no goat mafia is gonna get their horns into me and get me saved. I've heard all the 'come to Jesus' stuff before."

"Then you know they're after you?" rejoined Shamus.

"Sure they are. They always have been!" responded Hatch with frustration. "Like I said, it's nothing new. When *you* were around, I didn't have to worry about it.

"And who do you think you are, to think they're not after you? But no, you're up there hiding out in the mountains rustling goats and teaching them to talk instead of helping me fight off the wonky bad guys."

There was more fear in Hatch's eyes as he got louder. Dealing with Shamus' abandonment and betrayal must have been triggering emotions from childhood. For lack of wisdom Shamus turned defensive.

"I found love, Hatch. It's God's love. I just don't belong here anymore. I wish I never did."

"Well, *damn you* for finding love, James. You took what love I knew when you left. There ain't no more love around here!" Hatch was nearly shouting and leaving space between words. "You don't know what you're talking about!"

"Hatch, give God your anger and pain," Shamus pleaded. He understood the deep wounds he was unintentionally reopening, but inexperience couldn't bring healing to them. The conversation was getting out of control, and his anxiety was going there, too. Ignorantly, he leaned harder on what he understood. "I can *show* you God's love. These goats can show you God's love. It's more powerful than all the stuff you're feeling. They've *seen* God and can tell you all about Him. I've seen Jesus face to face. He's *real,* Hatch. Real."

Finnegan stepped forward and said big heartly, "It's *true* Hatch. Jesus is real, and he loves you. My ability to talk to you is proof of that."

Hatch snapped, and he screamed, "Nobody loves me, and nobody loves you. If there's love in this world, I've never seen it."

"We are here to love you, Hatch." Finnegan responded vigorously. "Trust us and let us in!"

"You are kidding, right? Trust you? You're a freaking goat! Noooooooo."

Nobody saw Hatch take the gun out . . . He fired twice and Shamus was on the ground. He turned the weapon on the goats with one shot each. Then the stubby revolver was empty and five bodies were on the ground. Everything went black for Shamus.

* * * * * * * * *

"Hi Jake," Roee spoke into the sat phone. "What's up?"

"My brother is on his way to pick you guys up. There's been a shooting. Shamus has been shot, and it doesn't look like he's going to make it. He's lost a lot of blood. Two of the goats are dead and the other two are at the vet's getting patched up. I'm sorry Roee, but we have a mess."

Dodee saw the tears and went to him. "What happened, Roee?"

* * * * * * * * *

Del had left for Wonder Valley before the full story was known. He only knew that Shamus was flown to a hospital in Burnus.

Jake stated on the phone that the sheriff could not release a full report until their investigation was complete. But, rumor was that Shamus provoked the attack. The shooter was arrested without further incident and taken to the Burnus jail.

It was late in the evening when Del, Roee, Dodee and Rachel arrived in Little Faith. Roee and Dodee's only thoughts were of life without Shamus and the goats. Grief and guilt gnawed at them. They should have seen it coming. They agonized. They could have prevented it by being more discerning. Where was Papa God when they needed his warnings?

"Take my car," stated Del, "and you three get up to Burnus. Find out what you can and get back to us. Take my cell phone, and here's a credit card in case you need it."

The Wait

The minutes were a monotonous trudge and emotions exhausted. The steady stream of drama from the waiting room television sucked hope from the atmosphere. Seattle's Best coffee vended caffeine to visitors waiting for reports of family and friends in various states of repair. Only an occasional smile warmed the room.

Roee and Dodee fidgeted, sitting in chairs rated for short durations and a restless Rachel fussed with being stuck in a stroller longer. A minute to minute dose of patience warred against the insistent waiting.

Several hours had passed since their arrival and Shamus had been there several hours before them. According to the first doctor, Shamus flat-lined after he left the ground in a medevac flight from Lawless to Burnus. There had been no word from the people working to save his life since.

"Roee, help me! . . . This waiting . . . and not knowing . . . and it's so stuffy in here."

"Let's take Rachel for a walk," He responded. "The fresh air will help us all."

They headed for an exit.

The moderate night had an immediate effect. "Ah, that's better," Dodee stated as they left the building. "I really feel the ailing of human spirits in there. It's suffocating me."

"We are all ailing, Honey," Roee responded.

"Losing Finny and Rosie is hurting my heart so deeply." Dodee teared up thinking about the loss of her friends. "And the thought of Scampy and Maria hurting from their . . ." She couldn't finish and looked at Roee for support.

He put one arm around her while pushing the stroller. "You know what gets me the most, is that Papa supernaturally rescued Finny. And then we lose him in an act of violence. He was destined for so much more."

"I know you feel responsible . . . letting him go when you weren't really at peace about it." Dodee stated.

"I know we've hashed this over already. But it's hard to escape the fact that I didn't feel right about it." Roee said forcefully. "I let the others influence . . ."

"Stop right there, Roee," Dodee interrupted. She stopped walking and turned him to face her. "We've seen resurrections. We've experienced interventions of all kinds. We can talk for hours about the miracles we've seen . . . This isn't about you or me. I feel the weight of it, too. I could have spoken up if I wasn't comfortable with your decision. All of what happened here lands squarely on Papa's shoulders where it belongs. There is something going on here that only he has the big picture of for now. Finny and Rosie gave their lives for one of the highest purposes God has on this planet. Let's not steal that honor from them by blaming ourselves."

Her words moved Roee. "You are so right my love. In Papa's eyes, they're heroes. And regardless of how hard it is for us, were told to offer him praise. These are sacrifices we can't give when everything is going good. We've faced things like it before when we didn't have children and when we lost everything we owned back in our big city days. We never knew how it would turn out. But we wanted heaven's best then; the gold, the silver and precious gems; even if it comes by fire."

"And it's still what we're after today" Dodee added touching his cheek. "Isn't it?"

The cost of their commitment stirred in their hearts a few moments.

"I'm so glad I chose you," Roee said. "This path hasn't been easy. And I wouldn't change a thing. But you treat hardship like it's nothing."

Dodee laughed heartily, which got Rachel laughing as well. "Ohhh, it's something, Love. Trials need to do what they're supposed to do. They're meant to change us inside. Complaining would make it last longer, and I've never known *anyone* to be transformed by complaining."

"Besides, he will bless us when the blessing doesn't distract us from our pursuit of him. It's always worked that way. So, let's just wrap our hearts around some gratitude and move forward."

Roee's smile was warm and connected with Dodee's heart. As they held each other, praise and gratefulness filled the air around them.

* * * * * * * * *

He was surrounded in a cloth room of azure and beige that was drooping and pinging and swooshing. The ceiling was a fuzzy light surrounded by clouds. As his vision cleared, Shamus saw hot air balloons in a rectangular brightness; their colors brilliant red, yellow and blue. He closed his eyes slowly and opened them again. There was a t-shaped tree with two bags of fluid hanging from it. One was a dark color and one clear. His tongue was stuck and he smacked his lips to loosen it. *I can get a drink from one of the bags,* he thought. *The other one must be root beer.*

Why am I here? Where is here? A muzzle blast flashed and his body involuntarily jerked. He groaned with the sudden pain. He was supposed to remember something. *What was that?*

He was clothed in a long shirt that opened at the side. A

snake was attached to the front and breathing warm air over his cold skin. The sight of it made him snigger. The mama snake was outside the curtain and it parted quickly to save its baby. He gasped, then groaned in pain.

The woman that greeted him turned on a comforting smile. He couldn't remember ever seeing a smile like that. She was beautiful like a princess in a story book. Her name tag said "MiSeon." Dark, Asian eyes contrasted with her pearlescent teeth. Her long, black hair framed her innocent features.

A warm harpoon poked through his chest and out the back. *That's . . . that's cupid's arrow*, he thought and slowly reached for the spot.

"That's where one of the bullets entered your chest Shamus. There's another slightly larger hole in your back, which will leave quite a manly scar," MiSeon said lightly. "It should make for impressive bragging rights."

Shamus laughed, revealing another pain in his upper leg.

"Ohhhh, what happened there?"

"That's where the *other* bullet found you . . . You should cherish that one. Given all good probabilities," MiSeon continued smiling, "you should thank God you are still alive and, in this world . . . And, someday you will have children."

"Only if I can have them with you," he said without thinking. He winced, but not in pain. "I'm sorry," he added.

"It's the medications, Mister Breen. It may be a while before you regain your dignity. You will be in here for a couple hours or so and then we'll put you in a shared room. Depending on what happens with infection, you might be out of here in a week or so."

"Okay. That didn't make sense."

"You'll get your mind back when the meds wear off."

"How do you pronounce your name?" Shamus asked.

"It sounds like *me*," she said pointing to herself then pointed up. "And you will be out of here soon to enjoy the light of the *sun*. Me . . sun."

"That's beautiful. What does it mean?"

"It means," she said laughing, "you have visitors waiting to see you. They can stay for only a short while, and we will need to keep close watch with you until you get moved."

"Seriously Me . Sun, what does it mean?"

In Korean language it means "beauty and kindness."

"I'm sure it is very true of you, MiSeon."

"Thank you, Mister Breen," she answered politely. "So, do you want to know how you are on the inside?"

"Well, so far it feels like I'm okay."

"The meds are helping you with that. You had some minor organ damage. The surgeons have put you back together quite well and you should live to a very old age. You lost a lot of blood. But we found it and put it back in. And when the time is right, we will return the use of your super powers. Until then you will feel tired."

Shamus couldn't stifle the laughter and punctuated his laughs with ohs and ouches.

"Everything considered, though, you have a future."

"Thank you, Jesus," responded Shamus with watery eyes. "I guess my work here on Earth isn't done yet, MiSeon. Thanks for taking good care of me . . . And, please forgive me for my earlier remark. I don't talk to women like that anymore."

She smiled and said, "Your friends are waiting Shamus. Are you ready to see them?"

"Not really. . . . All this didn't have to happen. It was stupid . .

. Is it normal to be this emotional with the meds?"

"There are different reactions. You will be prone to waves of emotion for a while."

"Is that why you make me laugh?"

"Laughter is a good medicine. Contrary to all that you've read, no one has died laughing . . . at least not in this hospital."

Shamus chuckled painfully then sighed as if searching for courage. "I shouldn't keep them waiting. Have them come in."

MiSeon found Dodee and Roee in the waiting room wrapping up a chat with the surgeon. She got acquainted with Rachel while the doctor finished his remarks. When the doctor walked away, MiSeon introduced herself and prepared them for Shamus' physical and emotional readiness to see them. When she was satisfied that they understood, she walked them to Shamus' post-op cubicle.

Upon arrival, the surgeon was giving Shamus his full report.

The three stood exchanging hearts while the doctor and Shamus took care of business. Dodee and MiSeon bonded immediately. Roee looked Shamus over compassionately. When the doctor left, Roee went in while the ladies continued their exchange.

"Well cowboy, how does it feel to be on the losing side of the OK Corral?" said Roee. "It's possible you won't make a good marshal."

"I better take up a different occupation, Papa Shepherd," returned Shamus. "I didn't pull that off very good . . . I have a mind to go back to goat herding."

MiSeon interrupted, "I have other patients to see. I'll be back in a while."

She left without waiting for a response.

Dodee was smiling. "Nice girl, eh Shamus?"

"She's gorgeous," he responded with a deep breath. "And she just lights up the room." Shamus gestured as he spoke, which gave him a wave of pain. Wincing, he continued. "I embarrassed myself by talking stupid while I was waking up. I hope she won't hold it against me."

Dodee and Roee exchanged sidelong glances.

"I wouldn't give it another thought, Shamus," Dodee said.

"Wow," said Shamus giving them a blinking look. "I'm glad to see you guys this side of heaven."

Roee was holding Rachel while she napped. And choking back a response, Roee touched Shamus' foot, not knowing where he could touch him without causing pain. "We almost lost a dear friend, Shamus."

Dodee nodded in agreement and gently fingered Shamus' shoulder.

"So tell me, how did things go after I left? I don't remember anything until I woke up here."

"It wasn't good Shamus. This may not be a good time to talk about it."

"Come on, I have to know."

Roee sighed with reluctance. "Hatch shot the others after he shot you . . . We lost Finnegan and Rosie. Scampy and Maria were wounded, but they'll recover."

Shamus wasn't prepared for the news of Finnegan and Rosie. They had been a major part of his early growth and taught him about love and hope, almost as if they were family. They were good friends.

Through tears he asked, "I know you must have prayed for them. What happened?"

"Papa heard us Shamus," Roee stated. "We know that much to be true. But he didn't give them back to us this time . . . We'll know why when it's time.

"Hatch is in jail for attempted murder. It's odd, Shamus, but he didn't run. I was told he just sat down and waited for the Sheriff to show up. He's here in Burnus for arraignment."

Shamus looked into Roee's eyes and said, "It's hard to have friends on the streets, not like you and I are friends. But Hatch and me, we had each other's backs when there were threats against our turf. In those days, I saw people like Hatch and me through very different eyes. I knew what he was thinking. And I definitely knew what he was feeling. I should have known better, but I wasn't thinking. I'm afraid I didn't handle the situation very well.

"There was a way out for me and I *knew* there was hope for him. I kept pressing the issue and I pressed too hard . . . But I won't give up on him. And Papa won't give up on him." Shamus smiled. "And the goats won't give up on him. You'll see.

"And I know . . . I'll have to be here when he goes to trial, so I can visit him before he gets out on bail."

"We'll figure out a way to do that when you get released from here," Roee stated.

Dodee cleared her throat gently. "I think MiSeon would like it if you came back for a visit."

Shamus looked at her and said with a sigh, "I'd like to believe that."

"Papa can do anything, Shamus," Dodee declared. "With that in mind, let's pray for your healing."

JAILHOUSE

"Your Jesus is a funny one, Shamus," the doctor opined. "To heal your leg and not heal your torso just isn't logical. Think about it, you could have been released a week ago instead of today. This miracle business is a mysterious wonder."

Shamus had his own opinion and wanted to speak out. Truth was, he got to stay longer and have time with MiSeon. He resisted the temptation to straighten the man out and rejoined instead, "Doc, some things only Jesus can explain."

"Next time *I* see him," the doctor stated skeptically, "we'll have a chat about it. But in the meantime, MiSeon can wheel you out of the building since she's not on duty. I'll see you in a week or so." His face said he was satisfied with having the last word, and walked away.

"Well," MiSeon sighed with a chuckle and grabbed the wheel chair. She pushed it in front of Shamus and set the brakes. "Let's get you out of here. Have a seat and buckle up. I like to get a little speed on these things."

Outside, half a dozen cheery smiles were waiting when the automatic doors opened. Well-wishing questions and comments muddled together in a joyful noise as MiSeon rolled him to Shamus' Jeep at the porte cochere. He stood to the extended arms of offered hugs then stepped back and took a deep breath. Hi grimaced with a little reminder of his wound then said, "Oh that fresh air smell is worth the pain."

"Eau de sanitary is a great perfume, Shamus," MiSeon quipped. "I've been thinking of starting my own line with that fragrance."

"Yeah MiSeon," Shamus reacted with an arm sweep spreading a fake banner in front of him. "'Preferred by eight out of nine Himalayan Sherpas and their llamas.' The marketing strategy has enormous potential."

"Ha," reacted Jake. "You guys have been practicing. Great come-back."

"Well Shamus," Roee set up. "We took a poll and everybody figured you were ready for a nice meal. Is there any place you want to go?"

"I really would like to see Hatch," Shamus responded. "Can we do that?"

"I think everybody's hungry, Shamus," Dodee stated. "Besides, don't you have to make an appointment?"

"I have to try," pleaded Shamus. "Please. I can wait on the food."

* * * * * * * * * *

Hatch sat on the lower bunk with his back to the wall and his arms wrapped around his thin legs. It wasn't his first time in a jail and he was brooding about the social challenges that had closed in on him. With a half-million dollars bail for a second degree attempted murder charge, there was little chance his cell door would fly open any time soon. There was no clever magic that would make the concerns about his future vanish.

Nagging doubts chatter boxed his time with the idea that getting a competent public defender was unlikely. He fought the incessant looping thoughts with hopes for a plea bargain that would reduce the charge to aggravated assault. Then there were the animal cruelty charges and the concealed carry violation and, and . . . and. And maybe there were extra-terrestrials hiding in a rainforest nearby that would zap a hole in the building and abduct him. He was tired from endless thinking.

He had heard somewhere that if he pressed his tongue hard against the roof of his mouth, the internal monologue would stop. As soon as he tried that, his cellmate started an abusive denunciation of the current Department of Justice head. Bones would lobby for bigger cells and better meals and thicker mattresses. He was entitled as a citizen.

His wonky over grown cell mate puked a constant flow of negativity and insisted that he be called Bones. He said his real name sounded weak, so he used the nickname to intimidate would be predators . . . like Hatch.

Bones was annoying, constantly prying, clueless about respecting boundaries and touted jailhouse lawyer status. Bones took up a lot of invisible space and made the cell feel smaller than it really was.

The atmosphere was draining him like a krypton cape. Time would force him to accept the idea that he wasn't going home, so he was trying to make up his mind to resist the downward spiral and suck it up.

Considering what James said just before he shot him, maybe it was better to be in the slammer than on the streets where nefarious people had access to him. *Now there's a wonky outlook*, he thought with ironic amusement. *The bad guys want me dead and the only safe place I got is in this freaking cell. That's poetic.*

He still didn't understand how it all happened. Something was said that blew down his steely composure like a house of cards in a wind gust. He was jealous of one of his own tribe for actually finding a way out of the hand from hell they all had been dealt. Card one.

James and the goats had more real love than he could draw from. What he had was trumped. He was lost and he knew it. That realization was intolerable. Card two.

Hatch did not understand where the old street thug named James had gone, but now that he had time to think, he realized Shamus had really changed. He wasn't playing hidden cards. Even his face was different. It was ugly with tenderness. His eyes had warmth, and he scanned Hatch's face as if he knew something about Hatch that Hatch did not know about himself. The cold, hard eyes were gone.

Having a talking goat tell him about God's love was the squall that toppled his house. Hatch had to stop the penetration; it hurt and he didn't know why. Card three. He pulled the gun; he had to win at any cost. His body jerked at the remembrance of the revolver's first shot. He doesn't remember emptying the gun. But when it was over, the pain and loneliness was still there. In despair, he sat down and waited.

I wish I could stop thinking . . .

"Vincent Williams, you have a visitor."

The second call on the intercom caused Hatch to realize they called his given name. He left that name behind years ago to hide his identity. No one in Lawless knew it . . . except for James. As deep in navel gazing as he'd been, he probably wouldn't have heard his street name had it been called.

The guard came and escorted Hatch to the visitor center.

Their walk was filled with shallow chatter. Hatch's opinion was that the guards weren't allowed to say anything useful. No matter how you cut it, to see a *real* person behind the badge wasn't safe. It was jailhouse protocol to maintain distance with correctional officers.

As he entered the room, reflections off the partition glass prevented Hatch from seeing who was waiting for him on the visitor side. As he approached the cubicle, the glare diminished and he recognized the face sitting in the freedom chair. He picked up the intercom handset.

"You don't wear *dead* very well, James. Somebody's gotta learn to lock and load a little better."

"You just knocked the wind out of me, Hatch," responded Shamus.

"Cute, James . . . Yeah, you Irish can take a roundhouse and stay on your feet. Tough guys you are."

"Eight hundred years of oppression has made us wee folk very tough, Hatch."

"I see . . . I think they call that *blarney* in your old country," Hatch continued. The banter reflected on old times they had. "We English have another perspective."

"That depends on whether you're reading Irish history or English history."

Hatch combed his hair with his fingers, and looked at Shamus like he was from another galaxy. He took his seat and said trying to sound annoyed, "You didn't come here to chat history with me, James. As lovely a time as I'm having with our Irish and English drama, I don't see why you're here."

"You're still alive, Hatch," Shamus said warmly.

"I tried to ki . . ." Hatch caught himself. "See, I won't make a confession here, James . . . Let me remind you . . . you're still alive too, and I'm in the slammer. What's changed?"

"You're in this cozy retreat center and away from the mafia hitters who wanted you dead. That's changed. What I'm hoping for, is that with you off the streets, they'll just take over your turf and leave you alone. And as long as you're here I want to do what I can to keep you company."

"Ahhhh, that's sweet of you," rejoined Hatch rolling his eyes. "You know they only allow two visits a week. So what are we going to do in between to keep this romance going?"

Shamus let the sarcasm roll off with a shrug and a smile.

"I appreciate your positive vibes and all. But do you realize," Hatch continued, "the mob has people in here too?"

The conversation stalled.

"You know, James, you might have a point. I heard Guido and company, or whatever wonky name they're using, came looking for me the day after . . . our event. If I had been in Lawless, I might be sleeping on a coroner's slab instead of this cozy retreat center . . . Isn't it brilliant? I get myself incarcerated for attempted murder to escape getting killed, see. And in some weirdly twisted sort of way, I should be thanking *you* for getting in front of those bullets."

Shamus smiled, took a breath, and let it out. "I've been praying for you Hatch. And I have it from a reliable source that you will not die until you find real life."

"You're talking like your goat peeps. They're a cute bunch of talking heads."

"No, I'm talking about my friend Jesus. He knows who you are, Hatch. Or should I say he knows the Vincent you were created to be. The real you. He loves who you are with more passion than you can possibly comprehend."

Hatch scrunched his eyes and rubbed the back of his neck with his right hand while cradling the receiver with his left. He sighed at Shamus trying to be patient . . . then he softened.

"James, if this Jesus could find the likes of what you used to be and turn you into this . . ." Hatch raised his free hand and extended it toward Shamus. "this freaky spirit of kindness, then maybe . . ." He took in and held a breath and for a moment felt hopeful.

His persona of holding his own with James had been an emotional exercise of treading water since the beginning of the conversation. But the pain of a childhood monstrously off-center flooded his hope and drowned it. His resignation to a victim's existence without a life line was familiar; it's what he knew how to navigate. For now, he just couldn't see how to get where James was.

Shamus watched Hatch's thoughts play out in his facial expressions and searched for words of consolation. He understood Hatch's conflict and wanted to fix it. Hearing Roee's instructions to avoid forcing a decision, he knew Hatch had to choose life for his own sake. He let his countenance express the love he felt for this man.

A Corrections Officer opened the door and interrupted the moment with something Shamus couldn't hear. Hatch looked up, listened to him, then turned to Shamus and said, "I gotta go, bro."

"Unless somebody else tries to kill me," Shamus said leaning into the glass, "I'll be back.

Hatch's stare held Shamus while he hung up the receiver. Without looking away Hatch headed for the door, then turned and nodded his head at the officer. Shamus watched him until the door closed. He felt Papa's love in the atmosphere. *Everything's going to work out just fine*, Shamus thought.

"Papa," Shamus interceded quietly, "clear out all the lying voices so Hatch can hear you plainly and choose you without reservation."

He winced as he rose, then walked to the steel doors. He waited for the electronic click in the lock and pushed the door open into the sunny brilliance coming through the picture windows of the visitors waiting area.

* * * * * * * * * *

Hatch returned to his cell quieter of mind than when he

left, but felt a listless resignation about his future. Bones was snoring on the top bunk. He turned as the jailer locked him in then stared through the small window in the door as the guard walked down the stairs to the lower level of the pod.

He closed his eyes and turned, leaned his back against the door and reflected. The low growl jerked his eyes open to what he expected to be Bones, the assassin. What he saw instead unnerved him.

"WHOA! How did you get in here?" Hatch squeaked as his knees buckled.

"Don't be afraid, I won't be long. While you were away I cleaned out your man cave of all the invisible riff raff, and left you a present."

The mountain lion smiled then bounded once toward Hatch, causing him to duck involuntarily, then leapt through the small six inch by twenty-four inch glass in the door and disappeared.

Hatch's heart beat wildly.

"WOW!" he screamed without thinking. "What was *that*?"

Bones bolted upright on the top bunk, the whites of his eyes exposed around his pupils. "Dude . . . you got *serious* issues! They gonna take you to the loony pod."

Raucous laughter echoed from other cells in response to the noise. "The new guy's losing his mind!"

He decided to keep his mouth shut. It wouldn't end well if he responded. Who would believe him? It happened so fast and it was so strange, he had to be hallucinating. Hatch sat on his bunk with his back to the wall and took deep breaths. The experience replayed vividly. It was real, and it was scary. And it was from another world.

"That was crazy," he said to himself.

"You can say that again," Bones rejoined. "You're nuts Hatch."

For an hour Hatch revisited what happened a dozen times. Diverting his thoughts, he lay down and reflected on why someone he'd tried to kill would visit him. Revenge was out of the question. But that's what he would have done. He would act like everything was okay between them, then look for an opportune payback.

"Having a mountain lion in your jail cell," thought Hatch out loud, "isn't normal."

"And goats that talk and have feelings," he continued after a pause. "That ain't normal either."

"Dude, you're talking out of your mind," injected Bones loudly. "What did that guard give you, man?"

Hatch chose silence.

When the adrenaline rush of his encounter wore off, and he was wrung out. He closed his eyes. A nap would be a welcome break from this world.

Maybe I am nuts, he thought to himself and drifted off.

A Home Restored

He was four years old, but didn't know why he knew that. Everything had the sepic hues of antique photographs. He stood in the kitchen within the house where he grew up; the furnishings broken, the odors and their mess familiar.

A drunken war was raging in another part of the house. That was familiar, too.

He was reenacting a documentary of his typical family experience, only he was viewing the aftermath. Angry tirades flashed by as historical battles ran their course. He saw the hiding places that he hoped would protect him but didn't. The scenes lacked the black line and white blip particular to old film, yet a virtual experience.

Vincent wandered the wreckage of his life that was clothed in years of neglect. Fear wrapped around him like a shadow. Now he was ten. He felt nothing. No love, no joy, no peace; he was dead inside. There could be hate; he didn't really know. The light coming through the broken window was as grubby as the unkempt floor. His spirit longed for sunshine. Scars from self-induced cuts were as jagged as the remaining glass in the window frame. He didn't have a good reason for their existence. It was just a reflection of how he used to feel.

An archway led into the dining room. Windows were at the opposite end with the garage's common wall to the right. He went into the dining room in hope of finding food. Plates, glasses and serving dishes on the table were disappointingly empty and dirty. As usual, he was on his own to forage, beg or steal to satisfy his hunger. That's okay, he knew the ropes.

On his way to the other archway, he passed a mirror. Turning to look, it was a reflection of when he was fifteen.

Chair legs slid on the floor and pulled his attention back to the table. A man sat at the opposite end in a high-backed chair that looked like a throne; light brown wood with rich inlays of alabaster and gold. Its arms and back were covered in leather. A bow and a quiver with arrows were draped over one of two finials carved on each side of its back. The man wore camo clothing and a smile that reached for him.

"How long have you been here?" Vince asked quietly.

"I was with you the whole time, Vincent," the hunter responded. He stood, draped quiver and bow over his shoulder, then extended his hand. "Come with me."

Vincent accepted the man's hand.

The dining room led into the living room where the French doors were the main entry of the house. The Hunter opened both doors with a flourish. Fresh air and radiance poured in. Pine fragrance joined the gentle breeze floating through the door. The sepic haze ran away like fog chased by the sun. The brilliant outside colors beckoned him beyond of the gloom of the house.

The boy and The Hunter walked through the door hand in hand and into a world Vincent had never seen. A scene of yellow daffodils in a large green meadow spread out in front of him followed by a forest of pine and leaf in all directions toward surrounding mountains. The serenity ignited a hunger to know peace. When he took in the clean air, he inhaled the aromas of courage and hope. The fragrances infused his heart like a vaccine. His back straightened and he stood taller.

Long haired goats grazed in pockets amongst the abundant fauna of the large meadow. Deer a hundred yards distant raised their heads to inspect the sudden arrivals. Curious, they moved toward him. Fifty yards to his right was a pond where other goats drank quietly. To his left was a quaint log cabin with a woman sitting in a rocking chair on a veranda. She was nursing her child.

The woman stood and called a name he didn't catch. A man appeared from behind the cabin in response. He stopped at the side of the veranda and together the two headed toward the hunter and Vincent. It was obvious by the warm smiles they were good friends. Love colored in *belonging* flew at him like butterflies attracted to blossoms.

A sudden crash behind them caused Vincent to turn. The roof of the home where Vincent once lived had tilted and twisted. As he watched, it folded then fell inside the walls. The walls collapsed over the ruined roof. The ground vibrated then opened. It accepted the wreckage, then closed up without leaving a scar.

The Hunter faced Vincent and reached his hands for the sides of his face.

"Son, I gave my life to heal the damage done to you and the pain inflicted by others. Like this old house, your wounds are gone. I invite you to a new life and the opportunity to be with me forever. If you will believe in me, you will never taste death. Never look back to this, and I will give you a hope-filled future."

The Hunter waited for a response. Vincent felt no pressure. The moment seemed to stand quietly still.

Vincent didn't have to say yes, he just couldn't say no. He needed and wanted what the hunter had offered. The weights of fear and anxiety that had squeezed his chest and tormented his mind since childhood, was gone. He laughed then cried, then laughed again. Something splendidly weighty poured into him. Words he did not comprehend bubbled from his lips. He laughed some more.

"Before I send you back," the hunter said, "allow me to introduce you to my dear, dear friends. This is Roee and Dodee. They will be a father and mother to you for a season. You will come here and they will teach you about me and what has happened to you."

While Jesus made introductions, the goats approached to welcome Vincent. He sat with Jesus, Roee, Dodee and the goats at the edge of the veranda. The humans drank tea and talked with Jesus. The goats chewed cud and asked questions. Sitting on the edge of the porch with a handful of salted almonds, Vincent leaned against a post and closed his eyes to take in the wonder of the freedom he felt.

* * * * * * * * *

Hatch woke in the jail cell surrounded by a peaceful presence.

"This is wonky," he said to himself pleasantly.

He savored the dream, chuckled and felt something in his hand.

"Yes," he said, and popped an almond in his mouth.

He tried on some words to describe what happened; nothing fit. Stuff like that just doesn't happen, yet everything about it was undeniably real. When the house collapsed, the ground shook; he felt it. When Jesus, the hunter of lost souls, put his hands on his face, they were warm and loving. When Roee hugged him, it was fatherly and mountain-man strong. Hatch could smell the pine pitch that must have been on Roee's hands. There was no mistaking the baby's scent as he held her. There were almonds in his hand and crumbs in his mouth when he woke up.

"I was really there!" he yelled without thinking.

Bones lept off the top bunk, grabbed him by the shirt collars and screamed, "Get out of my jail cell! Vulcans didn't come and get you, Hatch. You're just a freaking lunatic."

Hatch smiled peacefully, held out his hand and said firmly, "Care for a space nut?"

Bones looked at the almonds, let go of Hatch's shirt and shook his head. "You're killin' me." He took them all and climbed back on his bunk. "Those are almonds, homey. You're the space nut."

He chuckled to himself at how calm he remained through the last two minutes of Bones' rant. *That's wonky,* he thought in marvel.

He remembered James telling about a valley where talking goats existed. *That's where I was,* he pondered. Although he saw the goats, he didn't get a chance to get close. He was ninety percent sure he heard them talking . . . maybe.

The house . . . the floors creaked where they did when he was growing up. The toxic communication and musty odor of untossed garbage had stirred aching memories. Life there was as it happened along with its emotional consequences. Then, all those broken structures got sucked out of him when the house collapsed. The hurts, the rage, the insecurity; he couldn't rehearse them back. They were gone . . . they were really gone.

Except for the French doors that led to the meadow, the house was identical to the one he grew up in. Although he had parents, he never bonded with them and felt like an orphan even at home. Belonging wasn't found there, but its counterfeit was found on the streets.

A picture of his mother and father flashed through his mind, and he wondered about their well-being. It was the first positive thought he had for them that he could remember. It dawned on him how messed up they were, and wondered what could have caused it. He never knew his grandparents, so he may never know. But now, he could forgive them.

* * * * * * * * *

For two days he wondered if the old familiar thinking would roll back in; it didn't. In spite of being locked up, he was content with it. Life in jail would be hard, but he was out of reach of the snakes on the outside and still breathing; that was consoling.

The loudspeaker in his cell popped his thought bubble with a message that James was scheduled for a visit the following morning. Considering that news, he looked forward to telling someone about his unexpected adventure. Anybody who had goats for friends would appreciate a story about a talking mountain lion.

He rethought the plan, then said to himself, "I don't know. There will be other ears listening."

"What you yammering about now?" Bones intruded impatiently.

Vince smiled. His cell didn't feel as crowded as it did a few days ago.

* * * * * * * * *

"Vincent Williams, you have a visitor."

Hatch stood erectly in the *tween cage* of the pod as an officer opened the door to escort him to the visitor facility. It was a small room with two doors designed to control inmate flow. The *in* door shut securely before the *out* door could be opened.

He was nervous and felt like a kid with a secret that had to be told. Passing through the door he put on a brave demeanor to appear calm.

Hatch picked up the handset as he sat down and said, "Hey James. It's good to see you."

Shamus gave him a sideways once-over. He looked . . . happy.

"It's good to see you too, Hatch."

Shamus could feel energy coming through the glass. It was

brilliant and weightless. He leaned in expectantly.

"I've been thinking, James. Hatch is my street name. You know, it keeps people from knowing who I *really* am. Or at least, that's what I thought it did. Who I was doesn't matter now, and I want to try Vince to see how it works. Could you call me Vince?"

"Yeah, I could do that . . . Vince."

Shamus considered Vince's appearance. There was a change. He studied the lines on his face; his features had softened. The worry lines on his forehead had almost disappeared. The dark mask Hatch had always hidden behind was gone. A more relaxed Vince was showing. Shamus smiled.

"Since you're doing a name change, let me tell you my real name; it's Shamus. It's the Irish version of James. I was probably using James for the same reason you were using Hatch. I had something to hide."

"Yeah, I kind of remember hearing your real name before. You might have told me that a long time ago when we were kids . . . So, it's Shamus for you and Vince for me. Yeah. . . Yeah. Like a new beginning, eh?"

"Yeah, like that," Shamus responded.

"So, *Shamus*," Vince said stiffly. "I've been thinking about those goat buddies of yours. You know, the ones that got shot? How they doing?"

Shamus was surprised by Vince's concern for someone other than himself. There *has* been a change, then.

"You know Vince, they're doing good. They spent a little time with a vet and made some new friends. They've recovered enough to go back to the valley where they have green grass, fresh air, and lots of family."

"You make them sound like people," responded Vince visualizing scenes from his dream. "Is that the same valley where you live?"

"Yeah, I have a tent set up there. But I've been away more than I've been *there* lately. It's a great place to learn about God and his love. And it's packed to the gills with his wonders. In fact, we call it Wonder Valley."

"It sounds like a nice place. Tell me more. What's it like?" Vince seemed giddy with expectation.

"Aside from all the goats, there's a big green meadow, a lot of pine and oak trees, a stream. . ."

"Is there a cabin?" Vince asked interrupting Shamus. "There's gotta be a big wonky cabin there."

"Yeah," Shamus responded with a chuckle. "There's a new cabin with a veranda on the front and a rocking chair by the door. I helped build the cabin."

Vince sat back and sighed with satisfaction then asked, "Is there a pond?"

Shamus leaned forward, smiled and ventured into Vince's space. "Vince, what happened? You're different. Something's turned a light on. You aren't the same guy I left here three days ago."

Vince fidgeted, then took a breath.

"I had a dream . . . In the dream, I was at my old house. And that house collapsed. My . . . the house where all my troubles began is gone. It's gone in my . . . I don't know . . . It's not like I don't remember, it's . . . it just doesn't hurt anymore. In here." Vince opened his free hand and touched his finger tips to his chest while holding the handset with the other. "Is that my soul? I don't see the shadows and haze anymore. I don't see the broken furniture lying around . . . I don't feel the pain."

Vince searched for more words by closing his eyes. Shamus waited.

"Yeah. In my dream, I walked out of my old house that I grew up in with this hunter guy dressed in camo. Then it just rolled up and caved in on itself. Then it sunk into the ground and disappeared. And all my past went with it. When I turned around, I could breathe and smell flowers. There was a pond and I could hear a stream in the background. I could feel the breeze on my face."

"Wow," said Shamus. "Wow, wow, wow. . . It sounds like you were at my place in your dream."

"No Shamus," Vince exclaimed a little too loud. Faces turned. "It was no dream. It was way more than a dream. I met Roee and Dodee and their baby. Her name is . . . I can't remember. It starts with an R."

"Rachel."

"Yeah . . . Rachel. And here's the kicker . . . I came back with a handful of almonds. Salty, roasted almonds. They were so good. You could ask Bones; he got the last of 'em."

"Vince, you think big brother might be listening?" Shamus was suggesting caution.

"Uh, yeah. I know they are. But I don't care." He pointed to his head and added, "They think I got a nutted almond anyway. But I had to ask you. I had to find out . . . Did I tell you about the guy in camo?"

"That would be Jesus, Vince."

"He saved me, James . . . uh Shamus. . . Does that make us brothers?"

Shamus' throat constricted and his eyes watered. "Yes it does, Vince," Shamus forced out. "I just have to tell you, if I had lost my life to hear those words, it would have been worth it."

"What do you mean? How could you have found out if you was dead?"

"Papa would tell me. He would have gotten word to me. But I didn't die. And I'm here to enjoy the rest of our lives on earth as brothers . . . How's that for family, Vince?"

Vince sighed then smiled. "I think I got a lot to learn about that, Shamus."

"You want a bible?"

"The chaplain will get me one. They're always good about that kind of thing."

Vince was about to talk about the mountain lion in his jail cell when the correctional officer informed him that his time was up.

"You gonna come back, Shamus?" Vince asked.

"I wouldn't miss it."

"Okay. See ya, bro."

Shamus watched Vince as he headed for the door and noticed his step was lighter than before.

"Papa, what are you doing?" He heard laughter in response.

As he walked out the main door, he considered the whereabouts of his own parents.

* * * * * * * * *

Vince returned to his cell feeling like an inner bottle of energy had been uncorked. Talking with Shamus about his dream and his encounter with Jesus confirmed that everything he experienced was real. He wasn't stuck on a starship trying to explain a worm hole.

He lay on his bunk and grabbed a book. He hadn't read in years. He didn't have the patience. Now he thought he could. That was a breakthrough.

He smiled, opened the book, and after a few pages, drifted off to sleep.

THE BASSMEANT

After Shamus' visit with Hatch, his remaining time in Burnus was short. Besides a scheduled appearance with the doctor, he didn't have a good reason to just hang around. Two weeks in the hospital provided intermittent opportunity to be with MiSeon. That time fanned a valorous resolve to pursue her. Well aware that he didn't know how and didn't have opportunity to ask for help, he risked it all with a simple question, "Can we do something together?"

MiSeon swung both hands out in front of her as she gestured, "I *love* this place. The mood is perfect, the music is quiet in the background so I can talk normally and their coffee is the best in Burnus."

"I have to confess that I'm not a coffee snob," responded Shamus, as he opened the glass door for MiSeon. "You're talking to a guy that recently graduated from instant to what Roee calls cowboy coffee. He just throws the grounds into the coffee pot and sets it on the fire to cook. I thought it was a huge improvement."

"You drink it with the grounds?" MiSeon asked wide eyed.

"Not exactly, we use our spoons to skim the big ones off the top and flick them in the fire. If you add a little cream, they're easier to see. The sludge simply settles to the bottom. Whatever gets stuck in our throat, we cough up and spit on the ground.

"That sounds a bit Neanderthal."

"Yup, knuckle draggers, every one of us. We aren't as sophisticated as people here in Burnus. But we know how to relax."

MiSeon roared with laughter while Shamus chuckled with admiration. "You're a different person away from the hospital."

"As a professional, I must always be attentive. The unexpected happens all the time. When I walk out the door, I get in the car and bring down my nurses antennae. So, this is me without my medical persona."

"You're amazing either way. But I like this person I get to share coffee with tonight. Now please help me grasp the finer points of a good cup of this stuff."

"As you will see the coffee mystique is not just about flavor. But it sounds like you might like the French Roast. It's roasted black, slightly bitter and it would be close to your normal."

"I can have normal anytime. Why don't you pick something . . . oh . . . something interesting for us."

MiSeon countered with a chuckle. "That's a big responsibility. What if you don't like what I pick?"

"I know it's risky, MiSeon. Surprises work along side adventures like this . . . Come on, it'll be fine."

She looked him in the eye and said, "Okay . . . One more question before I order for you . . . Do you like sugar in your coffee?"

"Yeah, sometimes . . . either way."

"Well my good cave man, you refuse to be fussy. Frequenting a place like this will change that."

At the counter MiScon placed her order for two mugs of caramel macchiato. Shamus paid the cashier then looked for a booth close to a window and away from the door.

"That looks like a great spot," He said pointing. "What do you think?"

She pulled down his pointer and said, "That's fine. They'll

bring it to us when it's ready. . . By-the-way, in Korea, it is considered impolite to point; just in case you were thinking of going there."

Shamus chuckled and responded, "Once upon a time in America, I think it was that way here. I've heard it said in an old movie or two . . . But, I am at a loss to figure out how I can get you to understand which booth I was talking about without pointing."

"There must be ways. Here, let's try this." She bent his arm, put her hand through the crook of it and said, "Lead the way." When they arrived at the table, she let go of his arm and curtsied. "How was that for a pair of cave dwellers?"

"Is 'regal' a stone age word?"

MiSeon shook her head and responded, "Splendid will do nicely."

"Then we are splendid cave dwellers in a regal world. It gives me license to be annoyingly sophisticated. I hope you don't mind. Please be seated. And just so you know, MiSeon. I don't get embarrassed. If there's something I need to know, you'll have to say it. My cave manners are a bit unrefined."

"Thank you, Shamus. That is very noble. But I was brought up to be subtle and honoring." She pointed her finger at him and added, "So, pay attention."

They laughed. After settling in across from each other Shamus started taking in the décor and watching people.

A wide wall was the focal center-piece of the main room. It was crafted from architectural rock overlaid with a three-dimensional, rust-colored metal sculpture with holes, gaps and layers that covered six feet of width and four feet of height. The design was an abstract that had meaning to the artist, but didn't register with Shamus.

At the base of the wall was a continuous upholstered bench with narrow tables in front of it and chairs that could be moved around to suit a variety of settings. A man of thirty-something was the only occupant on one end of the bench. His open laptop was connected by ear buds that stimulated his plunking of the keyboard. Shamus categorized his countenance as *confidently philosophical.*

"Are you a people watcher MiSeon?"

"I watch people all day at the hospital, Shamus," MiSeon said with a laugh. "But I'd guess for different reasons than what you're talking about. Why do you watch people?"

"In my old life, survival depended on it. There were looks in the eyes of certain people that revealed their intent and their feelings; if they still had any. There were people to avoid. People who have no regard for life have a look unlike any other. And I hope you will *never* have to know anything about that."

MiSeon responded, "In the medical field, we look for things that help *other* people to survive. It's the very opposite of what you are talking about. People don't often know they are in danger or how to describe a physical crisis. We have to read symptoms well and read between the lines of what people say. Our observations tell us what actions to take."

"We *are* a bit opposite there, aren't we?"

MiSeon nodded. "Not entirely."

"I learned a few things about ordinary people, too. Sometimes, I sense what kind of life people have. I *feel* their deeper thoughts, and sometimes what motivates them."

"Really? Are you a watcher or a seer?" MiSeon asked with a touch of wonder.

"I don't know anything about seers. I think I just have an old watcher's habit that's hard to quit."

"I understand, Shamus. I have to turn off my professional watcher when I leave work. Otherwise I find myself spotting sick people everywhere I go, but it never shuts off completely. Sometimes it feels like a curse and sometimes it feels like compassion. Maybe your talent will be used for something good."

"I can't imagine what that would be."

MiSeon looked about amused by what he said and subtly studied an older couple so as not to be caught staring. The couple sat together at the end of a booth near the order counter. The man was taking his eating seriously while the woman picked at the ingredients of her sandwich. The man boldly helped himself to her discarded pickle and tomato. Conversation was not happening at the moment.

"What do you see about that couple over there near the counter?"

"They're sitting next to each other instead of across from each other. That makes it easier for the man to avoid eye contact with her. They've probably been together a long time. And it looks like he might be here for the meal and not the conversation, judging by the speed he's wolfing down his dinner. He probably needs to be somewhere.

"But he's here with her instead of eating alone. So I would say he dutifully cares about what's important to her, but his mind is elsewhere."

"I'm not sure that's an accurate prognosis, Shamus. I have often seen my parents act like that. And they really enjoy being together. People act different when they're in public. They probably show more affection at home."

"You could be right, MiSeon. But, my knower is accurate for me most of the time."

The man they were talking about had finished eating, stood

at the edge of the table leaning with both hands on the surface and talking happily with the seated woman. He paused, touched her hand, looked around and left briskly through the north door. She smiled as he left, then sat with an unreadable expression for another minute appearing to sort through her thoughts. She got up slowly and walked with unhurried step out the south door.

"Hmmm," MiSeon commented playfully. She put an elbow on the table and cupped her chin between her pointer and thumb. "I'm not convinced about your diagnosis, Doctor Shamus. Try again."

Shamus was up to the challenge and watched another table briefly.

"See those three ladies in the corner chatting it up? It doesn't matter who's talking, the other two listen as if what's being said is important. I'd say they're good friends and have been for a long time. I'd also say they love each other."

"Now I would call that an accurate observation, Shamus. Sure, they're enjoying being together. It's a girl thing. But I would have to add, you're pointing out the obvious if you know *anything* about women."

Shamus laughed heartily. "Perhaps Doctor Shamus should retire from his practice. It's not something I need anymore. I've left the dangerous part of that behind, anyway."

Shamus appreciated MiSeon's honesty. She was no pushover for unimportant chatter or opinionated gossip. She handled it skillfully and kindly.

"You did that well, MiSeon."

"What did I do?" she asked.

"I talked like an ogre and you made me feel like a prince. I'm not only impressed, but you've given me a desire to learn how to do that with other people."

"I believe it is one of those traits that is caught, not taught. My parents always treated me like that. I don't even think about it."

"Well, I'm looking forward to catching it from you if I can."

The mood shifted as their caramel macchiatos arrived. Shamus pulled the oversized mug closer and beheld the design floating inside quizzically.

"That's called latte art, Shamus. And the people who make your coffee drink are called baristas. They actually have competitions called *throw downs* to challenge their creativity in latte designs using heavy cream."

"This is fascinating."

Shamus watched MiSeon pick up her mug with the fingertips of both hands and took a sip. The look of delight on her face stirred appreciation for her refined free-spiritedness. Using the palms of his hands, he felt the warmth of the cup. Assessing it suitably safe he raised it by the handle and took a sip. Holding the mug in front of his face, his taste buds savored the results. He smiled and nodded.

"Now that's a tasty cup 'o joe, MiSeon." He took another sip. "That's nothing like cowboy coffee." He took another sip, set the cup down and looked at the changed design inside. "I think I'm feeling my first fussy fit coming on."

MiSeon laughed.

"I'll have to tell Tom and Meadow about this latte art stuff. Tom's the coffee master at the general store in Lawless. He'd get a kick out of this."

MiSeon smiled. She was intrigued by this man across from her. Making repeated assessments was a big part of her professional life, yet she was free of foregone conclusions about him. Although he was honest about his stormy history, she understood God's transformation would calm the dark clouds from his brokenness. She chose instead to believe he was a treasure in the rough and would be a much different man in two to three years.

"How long have you lived the mountain life?" she probed warmly.

"I went up there more than a year ago to help build a log cabin with Jake and his brother, Del. But first, maybe I need to tell you how I met Roee."

"I think you should," MiSeon encouraged with a smile.

"The first time I saw him, I was making rounds in the Lawless neighborhood looking for potential clients. It was late at night and a man was standing where there had been no one just a moment before. The situation was weird enough to make me wonder. So I went up to him to see what was up. It turned out that he had never been around what was my world at the time. Some things started happening that clearly shook him although they were normal to me. He said some things that I thought naïve, and I told him so.

"He asked questions that made me think he was some alien life form. He gave me some yarn about his father dropping him off to learn or do some odd assignment. He said, 'When I have learned it or done it, I will return home.' I told him, 'You're an odd duck with a very weird family, Roee.'"

MiSeon laughed. "I probably would feel the same."

"His response was even stranger. He said, 'I wouldn't have it any other way.' In spite of the way he arrived and the stuff he said, there was a love and peace that came with him. He spent the night with me and my girls and just loved us." Shamus' eyes got moist. With a tight throat, he continued. "We were the bottom of the social food chain, and he showed us love that we had never seen before. We felt like he adopted us and it made me hungry for more.

"When he left in the morning I walked him over to Jake's store. I didn't know what he was doing at the time, but he prophesied some things about me that were too good to be true."

MiSeon wanted to hear more. "What did he say, Shamus?"

"He said I was an amazing man. I'm still wrapping my heart around that. He said that someday I would be a father and have grandchildren. He said my life would be a message and that I would see miracles and have spiritual encounters with God. I've seen a little bit of that. Most of all, he said I would know freedom and what it's like to be loved and what it means to be a son in the Kingdom of God. That has been the best part of all of those words. I'm experiencing that.

"The last thing he said was, 'When you're ready to walk away from the streets, call on Jesus. He will hear you and help you.' When he said it, I felt hope pour over me like a liquid. I had been wanting to leave the streets, but didn't know how. I *still* didn't know how after he was done talking." He chuckled with a raised finger. "But now, I had hope."

MiSeon chuckled with him.

"I need to make this story shorter. So I'll cut to six or eight weeks later when Jake and his friend Rigo visited and brought up an idea to go to Wonder Valley and help Roee and Dodee. They were living a primitive lifestyle at the time."

"Neanderthal?" MiSeon asked.

"Yes," Shamus exclaimed with a laugh, "Neanderthal with tents and talking goats."

MiSeon got wide-eyed. "Talking goats? Like the ones who were shot when you were?"

"I'll have to come back to that, or I'll never finish."

"Okay. But I won't let you forget."

"So I invited myself along. I really wanted to see Roee again. And I was ready to leave the streets. But I felt locked up. I couldn't just walk away. The guys wanted to help Roee build a cabin, so I went with them. That night, I met The Hunter."

"Who's The Hunter?"

"For some strange reason still unknown to me, that's how I've experienced the manifestation of Jesus. He appears in camouflage clothing and carries a bow with a quiver of arrows over his shoulder. I think it has something to do with the mountain setting. It seems so appropriate for him to dress that way up there. He's probably been doing it for centuries."

"You're telling me that Jesus shows up in Wonder Valley." MiSeon stated with a little envy, then put both hands flat at her heart. "I want to experience that!"

Shamus responded, "I don't know how to make that happen. It just happens.

She sighed and said with reluctant resolve to move on, "Okay. What happened next?"

"That night we were sitting around the campfire. Roee and I were talking about Jesus, my history and making choices. I told Roee that I would like to meet the Jesus he was talking about. And this voice outside the light of the campfire says, 'I've been looking forward to this moment, Shamus.' The Hunter steps into the light and says, 'Give me your history, and I'll give you more life than you know what to do with. I'll be the Dad you never had and teach you the ways of my Father.'

"He made me an offer I couldn't refuse and held out his hands. While he held me, my old life fell off in pieces. And when he was done, I was different.

"I didn't go back to Lawless for several months. During that time, Roee and Dodee became my spiritual parents. They call it discipleship, but spiritual parenting is easier to understand. Also, I'm learning to be a goat herder. And goat herding is an education about people unlike any other."

"Tell me about that," said MiSeon.

Shamus scanned the big rock wall as if looking for an inspiration. His eyes sparked and he raised his idea finger. "I got one," he said.

"The male goats play a head-butting game. They rise up on their back legs and come crashing down," Shamus brought his fists together, "head to head, horns to horns. In a way it's practice, because when mating season comes, it's the real thing. In some way, it's a training fight for the real contest of who will get the prettiest girl."

MiSeon involuntarily howled then pulled her laughter to a quick halt by putting her hand to her mouth. It was too late to avoid the affect of drawing attention. But she continued to chuckle. Shamus caught the spirit of it and laughed too.

"That is so funny, Shamus. I just had this hilarious picture come to mind of you and another man lowering your heads and running at each other, vying for my affections . . . that would be good content for a Renaissance story book.

"I'm sorry to interrupt. Please continue."

Shamus was captivated by her animation. What flowed from her was beautiful and spontaneous. He forced himself to shift from admiration to conversation.

"Actually, I could kind of picture it being romantic." Shamus said, hoping to provoke more laughter. "Like you said, two medieval knights dueling for the honor of the fair maiden."

MiSeon chuckled and said, "If this were the medieval times of chivalry, such acts of bravery and honor would be considered

. . . . stylishly gallant. But I would prefer flowers and something more peaceful."

"Of course, I was jousting," he rejoined.

MiSeon laughed at the word play, grabbed her spoon and licked it. Touching each of his shoulders she said, "Then you shall be my knight, Sir Shamus. I look forward to our first head butting games. . . I will make an excellent spectator.

"Now, this would be a good place to tell me about the talking goats. What *is* their story?"

"According to Tanny, the goat historian and story teller, they've *always* talked." Shamus squared his shoulders, put on story teller persona and cleared his throat. "It all started when Roee went in search of his lost goat, Maria. He tracked her into the forest and up the mountain. And at the end of the first day, he lay down to sleep and had a dream of an angel that came to bestow a gift. The angel said it was a new tool for his new assignment.

"Then he was awakened by the sound of talking. But the forest was dark and he groped around to find the source of the voice. He was shocked when he discovered a raccoon grumbling about having a hard time getting into Roee's rucksack for food. The experience revealed to Roee that he was given a gift for talking with animals."

"So the talking happens between Roee and the goats?" MiSeon queried.

"It started with Roee talking with all the animals," Shamus responded. "But there is more to the story."

"Well come on, Shamus. What's holding you up?"

They laughed as Shamus continued. "After Roee discovered Wonder Valley, he found a wild goat herd that had been there since settlers had left them generations before. God used that experience to call Roee to be the shepherd of this wild goat herd. So, when he went back down the mountain to get Dodee and move to the valley, Dodee had her own experience and received the gift as well.

"The next part is very important to know."

MiSeon leaned forward, put her elbows on the table and folded her arms. "I'm listening."

"The night before I came to the valley, everybody including the goat herd was transported to heaven and had a supernatural encounter. Up to that time the only humans the goats could talk with were Dodee and Roee; whom they call Mama and Papa Shepherd. When people started showing up from various places to help build the cabin, the goats were stunned that they could understand everybody else. They couldn't before that. I was there when it happened.

"There's a lot more to the story. But that's how talking goats got started in Wonder Valley. You need to come up to the valley and get the big picture from Tanny. He's an amazing story teller."

MiSeon looked overwhelmed and was shaking her head. "I just stepped into a dimension of God I didn't know existed."

It was Shamus' turn to be dumbfounded. "Wow MiSeon, I thought the supernatural side of God was normal. The scriptures are full of it."

"I believe in the supernatural, Shamus. I've seen healings and had assorted revelations. But what *you're* talking about is a considerable upgrade from what I am used to. This is exciting, extravagant and endlessly creative. I would like to meet your goats and have a heart to heart chat. Your story is a lot to process.

"So, tell me more about your goat education," pressed MiSeon.

"Okay," Shamus thought while looking at the table top. "This one will give you a picture of goat parenting wisdom. It's about how the baby goats learn.

"Young goats love to climb and be on top of things. Small sheds, big rocks or boulders, leaning trees and fallen logs are fun places for them to play king on the mountain games; where they acquire their balance. The adults don't interfere.

"I've seen six kids lined up on the same leaning tree that ended twenty feet in the air, where there's no room for mistakes. Falling is unforgiving and injury is certain in that respect. But, they never fall. They learn balance by climbing on their mother's back first. It's supervised. Then they work their way up to more difficult things. If they fall, it's in places where it is safe and they learn how to land."

"How does that work for raising children?" MiSeon asked skeptically. "That seems like a rough way to learn."

Shamus was ready with an answer. "As children grow up, they need difficult, real life encounters with choices that are not critical to their future. They learn fairness, leadership, practical skills, how to get up from failure and how to succeed while supervised. They eventually learn in uncontrolled opportunities. It's training at a young age for grown up situations. It makes them powerful and confident."

MiSeon put her elbows on the table, cupped her cheeks in her hands and smiled. "You are a wise one, Sir Shamus. You are going to be a good father."

Shamus put his fingers together at the tips, nodded and said, "I hope to get my GHD someday in goatthropology, Lady MiSeon."

MiSeon chuckled, "Those are high aspirations, I'm sure. But, what *is* a GHD?"

"It stands for Goat Herder Dude. It's the highest order of the realm. I would wear a fur hat with goat horns attached to it. I could take the hat off and blow either of the horns to call the goat herd." Shamus sighed longingly. "It would be an incredible honor."

By the time he finished his description, MiSeon was doubled over in laughter. Shamus joined her briefly, but sensed it was time to leave goat world and put an intentional pause in the conversation.

"Were you an orphan?" asked MiSeon.

"Not exactly. Both my parents were drug addicts. My childhood was a prison of fear and a school on how to survive. My Dad was abusive and my Mom was so absorbed in her addictions, she never had time for me. When I was fourteen I hit the streets to make my own life. Where it took me and what it made of me doesn't have a happy ending . . . until a met Jesus."

Shamus was aware from talks with Roee that he should leave nothing hidden from MiSeon if they were to have any future together. The thought of telling her everything unsettled him. But she knew so much already from their talks in the hospital and she still came with him tonight. That said something about her courage and integrity.

The old James was a shroud of deceptive suavity. But the new life he longed for would have to leave that behind. Transparent honesty looked risky. The knight's status she gave him was undeserved. He drew long from the macchiato then looked at MiSeon with a courageous smile as he set the mug back on the table.

MiSeon read his struggle by the lines on his face and reached out to his heart.

"I'm not going to judge you, Shamus. We have plenty of time. Start where you're comfortable."

"Thanks MiSeon." He paused then chuckled at the picture that came to mind. "Did you ever see the movie Shrek?"

MiSeon laughed in delight. "Oh yes . . . and the two sequels as well. I love those movies."

"There's a scene in the first one where Shrek says 'Ogres are like onions?'"

She nodded smiling.

"Well I feel like an ogre with lots of layers that have to be peeled back gradually or you'll think me a very stinky ogre that'll make you cry."

"I'm sure your analogy is misguided Shamus," she responded. "Cakes have layers too."

Shamus recognized Donkey's re-directive statement from the movie.

"Shamus, you're not an ogre and I'm not a donkey." MiSeon said kindly. "We are human beings with two lives that have two very different histories. I've known Jesus all my life and you have only known him for a short time. I have wonderful and loving parents and you don't. That doesn't make me better than you. And that doesn't mean we can't have . . . a good relationship."

The sound of instruments practicing drifted in from somewhere. Shamus thought it could be a club next door.

"I wasn't born in Korea but my grandparents were. And they have passed on some important Korean observations about the American culture that I think are true. The one that I think is important in this moment is that most Americans do not know how to build patiently for enduring relationships.

"Shamus, I can see that you are attracted to me. And quite

honestly I am attracted to you. But love is not like a Hollywood movie filled with physical and emotional carelessness and disregard for the values of the other party.

"I am simply saying, and with no arrogance or pride, that I love who I am and value what I have to give. I am a virgin and will be one on my wedding day. I love myself enough to know that I am worth waiting for," she began to laugh. "And worth knowing for the treasure I am on the inside as well as for my good looks and charming smile."

Shamus laughed with her, captivated by her loving frankness.

"There is a rich treasure in you, too, Shamus. Jesus is making you a shining light that will create a magnificent legacy for your children and pass on a brilliant and rich inheritance. We can't afford to go forward without patiently looking at how that works and what needs to happen. There's a lot involved.

"And with Jesus, there is no way you can fail. He will always be with us and guide our lives in the right direction. With faith, perseverance and love we will see everything he's purposed for us.

"The man I grow to love will learn to see the person I am on the *inside* and be secure with his own identity. Maybe you will be that man and maybe you will not. You are getting rid of who you *were* so you can find out who you *are*. If *you* are patient and do not give up, we will have a lifetime together."

MiSeon paused, took a breath and waited.

What MiSeon shared about building slowly with patience reached deeply and stirred him at a level Shamus had never experienced.

"MiSeon, you give me hope. As you were speaking, I could see a picture of what you were saying as if it were a movie. It was clear, and in some way, I understand what needs to happen in me. And I know it may not be easy and it won't happen quickly. But I'm determined to never give up.

"Fear, self-protection and doubt float to the surface at the strangest of moments. Roee teaches me to take those things to the cross where that old nature belongs. But I don't always understand what that means and how it changes things.

"I suppose I'm a little like this latte art thing we're drinking. It takes practice to know how to make it beautiful. But then when you drink a little, it doesn't look the same. So you get another cup and do it over again. You don't deserve a man who is constantly being redesigned."

"Like all allegories and metaphors," MiSeon rejoined knowingly, "they're incomplete representations of the whole picture of life. People change as they get transformed by God, sometimes radically. And I will change, too, because I'm still growing. But commitment is what gets people through restarts and redesigns.

"I think we are off to a better start than most people." MiSeon chuckled. "We have the goats to thank for that, I think. They have made you wise."

As they laughed, the band that had been warming up in the background kicked off a rendition of a Miles Davis song.

"Is this why we came here?" Shamus asked.

"Yes. That's my surprise. There is a jazz club in the basement that's owned by the people who own this coffeehouse. It is called The Bassmeant[a], spelled with b-a-s-s like a bass guitar and m-e-a-n-t like what jazz is meant to be."

"Hmmm, I'm going to like this place. I might even learn to be fussy."

They paused to drink in the quality of the music. It had the magical effect of calling them down to the club.

"MiSeon, my life's history was one of violence, lust, and deception. When Jesus found me everything changed. And I don't know how long it will be before all of that is wonderfully healed and in the past. But, there's more I need to tell you.

"But, I'd prefer to talk about that when we can be outdoors where the weight of regret isn't so heavy. I've seen it happen when I've talked about it with the shepherds. And I don't want that to happen tonight."

"Do you like to go hiking?" MiSeon asked.

"Oh yes, there are some excellent trails we can explore near the valley."

"There are several near here as well. Burnus has some nice views not far from here. But I want to explore some good jazz music with you tonight. Shall we go downstairs?"

They picked up what remained of their caramel macchiatos. MiSeon poured what was left of hers into Shamus' and took her mug to the bussing tray before heading for the stairs.

"You don't mind sharing do you?" MiSeon asked with a smile.

Shamus bowed regally, offered his arm and stated with an aristocratic British accent, "By no means m'Lady."

Endnotes

a   Styled after Talia's Espresso and Talia's Bassment Club in Wilkesboro, NC.

Advancing

Intercessors milled about in open fields to the south of Lawless while Nara paced, keeping a distance between himself and the group. Their discomfort with his presence distracted his focus. He was already preoccupied with thinking about Kefirah[1]. She was so beautiful and fun to be with. He reluctantly left her when The Hunter showed up with instructions for another assignment.

He could watch the crowd without seeing it while thinking about her. Then a picture of romping lion cubs yet unborn bounded across his imagination. An inner voice interrupted his wandering thoughts. "Remember, expect the unexpected. I will be with you." *At your service*, he thought in return. The alert brought his focus to battle-readiness and turned his mind to training maneuvers instead.

Pacing fifty yards from the contingent, he waited until the unintelligible buzz and song of intercessors reached his ears. He kicked up a bounding run toward the northwestern side of town, then accelerated to a sprint. He leapt through the veil and into the second heaven above Lawless. His paws grabbed unseen turf that took him to an altitude above the town for clear observation. The fortress-like wall that he saw during the battle for Little Faith was below him. Guardian demons who kept watch on top of the wall were on nervous edge. They had seen the brightness of the people occupying their turf on the south side of town and were expecting trouble.

They were winged yet rat-like with pig snouts and talon claws. The eyes were a feverish redness. Their repugnant faces bore moth-like antennae and scowled lunatic malice.

On the ground were ugly bipeds with crocodile features, elfin ears and spiked head armor. They carried swords with serrated blades of what looked like bone. Some pointed at Nara with their swords and laughed.

Others were simply fat bodied imps with bullish heads and many hands that gathered and groped. Another was a muscular dwarf with the head of a vulture that carried chains and taunted Nara. These appeared to have purposes other than fighting.

"The worst of them keep the poison of rejection alive and stir up the pain of woundedness. The others you see are spirits of lust and greed. They are relentless and heartless beasts." Carrie's commentary announced her arrival.

"There must be lots of those hairball liars down there, too," Nara responded, breaking his focus. "I see you've added some shiny stuff to your armor. Is that gold?"

"I have you to thank for that nice addition, Nara. It was a reward for the victory we fought for in Little Faith . . . How do you like it?"

"Hmmmm, don't know that I would have any use for it," Nara said absently while he kept his eye on the activity below.

"It's a girl thing, I think," Carrie responded.

Carrie glanced behind her and stated with zeal, "I brought some help with me, Nara."

Nara turned and saw two goats clothed in leather armor like Carrie's, only without the gold.

"Hi, Nara. I'm ready to kick up some hooves!"

Nara was surprised and gave Finnegan a sloppy lick on the face.

"Finnegan, it's so good to see you. I heard you were dead."

"Well I . . . I am dead," he chuckled . . . "At least as far as the earthly life goes."

"Oh yeah . . . This heaven stuff seems so real."

"It's as real as earth, Nara." Finnegan responded enthusiastically.

"It's hard to tell the difference . . . And you must be Rosie. I heard about your bravery from Jesus. He speaks highly of all of you. I am honored that you chose to be here with me."

"I am pleased to fight on the side of such a valiant warrior, Nara. You have a marvelous story among my circle of friends," responded Rosie.

Nara bowed his head as a courtesy and replied, "Thank you, Rosie."

When he returned his attention to the situation below, he chided himself. His sentimental delay allowed the enemy to gather and prepare an offensive.

"They're ready for us . . . Jesus, what do you want us to do?"

Beyond the dark forces that faced them, Nara saw a small puff of light turn on. It seemed close yet far away, and the demons were unaware of it. He wondered what it could be.

Holy Spirit spoke, "I have gathered other warriors. They will ambush them from behind and cut off their supply of reinforcements."

They all heard the voice and looked at each other. In their composite purpose, they were of one mind with their commander. Nara understood the advantage; they could move and respond as one. "Spread out some," he said.

From the gathering of intercessors in the field below the volume and intensity of singing and praise increased.

The horde from Lawless made a frontal attack while a demon from the wall flanked and scraped Nara's side with its claws.

The affect was painful and bloody. Nara cried out but ignored the sting and reacted by grabbing the rat from behind before it got away. It slowed the creature's momentum enough to allow Carrie to pierce the creature with double swords.

Nara discarded the useless body and forgot his pain with thoughts of praise.

A biped was barreling full speed toward Nara with a spear that belched flame like a torch. He looked like a knight in a joust, but without a horse.

He side-stepped the dark warrior but was unprepared for its nimble reengagement. Nara sped between the creature's legs and climbed its back before the spear's flame could find his fur.

Finny zipped by at a charge. The razor edge of his silver horn covers separated its head from its body and the two were off to help Rosie and Carrie who were almost overrun by a v-shaped formation of enemy. While Finny attacked from the front, Nara's claws pulled down from behind. The move allowed the three goats a quick counter-offensive. The result let one demon escape to regroup with others.

While the four were engaged hoof and claw above, they drew enemy forces away from town. A contingent of saints from the lighted cloud descended into the vacuum with overwhelming numbers and forced the remaining demons to abandon the city like a swarm of flies swatted from a carcass. They hovered like a fog of darkness.

Carrie saw the swarm leave the disengage the battle. The saints from behind had gained a strategic position and were widening their swath of occupation. She darted from the engagement to get a clearer perspective and called to the others who were hammering out a tough fight.

"Disengage and step away!" she yelled. Their sudden departure left the enemy swinging at each other and empty space. It allowed the dark forces to see their stronghold had been broken. With the possession of Lawless now out of their hands, lesser minions fled to the north. Those focused on the fight raged at being outmaneuvered.

A shout rose from the field below. The intercessors danced like they had seen everything first hand. Increasing numbers of saints surrounded the demons in a Jericho march. When they shouted, the second heaven thundered and the demons wailed in defeat.

"It is one thing to win," howled a ranking fiend, "another thing to occupy. We will be back! You Christians will let your guard down in time."

With their departure, the atmosphere shifted. But it was not a quiet peace. The shouts and singing of victory continued to rise from the crowd of intercessors on the ground and mingled with the voices of the saints that surrounded and filled the city.

The saints moved toward the wall and stood above it. Without knowing why, the gathering on the ground turned toward the railroad tracks. Both groups raised a sustained shout.

The fortress wall above the tracks shook violently then collapsed into dust. A brief but tempestuous wind carried the dust north to the wilderness. Although the crowd below could not see the wall, they experienced the wind.

Nara fell into laughter, ran to Finny and scooped him onto his back. He then retrieved the rest, leaving his back now full of balancing goats. He stopped suddenly and deposited the laughing brood in front of him and pounced on them. They romped and squealed without restraint.

"You can't wear us out Nara, we can do this forever!" howled Rosie with delight.

"I don't care," roared Nara. "You guys are the best. I'm so

proud of you!"

"And I'm proud of all of you, too."

Jesus appeared, laughing at their antics while Nara settled into a pant. He was tired and the pain of a wound on one side returned. Although bleeding, he'd forgotten the bashing he took from the spiked rat.

"It looks like Nara could use some help here guys," Jesus pointed out.

Everyone including Jesus touched noses with Nara and spoke healing to his torn fur coat. The results were immediate, and Nara felt relief and a surge of energy that jerked his front shoulders.

"Ahhhhhhhhhh, that feels good. Thank you."

"You're welcome," they said.

"Those are interesting stripes, Nara," joked Finny. "They could be fashionable in a rugged liony sort of way."

Nara looked at his side. He could only see a portion of the new white streaks through his peripheral vision. Against his tan fur, they stood out sharply.

"What's with the new fur job?" asked Nara.

"It's a reminder to always be alert in a battle," Jesus responded while rubbing Nara behind his ears. "You got careless back there in the beginning.

"What's rule number one, Nara?" Jesus asked with a smile.

"Expect the unexpected," he replied. "I suppose that carelessness could have cost me my life."

"I want you alive until I'm ready for you to be with me. Those guys are seasoned fighters . . . Stay alert."

It was loving correction and Nara took it to heart.

A song drifted up from the earthly realm.

"You ready to go back?" Jesus asked.

Nara thought for a moment and a silly grin covered his face.

"She's beautiful Jesus. Thank you. She's . . ." Nara said.

Jesus started laughing before Nara could finish, because he knew what was in his heart.

"She's perfect for you in every way, Nara," responded Jesus. "Now get going!"

"What was that about?" asked Carrie.

Jesus replied with a chuckle, "It's a guy thing."

* * * * * * * * * *

Nara's return from the second heaven was slow. He had little enthusiasm to go back and face the humans. He knew they would be excited about the battle and want a report. But he wanted to get back to Kefirah.

He put his negative thoughts aside and kicked up his speed. In a moment he was on the ground and loping toward the waiting crowd. He singled out Papa Shepherd and headed toward him. News of the three goats would be a good thing for Papa Shepherd. Using that name was getting easier.

Nara's report to the people included mention of the extra goat helpers along with the saints that made up the fighting corps. By end of the discussion, the tension between him and the intercessors had changed; a bonding occurred.

The Kingdom's revolution of healing moved forward. With skirmishes won and the opposition in retreat, it was time to liberate those imprisoned.

The prayer warriors spread out in groups of two and three taking to the streets of Lawless. Their purpose was simple . . .

stir up friendship with the citizens of Lawless and seek to be a source of their wellbeing. They cared, they prayed; miracles happened. Love found hearts that were hungry for life.

Momentum built throughout the day and an idea spread of having a street party. A spontaneous barbeque was suggested and the community took it on. A love feast was in the making.

* * * * * * * * *

Shamus sat with MiSeon on a bench under an antique street light. It was twilight and the festivities on Main Street were quieting. MiSeon was watching two pockets of activity still going after the long day.

"MiSeon, it's just like Nara said. The wall between the people of Little Faith and the people of Lawless is really gone. To have a party like we had today was unheard of this morning. This has been an historic day, and tomorrow the sunrise will be filled with something different for all of us. It will shine with hope."

"The love in the atmosphere is tangible, Shamus. I can almost taste the flavor."

"Tastes like chicken," Shamus cracked. And they giggled at the quip. "Rosie said that when we came to town to talk to Hatch. Those are some good moments to remember. And to think she and Finny were involved in the battle is poetic justice for what they suffered."

"I overheard," MiSeon continued, "a couple invite two girls to their house for dessert tomorrow, and the girls accepted the invitation . . . You know what one girl said?"

Shamus looked at her and waited for the answer.

"She felt like she . . *belonged!*"

Shamus took that word in with understanding. He knew the depths of what that meant.

"I was with some guys that were talking about taking some of the unused land around Lawless and creating a farm or some kind of industry. I've *never* heard that kind of talk. The people who do what I used to do don't own land, at least not in their own names. Their identity gets stolen on so many levels that just making it through this life of hell *alive* is uncertain. Nobody here plans for the future . . . History was made today, MiSeon."

"Shamus . . . with the breakthroughs today, have you given any thought to settling down here? There's so much you could do to help give these people a future."

"What I have been thinking about is the idea of moving to Burnus and getting a job there."

MiSeon asked with persistence, "Why would you do that?"

Shamus looked at her like she had asked a dumb question.

"Really, Shamus," she encouraged. "Listen to what's in your heart."

He looked away a moment as if searching.

"I believe with all my heart that you are the woman *I* want to spend the rest of my life with, MiSeon. Papa is repairing the brokenness I grew up with. And I think in time I can be the one that *you* want to spend the rest of your life with also.

"I want to invest whatever time it takes to get the job done and explore every facet of the jewel that you are. You're worth waiting for. And I'm in no hurry to settle for something less than the best. I just want to be near you during the process."

He paused then sighed.

"Yes, in some way, I belong here. They're a part of my history and I could be a part of their future. It would almost seem natural to grow with the changes. But I resist those thoughts taking root MiSeon. My future is with you."

He looked at her and waited.

Tears trickled down MiSeon's cheeks.

"It makes me happy," responded MiSeon, "that you are willing to take such risks with no guarantees. But it will be worth being patient now, so we can have the best later. I don't want you living for me; thinking I will make you happy. You must live for God and the destiny he has designed for you. You should first learn to live for what makes *him* happy. Please be careful that you don't make me an idol that gets in the way of learning that important lesson."

Leaning toward him, she took his hand and kissed him on the cheek. Sitting back, she looked in his eyes and said, "You are an amazing man, Shamus."

"MiSeon, no human has ever believed in me like that. You've turned on a switch in my heart and light has flooded in like a sun bursting out from behind storm clouds. You give me hope and love and . . ." He could not speak.

"Thank you, MiSeon," he said after settling the lump in his throat. "The gift you have given me is more than anything I could ask for . . . When I find better words that will express what has happened inside, I will share them with you."

He smiled, looked in her eyes and continued, "Maybe I can write a poem about it . . . maybe two."

"I know you will, Shamus."

Her smile exuded the warmth of affection she felt and knew she could not let the emotional tide rise further; there are no shortcuts to doing the right thing. "I need to head back to Burnus tonight. I work in the morning.

"But, I want to leave you with an assignment. I want you to ask Father what he has in mind for your future and that you will commit to hearing the answer. What he says regarding any part of life is what we live for. He can be trusted without reservation."

Shamus walked MiSeon across the tracks to the parking lot near the train station. They prayed, and then Shamus took her hand and kissed it.

With his hands in his pockets, Shamus watched as she drove across the tracks and headed north. He breathed deeply until a dull pain reminded him that gunshot wounds don't heal quickly. He looked up for the night sky to reveal a cosmic wonder. "Life is good, Papa. Thank you . . . Thank you so very much."

Endnotes

1   Pronounced Ka-feer-a.

RECONCILED

Pine and oak trees surrounded him, the sounds of forest a chorale accomplice. A gentle breeze carried tree whisperings. Birds piped their fife and flute opera. Fingers of late morning sun probed through the branch canopy to touch his face and embrace his air-starved skin. He spread his arms, took a breath and inhaled woodland. Its mystic fragrance imbibed to loosen his spirit. He danced a slow waltz, taking in the panorama.

"Where am I this time?"

"This is our home it is," said a smallish voice.

Surprised, he spun around. Tilting his head curiously, Vince said, "I guess I shouldn't be surprised that a raccoon can talk."

"Oh yes, we speak the talk. But only recently have we spoke the talk with humans. Now everybody in this valley talks and speaks to everyone. It's a wonder isn't it?"

"Uhhh, yeah. A wonder."

"How did you get here?" rejoined the raccoon. "I didn't hear you come and I didn't smell you come. An angel you're not. You don't smell like an angel."

"I think I'm dreaming, Rocky. This doesn't happen in real life. And I'm certainly not an angel."

"Oh no, my name is Skitter, man of the woods. And I don't speak the talk about dreaming. And yes, this is very, very real. And this is very, very life. Many, many things happen here that don't happen elsewhere, you can be sure. Ask Papa Shepherd if you don't believe me. He speaks the talk about many, many things, he certainly does."

"Who is Papa Shepherd? Is he the king of this mysterious place?" Vince asked.

"Humph," replied the raccoon matter-of-factly. "Oh no, there is only one King. And Papa Shepherd is not he. You can ask about that too. He will be along. He's up on the rock, he is. And if you're lucky, the King might be with him.

"So little time I have, so little time. I have to go. Food for the family, you know." Skitter was off, sniffing in his search for whatever he needed.

After a couple contemplative moments Vince called after him, "Uhhh, who is the king?" Skitter kept walking, apparently focused on things to take care of.

"I hope I didn't offend you," he said a little louder. "Uh, bye Skitter. Um, good to meet you."

"Did I just say that?" Vince asked himself. "This is wonky."

He strained to see through the trees and underbrush and spotted what might be a trail, but no living creatures. The forest was dense in one direction and thinned toward another. The ground rose in front of him. Skitter had called him man of the woods. It was far from true. He didn't know which direction to take if he had to find his way out.

He heard a heavy thud on the higher side of the slope, followed by footfalls through leaves. Whoever it was, scatted a lively song that ranged from high to manly deep.

"Hellooooo," Vince yelled.

The song stopped.

"I heard you, keep talking," returned the other man with a laugh. "You sound like you're everywhere. Sing something."

Vince cupped his hands around his mouth and said. "I don't sing so good. I'll just keep talking. Can you hear me now?"

A moment late, he repeated, "Can you hear me now?"

"Yeah, yeah, yeah, I got a bearing on you. I'll be right there."

The man trotted through the forest along the path and adjusted his course once he saw Vince. Within minutes, Roee stood in front him with a hand extended.

"I've seen you before," Vince declared.

"You were here a few days ago, Vince. I'm Roee."

"Yeah, that was a dream I think . . . or something."

Roee smiled oddly and chuckled. "I'm not surprised. I had a similar experience when I met Shamus."

"Are you Papa Shepherd?"

"That's what I get called around here. How did you know about that?" Roee asked.

Vince laughed.

"I know it sounds weird, but Skitter told me to ask you if this is all real, because I'm not sure if it is . . . And who is the king?"

Roee chuckled. "Yeah, Skitter's a busy guy, always chasing down the food chain. It was nice of him to take the time to chat."

"I kinda popped in when he wasn't looking." Vince responded, feeling more at ease. "He was very, very surprised, if you know what I mean."

"Sounds like Skitter . . . Come on down to the cabin, and we'll talk over a cup of coffee. Feel up to a run? The exercise will do you good."

They jogged until they came out to a long and lush meadow that spread to the left then dog-legged away to the right. In the distance Vince could see a house, a couple of out buildings, and the log cabin.

Goats peppered the area, some grazing and some lying

around chewing contentedly. The appearance of the jogging duo didn't disturb their tranquility, but their curiosity was certainly aroused. A few ran in their direction in obvious competition to get there first.

"Ha! I beat them! Hi, my name is Scampy. What's yours?"

"My name is Vince," he said breathing hard. "I've heard about you guys from Shamus. This is quite a dream."

"You're not dreaming," replied Scampy with little boy enthusiasm. "At least *I'm* not dreaming. It's as real as a head butt. Care to try one?"

"I don't think so, Scampy. I just don't know what to call it. Somewhere else, I'm asleep . . . but I'm here, too. Any ideas?"

"That's simple," Scampy proclaimed. "You're as messed up as all the rest of us." Laughter followed. The answer is Papa God. He can do anything, even the impossible."

"Okay, you're right. That's simple. But what do we call it?"

"Why call it anything?" Scampy rejoined. "It just happens.

"Eye has not seen, nor ear has heard, neither has entered into the heart of man or goat the things that await those who love him. Mama Shepherd read that to us once, and I remember it. If it's possible to think it, it can be done, and beyond. You're making this too hard when it ain't hard at all."

Roee chimed in, "Vince, these goats have more faith than most humans. They believe with amazing simplicity."

"I don't know much about faith. But I've never heard *anybody* talk like that. Not goat or human."

A few goats walked with them as they continued toward the cabin and affirmed more than once that Vince wasn't dreaming.

"I think I got it," he finally had to say.

As they approached the cabin another goat limped up to

them. She didn't look like the other goats, but Vince realized there was something familiar about her. He slowed his pace to talk and stopped when he stood in front of her.

They looked in each other's eyes before speaking.

"Are you one of the goats I shot?"

"Yes. My name is Maria. Me and Scampy were the two that lived. Rosie and Finnegan died." Tearing up, Maria added, "And I do miss them."

Vince looked for Scampy and caught emotion on his face.

"Finnegan was my best friend," said Scampy. "And I didn't get hurt as bad as Maria. I'm okay."

Willie added, "And Finnegan was like a son to more than one of us."

"Yeah, that's true," affirmed Sully.

"Vince," Roee injected. "They're saying what they feel. They're not trying to make you feel guilty. It's just the way they are."

Vince felt the sentiment and had to respond, "I'm so sorry. It's hard to explain what happened that day . . . I felt lost and I was scared . . . Shamus had been my only friend in a very cruel world and I felt like he abandoned me. When all of you tried to love me, it seemed like you were from another world and something snapped . . . and then I started shooting.

Vince looked at Roee with pleading eyes and asked, "What can I do?"

"That's simple, Vince. If you really mean it, ask them to forgive you." Then Roee yelled toward the cabin, "Dodee, we have a visitor."

While Vince looked at the faces of Scampy and Maria, Dodee came out and stood on the veranda with Rachel. He glanced at her face and saw unconditional welcome in her face.

"I've never done this before," Vince said as he kneeled. "You know, I really feel the pain of your loss. And I am so sorry. Please, please forgive me."

Vince looked about from face to face, watching as responses registered in their eyes.

"How do you hug goats? . . . Can I give you all a hug?"

"Yes, you can hug *me*," Maria said with a smile. "I like hugs."

"Please forgive me, Maria," he said.

"You are forgiven, Vince. And welcome to our home. And we know that we will see Rosie and Finnegan again someday. So it's not as bad as it seems."

The healing continued until all had extended the mercy that is vital to life in Wonder Valley. Vince then stood and asked, "Is there anything more?"

"You might consider," said Dodee as she descended the steps of the veranda and walked toward him, "doing the same with Shamus next time you see him.

"And I forgive you too," she added extending a free arm for a hug. "I heard Maria call you Vince? My name is Dodee . . . But of course, I think we met a few days ago when that house came crashing down in our woods."

"You saw that?" asked Vince loudly and with big eyes.

"Yes I did. And I was standing near you when you suddenly disappeared. We expect the unexpected around here . . . it keeps us wondering."

Vince addressed Dodee's earlier statement. "I'll have a talk with Shamus about forgiving me. I hadn't thought about it when I saw him a few minutes ago."

Dodee looked at him quizzically, wrinkled her nose and giggled, "I see."

Roee stepped up to complete the reconciliation by putting a hand on Vince's shoulder and saying, "I forgive you too.

"Now, let's get that cup of coffee. I want to tell you a little of our story."

"Do you have any more of those almonds?" Vince asked.

"Sure, we have plenty." Dodee responded.

Minutes later the fragrance of brewing coffee filled the cabin along with the smell of fresh baked bread. Dodee served goat cheese, butter . . . and almonds.

"Let me share a little about our journey into the unknown," Roee began. "It's not a tall tale of any sort. But it has been quite a process."

Roee and Dodee talked briefly of their journey from Grindlay Village to the present, then went out and listened to Tanny's masterful storytelling of the flock's journey into the supernatural.

"This Jesus, God, Papa thing is pretty amazing." Vince said.

"Williams!" yelled a gruff and unexpected voice, "You gonna sleep the day away? It's time to eat."

The shepherds looked at each other in astonishment. The voice filled the air with rude intrusion.

"Wonky . . . It's time for me to go," Vince said wistfully.

* * * * * * * * * *

Vince opened his eyes and looked toward the cell door.

"You gonna eat or not?" Bones asked loudly.

The taste of good coffee and homemade bread was still in his mouth.

"No," he responded slowly. "I already ate."

Bones scowled at him and said, "You're a punk, Hatch. A flippin' crazy punk."

He chuckled, leaned back in his bunk and resumed reading, amused to be playing with Bones' limited capabilities. "Call me Vince, Bones. That's my real name."

"You're a punk . . . Vince." Bones had the last word. Vince didn't care.

Looking for work in Burnus without a permanent address had proven frustrating, as every encounter turned awkward. And after two unsettling days, Shamus bid MiSeon a good weekend. It was Friday morning and going to Wonder Valley for some quality time with the shepherds was the path to a new perspective.

Little Faith was a two hour drive from Burnus. He arrived before lunch and stopped in at Jake and Anna's store. They were busy with the Friday bustle of customers shopping for the weekend, so he jumped in to help with bagging and loading groceries into shopper's cars. In short order, he was engaged in conversations and banter and forgot his anxieties.

When customer flow paused, Anna offered sandwiches and chips. "I'm going to make something for Jake and me, would you care for something?"

"Thanks Anna, I'm famished."

"And thanks for your help, Shamus," Anna continued enthusiastically. "You fit right in."

"I agree with that," Jake exclaimed. "By the way, how was your job search in Burnus?"

"Jake," Shamus said. "Could you let me use your address while I look for work there? Not having a permanent home really created a problem."

"Here's something to think about. I was watching you . . . and you're a natural with making customers feel comfortable and welcome . . . That's what we want our customers to experience. Instead of going to Burnus, come to work for us. You could live at our house. And given time, we could train you to *run* a market like this."

Shamus didn't like the idea. "I don't know, Jake. I'd rather be with MiSeon."

Jake laughed. "Yeah, I figured that out . . . But I'm offering you a practical solution to your *real* problem. You have great people skills, but no market value. Anna and I can teach you retail skills and the work here will sharpen your touch with the community.

"While you're thinking about that, let me to give you some strategic advice; think longer term. When you were getting your life put together, you used up or gave away everything. While there's nothing wrong with being generous, now you need to focus on replenishing your reserves and building a résumé. We'll give you the opportunity to do that by working for us and living in our home."

Shamus sighed, "You're right, Jake. I need a starting place . . . But staying here means being away from MiSeon. My dreams include her.

"Your dreams might have to wait until your resources are big enough to reach for them, son. For what it's worth, we have a lot of years invested in that piece of advice."

"That must be what fatherly advice looks like. I hope I'm grown up enough to follow it. I'm heading up the mountain for the weekend . . . and I'll talk with the shepherds about all of it. They will probably agree with you."

Shamus made a call, but didn't reach MiSeon. He left a message about his conversation with Jake, then called the valley's satellite phone to inform them of his intention to visit.

Afterward, he found Jake and Anna, and told the two he was heading for the valley.

"Thanks for the food and the advice and the opportunity.

We'll talk when I get back in a few days."

"Tell everybody we said hello," Jake responded.

SHANGRI-LA

The Jeep knew the way, so Shamus reflected on the good things he'd been blessed with from a figurative auto-pilot; he didn't need to pay attention. Those blessings started when he walked into the arms of Jesus and away from his destructive lifestyle. He got a new heart and identity and healing in places he didn't even know were broken. He was happy, hopeful and humming with gratefulness.

At a familiar turn off the roadway, Shamus stopped the Jeep and settled back to absorb the healing balm of the mountains. This area had been home since he left the bad lands of Lawless more than a year before, and was the wellspring of everything that now is. This forest had invested heavily in his new life.

When Jesus rescued him from the streets, Roee and Dodee were there first to help him see the wounds inflicted by his parents and forgive. His hands and spirit worked and played alongside them and the goats while he learned the basics of God's ways. Over time the internal chatter of criticism and accusation stopped. Forgiveness became a valuable tool.

Through their lavish love, he found a course of life he could sail without wavering. Roee gave Shamus the anchorage of wisdom to help him find a true identity. And now he came seeking their help to navigate the uncharted waters of courtship.

While playing with the goats, he experienced being a kid; a point of growing up that got skipped in the intensity of survival. But something still lacked; he was longing for more.

He thought of MiSeon and the miles of the different influences that shaped their life stories. The challenge of closing that gap felt daunting and looked impossible.

But, if it takes years to bring our hearts together, he reminded himself, *she's worth the wait.* There were no examples of romance to help him understand what was required or expected; except what he saw happen between Roee and Dodee. Learning to build a healthy and enduring relationship was like learning another language. *I suppose there are books*, he thought. Then he remembered a prayer which seemed to work in most situations . . . He looked up, raised his hands, and yelled . . . "Help!"

He then considered his old friend Hatch. Correction . . . *Vince.*

An encouraging sign of his transformation included the compulsion to go back to the streets he walked away from and save the life of his friend because of a dream. His intent was supposed to be preemptive. He never considered that it would nearly cost him his life. And it didn't matter now if it had. Although Vince was going to prison for the shootings, he was alive with redemption because of it. If Shamus had not responded to the dream, Vince would likely be dead . . . and eternally lost.

His meandering thoughts drifted back as he stopped at a junction where the backwoods road to Wonder Valley went west and the lava flow he'd traversed from the east ended.

Taking a personal inventory wasn't the reason he'd stopped here. Something was pulling at him. Thoughts buzzed Shamus' mind like bees looking for flowers. His imagination wanted to explore, dream . . . land on an adventure and taste its nectar.

His good intentions had prepared for moments like this by putting a telescopic fishing pole with a small tackle box under the back seat. Months had passed without using it.

"All the fishing spots I know about are on the other side of the mountains," He reflected. "I'll bet there's something around here."

He eased the Jeep into gear and crawled over the undisturbed terrain. Occasional ruts spoke of an older history of visitors. For a mile or more the landscape was sparse forest on the left and lava formations on the right that had captured sporadic patches of windblown dirt from the east. Airborne seed germinated in these accumulations creating intermittent plots of shrubbery that rabbits and quail used for cover.

He reached a point where the apron of ancient lava was too narrow to continue. He turned off the engine, sat back and considered what to do next. The afternoon sun was high and warm, but not too hot. Its rays drew variegated color out of the surrounding life and quieted everything with vibrant radiance.

Shamus unfolded his stiff legs and got out of the Jeep. He pulled each knee toward his chest, wobbled his stiff shoulders and neck, then smiled. He reached across the driver's seat, grabbed his full canteen and clipped it to his belt. Remembering binoculars, he pulled it out of the case and hung it by the padded strap around his neck. He opened the tackle box and stuffed a plastic case with a lure into his shirt pocket and a put an extra light reel in his pants. He hung the pole case from a strap on his shoulder.

Scrounging two out-of-date protein bars from the glove box, he started north.

Shamus set a leisurely pace so he could watch for details in the surrounding mountainscape. A half hour passed, then an hour, and a bond to the land reached out and tightened its grip. The trail ran out as the volcanic flow disappeared below dirt and as it went deeper, gave way to dense forest. The small groves of manzanita forced him to find meandering ways around and through them. He gave thought to the compass he left in the Jeep, dismissed its necessity and kept going.

Breezes carried the fragrances from pines and cedars; a reminder that some things never change.

Scolding squirrels let him know he was a stranger, then chattered their permission to pass.

The sound of a churning creek increased as he drew closer to some unknown thing. The noise changed to the voice of a waterfall.

Scrub growth thickened, forcing a detour. Pushing branches aside he stepped onto a granite stage. Beyond the slab and to the right was a deep and shaded grotto with water tumbling from an escarpment ten feet over it. Although the inflow was no wider than fingertip to elbow and perhaps an inch deep, the sunlight refracting through the prismatic waterfall reflected primary colors that shattered into pallid mist when joining the pond below. Instead of a rainbow, the mist produced a dappled cloud.

Nature's creative genius had fashioned a bowl beneath the waterfall in an ancient time when hot magma was formative. A molten bubble skin collapsed sometime in the ages after it hardened. The imperfect roundness formed the shape of a cumulus cloud. The depth of the pool below the waterfall was obscured by the water's reflection. And oddly, there was no outlet.

The woodland was lush near the water's edge at the southwest end. Beyond that was wilderness and the direction home if Shamus had wings. *Someone would have to drive me back here to pick up the Jeep*, he thought.

He studied the escarpment that filled up the north landscape and a section of the western side. Holes the size of pine cones dotted the water line. "Maybe that's how the water leaves this place," he thought aloud. "I wonder where it goes."

The crashing surface water and the slurping of draining water created unique harmonics. Shamus thought, *That would make a great sound effect for a sci-fi movie.*

The water was clear but shimmered with a hint of purple. "How bizarre," he said.

He kneeled at the lip of the rock. Using his hand for a scoop, he tasted it carefully. It was unusually sweet and very cold. He lay face down on the slab's surface and stretched his neck so his lips could reach the water. He took a long drink. When the water hit the bottom of his stomach, a thrilling quiver hit him.

"This stuff's got some kick!" he exclaimed laughing.

He imagined himself getting pulled into a whirling fogish murk and being dumped out as a frog. Without thinking, he checked the skin of his arm for color change.

"The flavor is like the well water coming out of Jake's drinking fountain at the store. I'll bet this is the source!"

He looked at the top of the waterfall and was compelled to know its source.

He peeled off his extra gear and piled it on the rock slab, then circled around to the right to find a way to the top. Some back-tracking took him away from the dense undergrowth that surrounded the pond.

Purple shades of color in the vegetation caught his attention. He stopped to examine the leaves. *Is it reality or imagination?* he wondered.

He came to a spring. Kneeling, he poked his left arm into the bubbling swirl to feel its texture, rubbed his hands together to rinse off dirt from his climb, then cupped them to draw a sample to his lips. The flavor was identical, but the temperature considerably colder. Again he stuck his mouth in the water and drank deeply. The iciness gave him a brain-freeze and goose bumps. He feigned a reaction by holding his throat, then laughed.

Rising to his knees, he closed his eyes and let the sensations take their course.

"Ahhhhh, this strange elixir doth bend my visage," he said with a British accent. "I must harness such to analyze in my laboratory."

He poured out what was in the canteen, and sunk it in the spring to refill. He stood and drank from the canteen as he walked along the stream that headed for the escarpment. His view of the pond from the top of the falls had no reflection to hide what was below the surface. The water's bowl was a rock portal curling deeply like a twisted and scored funnel. There were no fish, but a pair of salamanders moved slowly near the periphery. A dozen or so water skippers scooted over the surface.

Alluring faces pulled at him from the textures of its sides. They affirmed another world dwelt below, just out of sight in the esoteric folds beneath them. *Come and see,* they called with their eyes. He laughed and waved at them. Flickers from a wind gust waved back and beckoned again. Its seduction gave him pause to make the plunge.

He picked up a walnut sized rock and lobbed it into the pond. By that he got an idea of its depth. He could have jumped from the top of the falls and splashed in without touching bottom. But the thought of making contact with the chilly water made him shiver involuntarily.

He raised the canteen to consider it with a side glance and raised eyebrows. What he imbibed showed no sign of affectation. There were no warts, scales, deformations or untidy hair growth appearing. At least . . . not yet.

He pulled his attention away from the water and listened. The neighborhood was unusually quiet. Frogs hadn't catapulted into the water when he appeared at the top of the falls nor did he hear croaking in the distance. It seemed odd. Perhaps they had succumbed to this strange brew from the depths of the earth.

From the vantage of this high point he spotted a cabin directly across the pond. Masked by dense growth, it was difficult to determine its condition from where he stood. He smiled, thinking of what treasures it would hold, then headed that way.

Outside, signs of wood rot and layers of mushroom-like fungus revealed integrity issues at the base of the old logs. Inside, a heavy snow load had broken rafters, leaving patches of sky for roof.

Above the mantel was a hand-carved sign that read *Shangri-La*. He could feel the boredom that had provoked the pocket-knife whittling on the end of a wooden crate.

A pair of rusted spring traps hung on a railroad spike driven into the chinking. They hung next to the fire place. The idea of taking them as souvenirs crossed his mind. But as he reached up to remove them, a picture of frowning, disapproving goats came to mind.

"That wouldn't go over very well." He reconsidered and pulled his hand back. "I'd have to explain what they're for. . . Nope, not the kind of thing my friends would appreciate."

Nature hadn't been gentle with the furnishings. What the rodents had started, elements and decay had continued. The table and chair made of woven branches and limbs had been busted and the twine bindings had been chewed through years before. He pictured a baby bear trying to sit in the flimsy contraptions, only to have them collapse. Without question, the whole Goldilocks business had taken place right there.

He kicked debris away to safely cross the room. Closing his eyes, he envisioned the kind of people who would choose this tough life. Vivid imagery fed him pictures of long-ago days. He saw coon-skin caps, deer skin breeches and shirts, buffalo coats, flintlock rifles, and he heard the language pioneers used to forge new frontiers.

That era was shoved aside and another slid into place. He imagined cowboy hats and bowlers, oiled slickers repelling rain, Colt six guns and Winchester rifles, stout men wearing shotgun chaps and cutting horses with roping saddles. These were coarse men fighting wars, exploiting resources and dreaming of striking it rich.

Long haired native bards and hippies sang their stories. Mystic shamans and pot-heads searching for light in mysterious and dreamy worlds. Mists reflecting utopias and time travel. Mind trips to odd and fantastical worlds. A white rabbit down a hole to inhale the remains of a smoking hookah.

He was caught up in scenes played like holograms in a glass house. *Were these pictures from books and stories vividly re-lived? Were they questions of curiosity being answered? Was there some message being sent that he needed to comprehend?*

What he now considered was the notion that a principle was being told by *all* of them over the eons. Generations made their presence known in times near and times far, but had left nothing written in this hidden backwoods cabin. Their social impact remained as untitled chronicles captured in opaque shadows.

He chuckled quietly at the thoughts this place inspired . . . *Or is it the water?*

"Why were you here?" he asked the phantoms. "Shangri-La? . . . . really? Did the water cause aging to slow and time to crawl? Who were you? What were you seeking?"

Shamus mused another moment then cupped his hands around his mouth like a megaphone.

"Did you find what you were looking for?" he bellowed through the busted roof. There was no answer, nor any echo.

Perhaps this is a moment formed in a parallel universe about why *he* was here; a pause on the way to somewhere more important. If that were the case, the quiet and the solitude would remain until the hourglass emptied. For this season, it was his hand flipping the bulbs again to get the sand falling in another time and unlock the question again for future visitors.

"Papa . . . why am I here? What will I leave behind when the days allotted for me have run their course?" He let the questions float away. An unexpected breeze bore them through the roof where they scattered. He looked around one last time and headed for the door.

Poking about the woods with a stick, he clanked into a trash heap nearly hidden by composting leaves and pine needles. He fished out old tins and relished the fragrance of ancient coffee. Sardine cans with winding keys wrapped inside their rolled-up lids were older than his experience. Broken canning jars, partial ceramic jugs with metallic labels that could no longer be read and assorted shards of glass and pottery were amongst the dig.

The moment was ripe with potential. And the air was surreal with the unrelenting scent of history that had created the debris. He doubted the dig would surrender its booty, when he spotted a chocolate colored apothecary jar with a lid wire securing the top. At first, the wire looked like nothing more than a metal band in the dirt. He dug around the band with a shard to release the find from the ground and reveal its identity.

It was double the size of a man's fist and rattled when picked up. The rusted retaining wire broke when he attempted to release the lid. Using a sardine can, he cautiously pried the lid by moving the can around the edge. The lid's rotted seal finally gave in to his persistence as it disintegrated.

Rotating the opening toward sunlight, he could see a trove of obsidian arrow heads and one spear tip. Shamus sat cross-legged and smiled with pleasure at the find. Carefully, he poured the contents onto his lap. He studied the gnarly specimens then wrapped them in green leaves and returned them to the jar. He put more leaves in it for insulation.

"That should keep you safe until we get home," he told them.

He sat quietly and ate the stale protein bars to celebrate. Along with water from his canteen, the moment was an appropriate sacrament.

Shamus saw what had gone before him. *Who's ever heard of the prophetic past?* he thought, then chuckled. *But one can learn and be inspired by those from the past.*

He felt like a thirteen year old with manhood on the horizon, exploring the what-ifs, curious about spiritual realities and looking into the future. Finally, he had come of age.

"Thank you, Papa. I will cherish these treasures you left for me. Even all those years ago, you knew I would be here today. You're amazing."

But, this appointment wasn't over. He was drawn to look at the tree branches around him. They're the minstrels of the forest when the breezes blow. Any place in this mystical oasis would hold secrets, even the trees with their songs. If they would only sing, their stories would be gems to retell.

A decaying hemp rope lay looped over a limb and dangled freely at both ends. It was high enough to be what could have been a food cache to deter animal raiding and yet low enough to be a hangman's noose. *Is it another silenced voice wanting to be heard?*

A black bear meandered slowly out of a dark patch in the woods, stirred tension in Shamus' gut. As it walked toward him, it stopped to raise itself on hind legs and sniff at the air near the tree where the rope hung. When it found nothing, it focused its rage on the man and kicked up a run in Shamus' direction. Shamus smiled and stared it down. If he ran, it would aggravate the bear even more and he could perish.

At long stride then a high leap, the bear evaporated. The tension relented and Shamus started laughing. From inside his spirit he heard a familiar response of laughter filled with love.

He had a playful and unexpected visitation. He had heard the voices of the past that were desperate to be heard. Who knows what these people may have contributed to the making of history. *Although their stories were never written, they left a legacy somewhere. Is that enough?*

Shamus declared with sincere affirmation to those who were still around to hear, "I heard you. You added your bit to the world. And it's floating around out there doing something still."

Today he also heard the voice of the one who guides history and gives legacies. And he was ready with his response. "Papa God, It's time for me to do the same. Whatever you want to do with me, have at it. It scares me to let you have that much control. But, I know how good you are."

His hike back to the Jeep was rich in the presence of the one who keeps a record of each life lived, who writes destinies for those whose hearts dare to read its content and have the courage to live it.

He hiked forward with awareness of the significance of those who will follow after him as well as the potential for the rest of his days on earth. For a few unexpected moments in the broad scheme of things, Shamus experienced a father and son treasure that completed a child that was becoming a man. In comparison, his spiritual pockets carried trinkets when he came. He was leaving with them full of golden meaning, and he felt wealthy.

He understood that imaginary "what ifs" can be what fathers and sons use to stir right choices in life. He stopped to consider what it might mean.

"If I ever get to be a father, Papa, I want to have lots of times like this with my children."

Shamus unloaded his gear, put his jar in a padded spot for safe-keeping and climbed into the driver's seat. He looked around one more time. And with a satisfied sigh, he started the Jeep.

GOOD ADVICE

Excited about being with special friends and sharing his journey, Shamus popped from the Jeep and trotted for the cabin. Instead of climbing the steps, Shamus made a hop –from the ground to the veranda. When his boot-heels hammered the wood deck, the resounding whump woke Rachel from her nap.

"Uh oh," he faltered with a sheepish stare at the door as if he could see his mistake on the other side. "I forgot."

"Now who's the forgetful varmint that woke you up, Rachel?" Shamus heard Dodee ask Rachel tenderly. "You just watch, we're gonna bust him to hard time at the wood pile for that one, aren't we?"

Shamus squeaked the door open cautiously. "You're not mad at me?"

"You can bet your Tony Lama's I am, Shamus," she said sweetly. "But you don't want your sweet little Rachel thinking I'm mad at *her* for waking up, do you? . . . You just come on in and make yourself at home while we consider your punishment."

Dodee handed still-crying Rachel to Shamus and punched his shoulder, "Now, you apologize to Rachel for your behavior."

Shamus laughed and said, "Rachel, you know what a thoughtless clown your Uncle Shamus is, don't you?" He rocked her a little before continuing. "Aaaah, I am so glad to see your precious face. I really didn't mean to wake you up." He smiled affectionately and made motor noises by flapping his lips together. She slowly stopped crying. He laughed, and Rachel giggled slightly. He laughed some more and she chuckled happily. Her response satisfied him. "I believe she forgave me. Now, where's that wood pile? I could use the exercise."

Dodee smiled warmly, "Welcome home, Shamus. Give me a hug . . . I was beginning to wonder if love hadn't whisked you off to another planet."

"Mama Shepherd, it might have. But I'm having trouble . . . I'm in love with her and she's in love with me. But she's a clear-headed woman who wants a whole man, not a broken boy. You think you guys could help me with that?"

"I know *I* can. I'm not so sure about Papa Shepherd," she smirked good naturedly. "But for a goat puncher, sometimes he's a purty smart feller."

"It may not be as bad as I make it sound. I just need a mom and dad to talk to and get a plan for fixing me."

Dodee smiled in return, "You just let us *fixers* arrange that."

"Where's the head goat cheeser?" he asked.

"I don't know. He stepped out when I told him it was nap time."

"I take it," Shamus chuckled, "he wasn't interested in a nap."

"Not at all . . . Let me take Rachel now that you have happied her up, and you can go find him. Maybe she'll go back to sleep.

"Rigo and Maria are here, too. You might find them at the house working on mohair stuff . . . And ask Roee about our recent visitor. You'll find it interesting."

Shamus kissed Rachel and passed her back to Dodee with an inquisitive look. He thought he knew who the visitor was. "Did Vince *really* show up here?"

"He told you about it?"

"He said it was a dream. I can understand a dream, but to actually come here and be asleep at the jail? That's . . . . . that's . . ."

"Kind of leaves you speechless, doesn't it?"

"Yeah, it's hard to get past the think about it to know what to say about it."

"Shamus, you won't figure it out. Don't even bother. Go find Roee and the goats. They'll give you the whole story."

It took Shamus an hour to attempt walking the short distance from the cabin to the house where Roee, Rigo and Maria were. Being missed by his goat friends warmed his heart considerably. And hearing the details of Vince's visit filled in the gaps that Vince couldn't mention under the circumstances. But getting through the onrush of friends was like wading through waist-high mud.

Shamus eventually made eye contact with Roee through a window. Shamus waved him out to join him. Roee ran out and gave him a bear hug.

"All right guys," Roee said to the goats. "You can talk with Shamus later. It's my turn." After a few playful groans, the goats went off to graze.

"It's good to see you, Shamus. Let's go up to the rock where we can catch up."

The dialogue caught up the latest news about town while they trekked to Vision Rock. By the time they arrived, Shamus was ready to get to the point of his trip.

"I need help, Papa Shepherd. I'm in love, but don't know anything about it. You and Mama Shepherd are great examples. But I need some shortcuts or I'll be an old man by the time I figure it out."

"There are no shortcuts on the path of life, Shamus. Every step is a walk with God. A man can plan his way, but God makes order out of it all one step at a time. You've got the basic ingredients. Let's just ask a few questions and we'll get some direction."

Roee asked those questions, then they prayed and Roee picked a starting point.

"You've worked a lot with me in the garden. Let's see how much of its secrets have found a home in your thinking.

"The Hebrew word, aikar, paints the picture of the husband-man of agriculture. He's someone who loves the soil and is connected with its natural and spiritual qualities. From experience, he skillfully nurtures his resources to create good soil that will produce the best results. Over time he intimately knows each vine, tree and field in his care. In the ancient days, that intimacy was passed on for generations as they lived on the same property. And if I may venture an opinion based in scripture, the land knew when it was well cared for and responded in harmony with the man.

"With that understanding, have you ever wondered why us men are known as husbands?"

"It's never come to mind," responded Shamus. "But you're painting a good picture. I think you're helping me to see."

"That's my goal, Shamus. If I can communicate a picture of truth and health, your healing and growth will be filled with hope. What do you see so far?"

"What I'm seeing is that a husband has the responsibility to love, connect and develop the environment, or soil, where a wife can grow well. Is that right?"

"That's a good snapshot, Shamus. Good start. There's a bigger picture to put together, so stick with me.

"When a man and woman get married, they become one. It's more than having physical intimacy. It's an environment where your protection of her, patient gentleness with her and your connection with her draw her into harmony with you. What do you understand about harmony?"

190

"I'm not a musician, Papa Shepherd," Shamus said while looking over the valley. "But I have heard some amazing harmonies in this valley that came from heaven. I don't know if I have the words to describe it."

"I'll bet you do. Take your time and think about it. Then give me what you have."

Roee waited patiently.

"My guess is when different notes are played at the same time, they make a better sound than when they are played separately. If we all played the same note, it would be one thing. If we played different notes they would have to be in *harmony* to have a pleasing sound."

Shamus smirked at Roee with his hands open. It was an expression that asked, *How did I do?*

"That's brilliant, Shamus. Unison is everybody playing the same note. Harmony is like you said. And they both have their purpose and strengths.

"Men and women have different bodies. When they come together in love and commitment, they make some wonderful music. But when Papa God says 'the two shall become one,' he's not just talking about bodies. He's talking about soul and spirit as well. There won't be good harmony in one aspect without having good harmony in the others."

Shamus laughed. "So, is that called three part harmony?"

Roee chuckled and responded, "You're getting it, believe it or not. That's exactly what it's about. Love in three part harmony; body, soul and spirit. You, your wife and Papa God. You your wife and children when they come. It's the harmonium of a healthy and whole family."

"Harmonium?"

Roee chuckled. "I think I just redefined that word. It's all the chordal elements working together. More simply put, it's when life together is producing a good sound."

Shamus smiled in understanding, then got a serious look on his face.

"What you said about the farmer and his relationship with the land is bothering me."

"What about it?"

"When a family lives on the same property, doing what they're supposed to do, each generation should see increase. Didn't you teach me that somewhere?"

"I believe that is Papa's design, Shamus. Some people may not agree. But it's an excellent principle for all aspects of life. Not just farming."

"Somewhere, that was interrupted in my family. My father and mother were broken people when they had me. I'm broken . . ."

"You *were* broken," corrected Roee.

"Compared to MiSeon, I feel broken. It's a lot of work to be in harmony with her. What do you call it when we're trying to play music and we don't have the same beat or the same color of sound, if that term makes any sense?"

"The music term is discordance or dissonance. It's when music sounds harsh, unpleasant and disagreeable. It happens along the way in every marriage.

"But let's continue with the musical analogy. Committed musicians improve in their skill of whatever instruments they chose to play. And learning a new song can produce an unpleasant sound until it's practiced into what they're trying to achieve. Over time, skilled people play variations of a mastered song according to their collective and individual creativity to keep the song interesting."

A light went on in Shamus. But Roee ignored it for the moment.

"In the book of Amos, a scripture asks the question, 'Can two walk together unless they make an appointment and agree?' The Hebrew picture for ya'ad is about choosing to join forces, with each player having roles for reaching a desired purpose.

"I saw a look in your eye, Shamus. What was that?"

"I was seeing something about unison and harmony. If I'm thinking unison, I'm playing to be in agreement with her, or to be like her. If I'm thinking harmony, I have the freedom to be different so long as I'm achieving the connection of good music."

"That's good, Shamus. I think that's one I can use. Do I have permission to quote you?"

"Only after you explain to me how to deal with this discordance thing."

"Practice and prayer, prayer and practice; it's a process. It's the nature of God to redeem if we don't become weary of an imperfect journey. Never give up, Shamus. Do you choose to walk with MiSeon? Do you choose to love her unconditionally?"

Shamus thought for a second. "Papa Shepherd, MiSeon said we could have a lifetime together . . . if I'm patient. I think that patience might be more directed at me than her. Yes, I choose her. I wonder if I will choose myself. How do I handle that?"

"You won't run when you get it wrong, or when your self-disapproval rating hits a low point. You won't retreat when vulnerability gets scary."

"I *do* get scared, Papa Shepherd. Sometimes it's hard to see me different than what I am. Sometimes it's hard to have people around me who know what I used to be, and I feel like they're thinking I'll never change. And sometimes I feel like running to some place where I can start over without the old me in the way of practicing a new me.

"And then, there's things that happen that show me how special I am in God's eyes. Have you ever heard of Shangri-La?"

Roee gave Shamus an odd look. 'That's a strange turn. Is this a rabbit trail?"

Shamus shared what he encountered on the way to Wonder Valley.

"How did that make you feel?" Roee asked.

"I felt like a kid on an adventure with my Dad. I was having fun. I was exploring. I was curious about things. I saw unusual things. I was somebody special even though I was alone. But I wasn't alone, if you know what I mean."

"That is something very special, Shamus. You'll never forget it . . . But what's the point?"

"Things happen that I'm not expecting that create a new me without me having to work at it."

"Papa is actively working to help you grow, Shamus. He does the work, you co-labor with him to let him get the job done . . . I think you're catching on, Shamus. Let God make you into the best man for MiSeon."

A late afternoon conversation with Dodee and Maria shed light about how MiSeon might see things. At day's end, he was encouraged and slept well.

The next day Shamus walked and prayed, processed and made time for the goats. Willy, Sully, Tanny and Scampy went with Shamus to the eastern end of the valley as he explained why he had come for a visit.

Tanny offered his bit, "Sully probably has a few goatisms that could help you."

"Tanny," Shamus responded with a straight face. "I've heard that goat wisdom is preferred by kings and rulers all over the known world."

"That doesn't surprise me," Sully rejoined matter-of-factly. "Us four-leggers have a good life. It's only natural to share our experience."

"You're right, Sully," Shamus said with his arms folded and fingers stroking his chin, "goat life has little complexity, no twists, no turns and no hesitations. It's just a straight-forward, go after it simplicity. There's something to be said for that approach."

"Yeah," Willie injected. "Mating is like a mountain lion hunting his lunch. All you need is a target. In little time after that, a new kid is born to the flock. It is very simple."

Shamus gaped in shock as he took in the comparison of goat and human courtship. "Yeah . . . oh yeah . . . I've seen you guys in action . . . Oh my goodness, yeah! I can just picture the reshaping of romance life if goats could write books."

"Romance?" asked Scampy. "What's that?"

"You'll have to ask the shepherds, Scampy. I don't think I'm qualified to answer that."

Monday Morning

How is it that Monday morning isn't just on Monday? Dodee thought. *What's the rush?* It was Sunday afternoon and Dodee said her farewell and gave her hug. Her child was leaving the nest and she was convinced that Shamus was not prepared for what was ahead. But Shamus' face lovingly told her that he had a lot to think about . . . without her help.

She understood that re-parenting a grown person is not the same as raising a child from birth. There will be things left undone. She knew that. As Shamus' Jeep rolled away with his tent and cot in the back, Roee sidled up and put his arm around her. "He won't be the last one we have to let go before we think they're ready. Papa will take good care of him."

"I know it'll get easier, Roee. But, he's the first. And I wonder if we've done a good job . . . and I guess the only way to find out is to give it time. But honestly, I would rather be more certain."

Dodee turned to Maria and said, "I hope it won't be like this when our own children leave the nest."

She retrieved Rachel from Maria's arms and headed up the steps. Dodee stopped at the top before going inside. She sighed as she stood on the veranda then turned around and looked down at Maria, Rigo, Roee and the batch of goats who had come to see Shamus off. "There goes the first of many who will come here and find a new life. Are we prepared for the next ones?"

"We're ready, Mama Shepherd," Willie responded enthusiastically.

"You guys are the unmistakable champions of this valley," Roee affirmed the goats. "You're amazing at what you do to restore people. And you do it without working at it. But I think Mama Shepherd might be referring to making the place ready for the ladies from Lawless. They need a place to sleep, besides the floor."

"Everybody's welcome to come out and sleep under the stars with us," proclaimed Scampy laughing. "And we rarely run out of food."

"That's great hospitality, Scampy," Roee responded warmly. "But, Mama Shepherd and Maria need to take care of that stuff. How about if we take Rachel for a hike and show her some butterflies and wildlife."

"That's a great idea," Dodee responded and headed down the porch stairs. She handed Rachel to Roee and turned to Maria.

"Maria, are you up for some tea while we talk about how we're going to do this?"

"I'm always ready for tea and good conversation, Dodee."

While men and goats went hiking with Rachel, the ladies heated water on the hearth.

"You know Maria, I'm uneasy about the way we're doing things. We've asked so much from people to help us prepare this place for what it's called to do . . . It's hard to ask for more. Furnishing the rest of the house won't be cheap. We have some reserves, but it won't be enough."

"Dodee," rejoined Maria, "worry will not find the funds we need. Faith will. And asking is part of faith. First we ask God. And he is always the answer. And when we ask people for help, we leave it up to their faith."

"Maria, I'm aware of what faith can do," Dodee said impatiently. "But people have limitations."

Maria returned a questioning look. "We have never obligated people to help. We simply ask them if they will . . . Are you okay?"

Dodee sighed, "Perhaps I'm still dealing with some post-partum hormones. For some reason, it's bothering me to let Shamus get out on his own."

Maria considered her response. "So this is really about Shamus . . . Take a deep breath, and relax."

Dodee breathed deeply and smiled. "I hate it when that happens. I feel like an idiot. I hope I'm not like this when the new women come."

"I think you feel like you have failed. Shamus is on a good path, and you have helped him to find it. It's time for him and you to move forward. Men must have great adventures while mothers feel insecure. It has always been that way."

They chuckled.

"You're such a good friend, Maria," Dodee said smiling. "I know the day will come when you will have the same experience."

"I am very much looking forward to it," Maria responded.

"Hopefully, I will exhibit the same patience you have shown me," Dodee responded.

"You will have that opportunity in the very near future, mí amiga."

"Maria!" Dodee exclaimed with a gasp. "You're pregnant?"

"The pregnancy test says we are. It happened when we were up here the last time. This place has so much miracle power. We prayed, and now estamos embarazdos; we are pregnant."

"Yaaaaaahooo!" Dodee yelled. "That is so flippin' cool. Can I tell Roee?"

"Of course you can. I have been waiting for this opportunity to tell you."

By evening their list of basic needs for the house was complete. Maria added some special considerations. They laid their hands on the list and prayed.

"You watch, Dodee, Papa will provide in wonderful ways."

The sound of laughter outside was an indication that Rachel was back.

* * * * * * * * *

The morning colors were captivating. Instead of the gold, orange, and purple tints of a stratocumulus horizon, the cirrus clouds were pink, yellow, and white. Roee was humming a quiet song, admiring his emerging sunrise and drinking in Papa's presence.

It occurred to him that Papa was getting his attention by showing him something different. The crack of goat horns coming together drew his eyes downward. As he watched the valley floor, he saw paved streets and unfenced estates spaced randomly. They looked real, but he knew it was a vision.

Jesus appeared and stood next to him. Roee leaned into his friend.

"Each house will be a house of prayer, Roee. Nations will be affected by the intercessors that live here. I want you to make a prophetic decree according to what you've just seen and the purpose I just told you. By faith, make this a reality. A future generation will live out another redemptive purpose for this valley that will affect the entire planet. Your daughter and her children will play a vital role in that plan. What you and Dodee have done here has prepared the way for it to happen."

Roee made a decree over the land, describing what he saw in the vision and using the words Jesus spoke about it. He released the valley's prophetic design into a future reality. Then, he wondered about the implications for him and Dodee and the future of the goats.

"All that you do is for our good, Jesus. And I know you will take good care of us wherever we go . . . What will happen with us?"

"You will laugh, son, when you see the things that I will do." Jesus looked in his eyes and added, "There will be a cost to be part of it. But your sacrifices will be greatly surpassed by your rewards."

Roee tried not to think about sacrifices. He would face those when the time came. He was content and he was in good hands.

"Look north, Roee. Look for Nara and look north."

"Where will I find Nara?"

"I will send him to you."

Roee looked at a home and valley he had grown attached to. "I love the land here, Jesus."

"And the land loves you. It won't let you go willingly. This land has longed to experience the presence of the sons of God. Now that it has, it does not want to lose you. That is why I had you make the decree. You are preparing the soil for its new assignment. Others will replace you."

GENERAL STORE

The décor of the Lawless General Store echoed the rustic flavors of Main Street. Outside were memories of the old west portrayed in board and batten siding and covered wooden sidewalks. Inside, modestly sprinkled wood shavings accompanied the peanut shells dropped by customers from the tables. Short plate rails that ran along the upper walls displayed blue and white decorative platters and plates. Varnished knotty pine beadboard wainscoting up to the chair rail enhanced the eating area.

Americana wallpaper of a spring prairie, stage coaches, farm houses and a small town with a church steeple finished the wall above the chair rail. Pictures were peppered about of happy festivities where crowds gathered. The ambiance invited connection and conversation.

Tom the store owner, occasionally drawled in Southern redneck to entertain his customers. He drew the line to not include a steady fare of country music for background. He claimed that whatever music he played, he would grow weary of it. So, from day to day, he provided a substantial variety.

He and his wife, Meadow, were two of few people in Lawless to use their real names. And because they weren't involved with the main trade of the town, their practical advice had listening ears.

Part of their store had grocery shelves that weren't filled to the brim with stock. But they carried what sold well. A wall of reach-in glass doors displayed a mere dozen brands of cold beer along with soft drinks, and dairy products. A few bottles of wine were available for sophisticated palettes. Snacks that satisfied the inner cravings were on hand in abundance. The markets of Little Faith carried everything else.

At the front looking onto the sidewalk through picture widows framed in roughhewn wood, were four ice cream tables with chairs for random arrangement. It provided a place where locals and strangers could enjoy Tom's gourmet coffee. Meadow kept the peanut bowls full to encourage appetite, chatter and shells for the floor.

Tom's a persnickety coffee master and expert sandwich maker. His reputation for great deli food and coffee has kept an adequate stream coming in for several years. He's treated his customers like noble citizens, and they've rewarded him with their business. Meadow's motherly kindness has been the social oil that made Tom's hospitality run well.

T and Zetta are engaged in an animated conversation at the tables while Tom putters about the store whistling and wiping dust from merchandise on the shelves with a moist cloth. It's Sunday afternoon and movements on the street are lackadaisical. Meadow is in Burnus picking up supplies.

"What do y'all have in mind this afternoon?" Tom asked with a bright smile.

"Ah'll have," drawled T, trying on her redneck-speak, "Y'alls famous bar-be-cued tri-tip sandwich with jalapeeños and holey cheese."

"You want that natural or warmed up?"

"Will ya warm that up for me and serve it with a salad instead of taters?"

"Watchin' yer figure?" Tom responded with a chuckle.

"Just trying to do something different," T rejoined dropping the cowboy English. "You know, changing my ways."

"Well there's a fine way to put that idea to work," he bantered. "I hear overweight women outlive the men who mention it, so I'll restrain further comment."

The giggles only affirmed that neither woman was overweight.

"What about you Zetta?"

"I'll have the same with lots of your homemade pickle slices instead of jalapeños. And hold the cheese; it ain't kosher, ya know."

"Well shucks, girls! Between holy cheese and kosher sandwiches, that's the most religion I've ever heard from you two!" Tom said with a straight face. "Would you like that blessed? No extra charge."

Zetta cackled and then Tom joined her, "Tom, you're a hoot! You should be a comedian."

"I couldn't stand the pressure. Ad lib is more funner . . . Want anything with it?" Tom continued with a glance at Zetta.

"Yeah, I'll take a salad too."

"House dressing for y'all? Salsa and chips?"

The girls affirmed both choices and Tom was off to the cubicle to prepare his specialties. The tri-tip was left over from Saturday afternoon's big cook-out. He carved the slices and put it in the convection oven to re-heat. T and Zetta's platters would be done in short order.

While building the salads and preparing the Panini bread, which he bakes himself, he reflected on T's story. He recalled when she first arrived and how over the years, bits of information eked out about how she got to where she was.

From another country, her parents were impoverished, and her father doused his hopelessness with whatever alcohol he could find. Having eight children forced him to consider her expendable. Desperate, T was sold by her father in childhood. The traffickers promised to take good care of her, train her for a profession, and send him money every month. He opted for a purchase price plus monthly stipend. Others where he lived had done it and were better off for it.

She was sold to be a servant, providing household services for the wealthy. As she matured into beauty, the climate turned dark and stormy when she became an object of pleasure for people she trusted. Her dignity and free will were caught up in whirlwinds beyond her control and sucked away as she was sold time and again. Living with abuse became normal.

Her name was changed from Gwenit to hide her identity. "T" had no meaning whatsoever. She worked hard for a time to re-member her name and where she came from in the event she ever found her way home. When the opportunity came, though, going back to her country was the last place she wished to take her shame, fear and hopelessness.

Zetta never opened up about her past. Tom and Meadow's probes produced tightness in her jaw with vague answers. But it was Tom's guess that Zetta's story wasn't much different from T's. Wounds and trauma were common ingredients in the sto-ries he knew about.

Both women were pretty enough they didn't need to be work-ing the sex trade. But the trappings were beyond Tom's compre-hension. So he and Meadow did their best to be friends and put a good face on it.

"Here's your grub, gals. And what're you fixin' to drink?"

"We'll have a little water for now," replied T. "Could you bring us some medium roast Sumatra after we're done?"

"Sure. Your usual French press for five minutes instead of four?"

"That's right."

"Your wish is my pleasure, girls." Tom said with a head bow.

When he returned with the water, Zetta asked "Can you sit a spell? We got something we want to talk to you about."

"I got a few minutes." Tom pulled up a chair and sat on the front edge with his arms crossed and elbows on his knees. "What's on yer mind?"

"What do you think about what happened Friday?" asked Zetta.

Tom leaned back in the chair, took a breath then let it out. He pursed his lips, rubbed the back of his neck with both hands and then stared at the ceiling.

"I think," Tom said slowly, "a space ship landed in that field and took everybody inside. They cloned them and let 'em loose on the town." He lowered his gaze and looked directly into their eyes. "Those guys weren't the same people *I* knew before. The judgmental and critical arrogance of religious people I've experienced in the past, went through a Vulcan mind meld."

"Except for that alien stuff, Tom, you're right," responded Zetta. "Something has changed around here."

"Remember when James first found us?" T asked Zetta. Zetta raised an eyebrow and nodded. "My view of life was about what didn't happen rather than what did. My glass," she held up her water, "was half empty rather than half full. You get my meaning?

"James had good street smarts and made a whore feel good about herself, so we didn't run off. He protected us from the bogies and gave us a sense of family. He gave me as much hope as a girl can have workin' this line. What we're looking at now is way beyond that.

"Tom, do you remember that freaky shepherd guy that

showed up in town one night?"

"I heard the story, but I never got to meet him until the other day. What about him?"

"He got James thinking about his life and it changed everything from then until now. The whole community has changed. Even them church people are changed . . . right?"

"Yeah," the others said together.

"James left and said he would be gone for a few days, but then didn't come back for *months*. He returned to pick up his stuff and released all us girls from any *further obligation* to him. He changed his name to Shamus and told us how he had been found by Jesus.

"Can you deny he wasn't a changed man? . . .You bet he was! And I got to thinking *then* that if he could do it, so could I."

"That's a lot of hope T," Zetta responded skeptically.

"Not really! Listen to the capper . . . James returns to bring God to Hatch, of all people. He claimed he had a dream that Hatch would be killed and his soul lost forever. Hatch lost it and started shooting. James and his goats were down before the smoke cleared and the screaming stopped. You can't tell me it wasn't a miracle that James survived.

"And get this . . . *next day* some dude shows up all smiles looking for Hatch and James. You gotta know that guy was a hit man. If Hatch wasn't in jail, he'd be dead today. James gave his life for Hatch . . . well almost!"

"You sure you didn't read that storyline in an Adventure novel somewhere?" Tom quipped sarcastically.

"Tom, think about it. That got *everybody's* attention!"

Zetta stepped in at this point to defend T. "Tom, with everything Shamus and that shepherd guy did, I think there's a lot of evidence to point to some kind of intervention . . . Everything that's happened, has affected both sides of the tracks." She held up the meal she had been enjoying and said, "It's as plain as a kosher sandwich . . . There is a God."

"I got one more point to make," T interrupted. "When James returned with that group of church people for a prayer meeting, they stood on our turf. That took balls. And it changed something. I can *feel* that it changed something! It was at that meeting," T poured out, "that Zetta and me got to meet love like we've never known it. That group walked through town introducing themselves and talking in real time, not looking down on us hookers. All the walls that had been there in the past were gone and a party opens up like morning glories on a spring morning. Barbecues were lit and food was everywhere. People cared. People prayed. Tom, that ain't no *story*," T said passionately. "That is real!"

"I'm still in shock about one thing," Tom confessed feeling ornery. "Shamus brought one of the most beautiful and loving Asian women I have ever met. After all he's done, he gets the pretty girl. I'm tellin ya, it's like an old love story."

"Tom, you keep tryin' to cool off my steam." Cueing each other with a look, the girls wadded their napkins and threw them at him. "I think it's time you brought the coffee."

Tom laughed and went off to brew a batch. When he returned, he poured coffee for the girls and for himself, then sat back down with a sigh.

"I got a suggestion," Tom declared. "I know it's Sunday. But when we're done with our coffee, let's go find that old market keeper across the tracks and ask him what all this Jesus stuff is about."

"Tom," rejoined T, "It's what they've been saying. It's about faith and love and all that."

Tom was looking back at her thinking and sipping his coffee.

"I guess what I'm saying is," Tom proposed. "Maybe we're ready for the next step. And I don't think we really know for sure what that is."

Meadow entered the back door with her hands full, laid it down at the cubicle and walked up to the table. "What's up guys?"

Tom's Chat

Shamus delayed getting back Sunday. Since he had his tent and gear with him, he spent the night at Shangri-La instead to think, pray and hope for another encounter. Nothing special happened. Monday mid-morning was sunshine and lazy warmth as Shamus approached Lawless at the northern edge. He pulled over at the field where they had waged a spirit war the previous Friday and sat to daydream.

Other battles have been fought here in the past, he thought. What inner battles will he fight to have a future with MiSeon? *Will my battle for transformation be won or cut short by my own sabotage . . . ?* After a weekend of tremendous encouragement, self-doubt and second-guessing knocked on his front door.

He recalled a legend about a tribal chief seeking peace with the rulers of his day. His efforts were secretly opposed by older men of his council, but open disagreement was seen as disloyalty. So when the chief and tribal council went to meet with the representatives of the government, those elders killed the chief and defeated his dream of peace. The council brought back a story of how the peacemakers had provoked an angry conflict, which left their chief the only casualty. The truth was revealed years later when the last of the perpetrators lay dying and seeking release from a guilty conscience for his part in the treasonous murder. The site of the conflict was named for that supposed battle, and its exact location was said to be close by. He could not remember its tribal name. Some locals simply called it the battleground.

He liked reading war biographies. Something about them drew his interest. Battle was unmitigatedly terrorizing. But the best of stout hearts could put a good face on it. Many a soldier went into battle risking their lives for what they believed. But facing death was unforgiving in its purification rights. And the longer a soldier lived, the smarter he fought to survive. What he believed was no longer a motivation. Those who returned home often found portions of their experience too painful to talk about. They understood that the real battle was the battle for courage. Yet more often than not, when the war was over the soldier never went home with the inner man that he took to war. Win or lose, for good or ill, his heart was different.

Spiritually, there is no turning back once the battle for truth and light is engaged. There's no quitting; it's every day, all day. There's no going home to a comfortable, care-free life. The restorative work of the Holy Spirit never ends. And from what Shamus understood, his battle was to become a new creation filled with enduring faith, hope, love, peace and joy. What he didn't understand yet was how it could be a finished work even when it didn't seem complete.

He sighed as he considered the choice he just made. *I feel like I just left my protective nest*, Shamus thought. *Am I being overly independent? I hope my new wings are strong enough. MiSeon is more than I deserve. What am I going to do with my life?*

"I refuse to keep replaying these dumb thoughts," Shamus said out loud. He was surprised when the tumult stopped and peace came over him.

"I will always be with you Shamus. My presence is your strength and confidence."

Shamus looked around hoping to spot The Hunter. The voice came from within. Or did it? "Thank you, Jesus." Shamus smiled and got back in the Jeep.

Lawless General Store came into view and with a nudge from Papa, Shamus decided to drop in. He parallel parked facing the opposite direction in front of the store and sat a few seconds listening. Shamus just knew it was important to Tom that he drop in and that was what mattered.

The store was empty except for Tom and Meadow, who were busy at the food cubicle preparing for lunch rush. Tom had just brought in hot tri-tip from the barbeque and was setting it up to shave slices. Meadow was filling condiment bins in the prep station. The waft of fresh-baked Panini bread drew a stomach gurgle from Shamus.

Shamus often wondered why Tom and Meadow chose this dubious town for a world-class deli. A difficult to understand brothel community, its history told of mysterious events that only the walls knew. The protocols of the street when Shamus was living here forbade asking about Tom and Meadow's story. Given his condition at the time, he wouldn't have cared anyway. He was incapable of a concerned response. Today, Shamus was a changed man. What was important to them, he would make important to him.

There was a different mood in the store today. Tom hummed a melody in tenor. Meadow wove a whistling harmony around it. Shamus waited and watched as they showed love in a way Shamus had never seen before. The song seemed mystical. Yet as they finished, Tom leaned over to kiss Meadow on the cheek. She reacted by offering her lips instead. Tom accepted then gave her a side hug.

It was Shamus's cue, "That was beautiful."

"Hey Shamus," responded Meadow, whose voice had the gravelly texture of a former smoker. "It's good to see you! How you feeling these days?"

Shamus stretched to check for an answer. He grimaced and

said, "I could stand some new body parts. But I've got a great life, and glad I still have one on this planet. What's going on with you guys? You look like newlyweds. And your song was beautiful . . . I've never heard you guys do that."

"That started yesterday," replied Meadow, "at Jake and Anna's."

Shamus smiled at the story potential in her statement. "*Tell me about it.*"

"I had just gotten home from Burnus after picking up supplies and Tom was about to close the store early. Him, T and Zetta decided to see Jake and Anna after having a conversation about what had been going on around here."

"You'll need to keep it short, Meadow," Tom interrupted. "People will start coming in a few minutes."

"No problem. So here it is . . . we unload my car and go to see Jake and Anna. We had questions and they had answers about Jesus and all that . . . And then, oh my gosh, we had a visit from Jesus. He *sang* over us, Shamus. Then he invited us to sing along with him. That's when something really odd happened. Tom and I joined in, and it turned into this *thing* of singing and whistling. And oh boy howdy, we got delirious with affection for each other." Tom looked at Meadow, twitched his eyebrows and laughed. She laughed and continued, "Here's the kicker, Jesus said that that is the way he feels about us all. Then T and Zetta started dancing with Jesus. Jake and Anna had never seen anything like it, and they laughed their butts off. We had so much fun."

"It's been real hard to be normal since yesterday," Tom said stifling more laughter. "Sorry Shamus, I hate to hurry things . . . Can you come back after the rush?"

"You couldn't keep me away, Tom . . . I'll be back about one and help you clean up. Is that okay?"

"We're usually fixin to wrap things up by two. But shoot howdy, if you want to lend a hand, y'all come. We've been thinking about you. We have questions and a lot to talk about. Please, make it back if you can."

Shamus climbed in his Jeep feeling like he just sampled Papa's vintage wine. Its flavor was the marvel that T, Zetta, Tom and Meadow were now a part of the encounters he has with God. Sitting quietly, he slowed his brain to consider the implications of their story. They had been the family of his former life. And now they were family . . . forever. With his hands held together and his fingers over his mouth, his appreciation for Papa's handiwork spilled over.

He walked into the store and found Jake and Anna at the check stands with lines waiting. Shamus jumped in to help, which let Anna talk with her customers. He really enjoyed making their country market a community experience. He enjoyed hearing the daily life stories each customer had to share. He enjoyed passing on encouragement when it was needed. An epiphany hit suddenly and he whispered to himself, "I actually *like* people." He stood without moving wondering where that had snuck in.

Shamus faced Jake at his register after the line thinned out, and Anna had walked away to speak with customers still shopping.

"I just came from Tom and Meadow's place, Jake. What happened yesterday?"

"God's bringing the harvest in Shamus," Jake said with an affectionate smile. "Friday's spontaneous love party got them talking and thinking. So Tom and Meadow and T and Zetta, came by to ask questions . . . and God showed up. I don't think *any* of us will be the same. And you can be sure there will be other folk from both camps looking for more of that experience because of it.

"So, Shamus what are you going to do? Are you going to stay and help us with the store? Are you going up to Burnus?"

"In the larger picture," Shamus began, "I it could be both. I just don't know the time frames involved. I'm going to stay here until my relationship with MiSeon shapes into whatever Papa wants it to be." He sighed and added, "Even if it takes years."

Jake looked into Shamus' eyes then said, "It takes a special man to be that patient. You're that kind of man, Shamus."

"I want the best for her, Jake. She's worth waiting for. And according to Roee and Dodee I should give Papa time to help me define who I'm meant to be. They say I'm going through a lot of changes, and will be for awhile. And ya know . . . she doesn't deserve a project husband."

"Well, we're all projects in progress on one level or another, Shamus. But, I understand what you're saying. She deserves a man who is whole and will pull a marriage together instead of someone with a lot of unresolved brokenness tearing it apart. You won't regret that kind of thinking, Shamus . . . So, are you ready to settle in? Anna has your room ready."

"Yeah . . . yeah, I'm ready. You think you might have time to talk?"

"Tomorrow night would be better. I don't have any blocks of time until then. Can it wait?"

Shamus laughed. "I'll probably have more questions by then. But I guess we have plenty of time . . . Are you going to start me working in the morning?"

"You could start this afternoon if you want to," responded Jake.

"I told Tom and Meadow I'd be back this afternoon if that's

okay. They want to share the whole story about what's going on with them."

"Go for it! I think you'll have a lot of influence on their future."

"Can I grab Anna and get unloaded? I'll be heading back in a few minutes."

"I'm sure she wants to give you all the details about the room and the kitchen and the rules about the house. But if she's tied up, I can show you how to get there."

Shamus grimaced. "Rules?"

Jake roared with laughter and slapped a flat hand on the counter top. Heads turned.

* * * * * * * * * *

"It was the best lunchtime ever, Shamus." That was Tom's response to Shamus' question about the afternoon. "There were lots of people in here from Little Faith. Some had to wait in line. That's a first . . . We'll need to add more tables if this continues. We had to add two from storage. That's all we have room for."

Shamus saw Tom's mind looking over the situation and considering potential changes. He saw that three of the four tables were still occupied. One needed clearing.

"Can I clear off that table for you?" Shamus inquired.

Tom came to attention and set Shamus up for the task. Then for the next forty-five minutes Tom, Meadow and Shamus cleaned and washed dishes as customers slowly finished.

With the work done and customers gone, Meadow asked, "How about a fresh cup o' coffee and a break?"

"That's why I'm here, Meadow," Shamus rejoined. "I'm *on my toes* with curiosity."

"Here come da the java!" Tom declared from the cubicle. He

brought a tray with three mugs, spoons, creamer, and a carafe. Sugar was on the table.

The three sat, sighed and settled into the peaceful afterglow of a job well done. Shamus's attention was drawn to a pair of mockingbirds squabbling in a badly stunted tree across the street. He thought about how the tree had been neglected for years without proper watering and pruning. *It's not as beautiful as it could have been,* he thought to himself. *This community could use some upgrades.* It was a random thought and Shamus wondered why he was even concerned about it.

"This is satisfying," Meadow thought out loud. "We have a record lunch rush and get to top it off with a good cup of coffee."

"Maybe you guys could bunch your shelves closer together," Shamus pointed out, "and make room for more tables. Have you ever thought of that?"

"Until today," responded Tom, "that wasn't something we needed to think about. We had the spares in storage and that was always enough; and rarely needed. Plus, we would need extra help to serve more tables. Attracting part-time people from around here with a normal wage is a little sketchy . . . And I guess I got lazy and didn't feel like working that hard anymore."

Meadow added, "But some of the girls want out of the trade. We could get their help and put them to work."

"That day may come, but for now I think the pimps might lean on you to discourage that," rejoined Shamus. "What about some of the young farming people? There's got to be at least a few that would like to earn extra money away from the ranch. And they could learn a job skill to use when they go away to college."

"You think," responded Tom dubiously, "that *those* people would want to work on *this* side of the tracks?"

"I think *this side of the tracks* is going to change. And the 'us and them' attitude about *us* will change, too . . . It's a new day, Tom."

Tom and Meadow looked at each other and smiled longingly.

Shamus caught their unspoken dialogue and felt compelled to probe.

"What brought you guys to Lawless?"

"Maybe ten years ago, Meadow's mother lived here, and her health begun to fail. We moved here to be nearby just 'cuz, if you know what I mean. You came a little while after that. And if I told you what her name on the street was, you might remember it. But in the interest of her dignity, I won't tell you that."

"I understand," responded Shamus.

"So, we left what we were doing and came here to help, like I said. We bought this building and created a store to give us a living. Then a few years ago, she passed away, and we had this store to run. With nowhere in particular that we could afford to go to, we decided to stay and make this work. And you know, we've done okay by it."

"I get the feeling," continued Shamus, "that you guys had other dreams. Care to talk about it?"

"Tom has always been a great cook," began Meadow looking into Tom's eyes. "He's the best at barbeque, as you know. But there is a lot more to Tom that nobody knows about. He has a wonderful mind for creative dishes. But the people around here have never seen his creations. His great dishes are too fashionable and sophisticated. In a big city people would pay good money for them."

"His creations are too sophisticated." Shamus repeated nodding his head. "We too red-neck for dat." They laughed at the implication that the people of the area were not *sophisticated* caliber.

"That's not altogether right," said Tom chuckling. "Most of the locals have never been around *that* kind of stuff. But we can raise their awareness to *some* kind of sophistication that's appropriate for them. That's just good marketing 101."

"So what would you do with your *about town* flare for cheffing? And what would you do to enlighten the populace?"

"Our original plan years ago," Tom continued, "was to open a grillroom where we were living. You get a picture of what that means by the name; steaks, prime rib and high-end burgers. Then I would add unique entrees and side dishes that we've created. We would do something different each day or week or whatever. You know, lots of room to change it up and make it interesting."

Tom was using his hands to talk. Shamus saw hope rising in his eyes. Then he sighed and looked at Meadow. He wanted encouragement.

"What would keep you from doing something like that here, Tom?" asked Shamus.

Tom scrunched one eye and gazed through the window. He put one elbow on the arm of his chair and his fingers over his mouth.

"Hmmmm . . . Well," he responded after a few seconds, "what we had in mind would do well in a big city, but not necessarily here. We'd have to start from scratch."

Shamus laid down a challenge, "What if you *rescaled* your design to be more suitable here? What then?"

Meadow leaned forward to share her thoughts.

"That's it, Tom!" she exclaimed. "If we created a unique place crafted just for this area, what would that look like? Instead of a grillroom, what if we created a bistro? It's just a slight shift in thinking . . . and it could be just as romantic."

Tom spoke slowly. "Meadow, we might be on to something. We have a passel of local resources for beef, lamb, chicken . . . and lots of vegetable fixins."

"I think Maria," interjected Shamus, "could come up with some recipes for goat. She's from South America where they eat it all the time."

Meadow and Tom looked at each other. Meadow wrinkled her nose.

"Don't throw that under the stage coach, Meadow," Tom responded, getting some traction for the idea. "I've eaten goat. It's delicious when it's prepared right." He laughed and added, "Tastes like chicken. . . The trick," Tom continued spreading his hands and arms over the table, "is presentation . . . on the plate and description on the menu. It could be just as big as all the others. And a nice change for those who like to explore new flavors."

"You'll have to convince me, Tom."

"I'd count it a pleasure and a challenge," Tom stated with his customary nod of the head. "And you know I can do it." He finished with a wink.

"Listen," Shamus interrupted. "What kind of obstacles would keep you from doing something like that?"

Tom looked around, "Well, the obvious would be some remodeling, new paint inside and out, and a new name. I might have enough equipment to get started. I would need resources for developing a good menu. There's probably new technology since we was mainstream.

"Shamus, you've inspired me to look outside this box I'm stuck in. It'd be worth giving a serious rethink to."

"You guys inspired yourselves on this one, Tom. I just asked the questions."

"Well, they were the right questions!" Tom proclaimed. "I'm getting a clear picture of this."

"Me too," rejoined Meadow. "Shamus, that statement you made . . . *about town*. . . it has meaning. The idea attracts, like we are the place to be. And it has subtle undercurrents of sophistication. It might be the perfect name for the people of this area. . . We could call it *About Town Bistro* and create an ambiance that attracts members of the community for a unique dining experience."

"I like the way this is shaping up," Shamus responded. "What would you guys think of involving the community in pulling the remodeling together? You know, volunteers to help paint and do some carpentry? You could give them complimentary meals after you reopen."

"I would be grateful for the help," Tom stated. "So long as people understand that I'm fussy about craftsmanship. I like paint lines straight; no drips or splatters and no ropey brush marks. And the carpentry gotta show excellence. You think that would be too much to ask of a volunteer crew?"

"What if we made that an upfront condition of service? I don't think there'd be any problem, Tom. After all, anybody can paint."

Tom looked at Shamus like he just blasphemed. With raised eyebrows, he shook his head. "That's a common misconception, Shamus. And if you ever seen professional painting, you'd know the difference.

"What I could do is hire a pro to supervise the volunteer crew and do the critical stuff. I want it done right. My customers deserve my best and I don't mind paying for it. But I really like the idea of getting people involved."

"Tom, I got a feeling this town may be getting to see a different side of you than we've seen in the past."

"He's got the goods, Shamus," Meadow added as she took Tom's hand. "This side of Tom has been buried for a long time. And it *thrills* me to see him dreaming again."

"This is more than dreaming, Meadow," countered Tom. "This could be reality."

A thought came to Shamus. He asked Tom and Meadow, "Would you guys allow me to talk with some key people about your idea? I think this could be bigger than what it appears to be."

Tom and Meadow looked at each other then back to Shamus.

"What's on your mind, Shamus?"

Prophetic Talk

Shamus had called a kitchen table think tank at Del's house. Jake was present, too, and it was getting into the evening hours.

"I saw something," Shamus began. "It was like a video, only real."

Del and Jake leaned forward. "Okay," Del said. "What did you see?"

"I saw Main Street! And it was made over with all new buildings. The lamp posts were new and the street was newly paved. All the trees were healthy and green, and there was a lot of traffic."

"That doesn't add up," stated Del emphatically. "We're at the end of the highway in a farming community. There's little commercial sense in that."

"But it sounds like something God would do, Del," countered Jake. "He's redeeming the people. Why not the land?

"Did something inspire that, Shamus?" Del asked.

"I was talking with Tom and Meadow at the General Store. And it came out that they've had a dream for more years than they've been *here* about having a nice restaurant. Tom's got some great ideas for a kind of barbeque thing that I think could help reshape the commercial thinking of our community. After we talked about it, I had this vision while I was standing on the sidewalk in front of Tom's store. I've never had anything like it before."

"So you're saying this is God?" Del responded skeptically.

"I'm just saying . . . I saw what I saw; it looked real. I don't know what to make of it. That's why I'm bringing it to you guys . . . So, what I'm asking is, if we act on this idea, what needs to happen?"

"Zoning and building codes have to line up with the idea to start with. That stuff is handled by county officials in Burnus," Del stated. "Somebody would have to spend some time with them getting all the particulars and making sure we can do it."

"I think," Jake added, "I know who that somebody could be."

Shamus smiled then said, "There's more to it . . . I want to stir people to help Tom and Meadow remodel their business once we get approval."

"You're already confident this is going to happen," Del challenged. "Why?"

"Because I see it as if it's done. I can't explain it, but I know it's where this town can go. It's like what Jake said, even this land can be redeemed."

Jake and Del looked at each other. Then Jake turned to Shamus and asked, "Do you mind if I have a talk with Tom and Meadow? I need more input."

* * * * * * * * *

Jake and Anna went to Tom's General Store the next day at the end of the afternoon rush. Meadow escorted them to a table by the window, devoted a few moments of personal attention and then left them with menus so they could choose their meal. She returned with a couple glasses of water.

"We decided on," Anna said, "a couple of BBQ chicken sandwiches. Jake wants fries and I'll have a small salad. And I think I'll just have water with that."

"Would you like something to drink, Jake?" Meadow asked.

Jake had been eavesdropping on a conversation going on at

the register between another customer and Tom about one of Tom's new creations. He pointed his finger in their direction and stated, "I think I'm going to change my order to what *they* are talking about. Instead of the BBQ, I want the Italian rub version. That sounds *really* good."

"That's Tom's latest creation," Meadow responded. "And we'd love to have your feedback on it, if you don't mind. If you don't like it, he'll make you something else."

"Well, I like trying new flavors," Jake said. "Anna and I could swap halves and she can chime in on that one, too."

"Mmmmm, I think I'll stick with the familiar stuff," rejoined Anna. "I might try a bite, but new flavors aren't my thing."

Meadow walked the order over to Tom, who brought it when it was ready.

"I am so glad you took the time to come in." Tom said with a smile as he laid their plates on the table. "Is anybody running the store?"

"Yeah," Jake said with a chuckle. "We left the cat there to keep everybody entertained with stories until we get back."

"There you go." Tom reacted. "Maybe he could call a hoe-down for me on Friday night."

"Sure, I'll see if he's up to it after a busy week at the office . . . Seriously speaking, Shamus is running things until we get back."

Tom smiled and nodded his approval, then said, "Well hey, you guys eat while it's hot and we'll get back to ya in a few."

"You got a little time to chat afterwards?" Jake asked.

"Sure," responded Tom with a smile. "The crowd is thinning out and we can take some time to talk in about fifteen or twenty minutes. Enjoy your meal."

Tom walked away and stopped at the other tables to chat with each customer.

As Tom arrived at the workstation, Jake exclaimed loudly, "Oh my gosh, Tom! That rubbed chicken is *heavenly*."

Tom continued to work, but responded with a pumped fist. Compliments were good, but he wasn't motivated by them. He just loved the art of creation.

Meadow came by their table after they had sufficiently eaten and asked if they had enjoyed the service. "Is there any way we could improve your dining experience?"

"I don't think you could improve on the food," Anna responded. "I like the atmosphere; I feel like a neighbor. Hospitable is what I'd call it. But if I ate here often, I might be concerned about my girlish figure, if you know what I mean."

"Yeah I do, Anna.

"What about you, Jake?"

"You should put a warning label on that sandwich." He held up hands like he was presenting a sign. "Warning! This food is known to encourage addiction in weaker individuals. . . That was a great sandwich."

"I'm so glad you guys liked it," Meadow responded sincerely.

"Would either of you go for a cup of coffee or some dessert? Desserts are where I get to do *my* thing."

"Maybe Jake and I can split a piece of apple pie if you have it. We gotta watch our sugar intake."

"And I'll definitely have a cup of Tom's coffee," Jake injected.

"Coming right at ya. . . Maybe Tom's at a place where we could join you." Meadow removed the dishes and disappeared into the back.

Tom and Meadow reappeared, each with a tray. Tom had a

carafe of coffee, fresh creamer and four mugs. Meadow's tray carried four half-slices of pie and a pressurized can of whipping cream.

As Tom spread the four mugs on the table and began to pour, Anna spoke up.

"Just a little cup for me Tom, I don't do well with caffeine. Maybe you could pour an inch in the bottom so I can have a taste."

"I can do that."

Setting the carafe on an adjacent table while Meadow served the pie, Tom offered whipped cream.

"Shamus tells me," Jake probed, "that you're considering a restaurant."

"Yeah, we're taking a serious look at the idea, Jake. We'd need a lot more space in here to handle any more business growth."

"I happen to know somebody that has some kitchen equipment. I can get a list and you can check it to see if there's anything you can use."

"Yeah, I'd consider any space-saver equipment to get started," Tom responded. "My main problem is space. If you could get me a list, I can do the research."

"I'd love to do that for ya."

The four carried on their round-table for another hour sharing ideas and raising questions. But the rest of that day's work was waiting to be done, so they agreed to come together again.

The four held hands to pray before heading off to their respective duties.

"Jesus," Jake began. "You know what we have need of before we even ask. And what we are asking for here is for blessings on Tom and Meadow and what's in their heart to do. We ask that you would go before us and find the right equipment and funding for their new enterprise. We ask that this place will be a place where your presence is experienced and people will find new life. And we offer up thanksgiving and praise for what you are about to do with their lives . . . Amen.

Tom, Meadow and Anna added, "Amen."

"What's the tab, Tom?" Jake asked.

"That's on the house Jake, no charge."

"Thanks Tom, that's generous of you."

Then he took out a twenty dollar bill and left it on the table as a tip for Meadow.

Meadow laughed and thanked him.

After they left, Meadow melted into Tom's arms for a much needed hug. "Tom, I just feel loved all over."

'Tween

Shamus entered The Bassmeant with the evening he and MiSeon spent together there on his mind. He smiled to himself. He had been at the county offices nearby and was ready for a break from the bureaucratic atmosphere. Coffee came to mind after ending a long detailed talk with one of the agents. His time spent had been encouraging, but he was not accustomed to thinking on those levels for that long.

"I'll have a brewed coffee, if you please." He further requested room for cream and paid the cashier.

Stepping aside to allow the man behind him to order, the customer smiled with warmth and said, "Thank you." He placed his order then turned to Shamus and extended his hand. "If you'll allow me to be a local politician, I'm Larry Cunningham. I'm the state representative for this area and coming up for reelection. Is there anything you want me to address as your representative?"

"My name is Shamus Breen, Larry. And I live down in Two Towns."

"Well, I'm still your representative, Shamus. Although I must admit I don't get down there. Not much happens except agriculture. And I can cover all that over the phone.

"What brings you up here?"

"We're going through what you might call an awakening. We want to bring Main Street back to life after nearly a hundred year sleep. I'm here looking at zoning and codes to facilitate the front end of all that."

"Well put, Shamus. Are you with the mayor's office?"

"No, I'm not. We don't have a mayor at this time."

"Who's casting the vision for this awakening? Who's doing the planning?"

Shamus reacted, "God is . . . He's turned the place upside down recently."

Larry smiled in appreciation and said, "You couldn't find a better builder."

The coffees were ready.

"I have a few minutes. If you have the time, I'd like to hear more. I can help you cut through some of the developmental red tape you're going to run into . . . Plus, I'd like to be a part of what's going on there." He laughed then added, "It'll make me look good you know."

Shamus chuckled and responded, "I appreciate your honesty, Larry."

"Now let me be clear. I'm not going to get in the way and take over. That's not what I mean. I have plenty to do and don't need any projects. But I can coach you through the political mine field and all the fancy footwork you're going to have to do.

"Does that sound alright?"

"You don't know me, Larry. Why would you do that?"

"I see something in you, Shamus. You're a leader. I can help you with your people skills and you can help me by being my eyes, ears and hands on what's happening in Two Towns. It's an easy exchange, and that's what politics is about. I can't do my job without help, and you can't do your job without help. You, me and God working together to build a better future. Are you up for it?"

Shamus hesitated, thinking about MiSeon and living in Burnus someday. But Holy Spirit nudged him.

"I can appreciate your caution, Shamus. If you want to . . ."

"Yeah," Shamus interrupted. "Larry, I came here to help the people I care about. If you want to be part of that, I'm open to it. And I'll be happy to help you in return."

"Beautiful, Shamus. . . Now tell me your vision for Main Street. What do you see?"

Shamus started sharing, knowing he had only a few minutes to do it. He rushed and Larry must have felt the pressure.

"Hang on a second, Shamus. I need to call my assistant." He took out his cell phone and made a call postponing his next appointment. "Now slow down, and don't leave out *any* details."

For the next hour, the dialogue focused on Two Towns, its potential and refills of coffee. Larry had insights that Shamus would never have thought of that would help save time and frustration later.

At the hour, Larry checked his watch and said, "I need to run. Here's my card. Call me in a couple days."

As he stood, he said, "Jesus said 'if anyone wants to be great among you, let him be servant of all.' Although it gets me in trouble with the politicos, I get as close to that as I can.

"Bottom line is, I can help your community if you will help my state. What I do for you will probably have to help us both so I don't get accused of favoritism.

"Honestly Shamus, I like what you guys are planning. It's a win-win for us both."

He extended his hand and Shamus stood and shook it.

"I'm looking forward to working with you," Shamus responded.

As Larry walked away, Shamus thought to himself, *Only God could have arranged that.* He picked up the cups, took them to the bussing station and left.

* * * * * * * * *

Shamus spent the late afternoon with MiSeon sharing their respective events of the day. Afterwards, he used the road time to plan how he would rally volunteers and skilled labor to get the job done.

The weeks ahead proved that planning doesn't go as projected. But with flexibility and repositioning, he could keep the community moving forward as Tom kept the remodel moving forward. Shamus was shaping up as a team player . . . and it felt good.

GRAND OPENING

The banner read GRAND OPENING. A white background with red letters was draped across the front of the parapet wall just above the roof of the covered sidewalk. Just in front of that and sitting atop the roof was a new sign with burgundy front and white letters that said *FINNEGAN'S ROSE BISTRO*. The *O* in *ROSE* was a radiant rose bud while the stem created the I in BISTRO. At night the letters, the yellow rose and the green stem were brilliantly backlit.

Months of planning and Shamus' networking, helped to move *Finnegan's Rose* toward a reality once the general store shut down. Tom, Meadow, and the community remodeled without stop until the day it reopened. Although it was Tom and Meadow's enterprise, their neighbors took personal ownership in the community's future.

It was the awakening to a new day purposed to let go of what was behind. From the start of the remodel, the wind stirred to rebrand the district. The former moniker of *Two Towns* would no longer be representative of its unfolding character. Lawless moved toward order while Little Faith grew in love and sacrifice. *Belonging* wrote a new core of values as the transformation took root.

The Saturday afternoon opening was light and festive with a touch of destiny. Many arrived in anticipation of Tom's barbequed tri-tips, chicken, and pulled pork. Customers said again and again that Tom's rubs, sauces and specialty seasonings would likely be famous. Tom took the idea with little seriousness.

A decorated platform put together from a farm trailer was parked across main street from the bistro so the person speaking could be seen above the crowd. Roee and Dodee, MiSeon and Shamus were standing together on the covered sidewalk across from it. MiSeon looked at her watch.

"It's time to start the dedication, Shamus." MiSeon nudged with an assuring smile.

He sighed and walked across the street to the platform.

Shamus was nervous. He wrote a speech with content he gleaned from the advice of others, and hoped he could deliver it without awkwardness. He got the people's attention by having one of the ranchers blow a goat's horn. Shamus pictured Robin Hood's horn sounding the call to his merry men to gather together in the Sherwood Forest. The vision distracted him. He laughed, shook his head and pressed forward.

"Today isn't just a dedication of a new idea, nor is it simply an opportunity to bring attention to Tom and Meadow for their investment in this community. Today we are setting a signpost, pointing toward the new direction of our community.

"*Finnegan's Rose* is Tom and Meadow's tribute to keep that signpost visible lest we forget to look out for the well-being of each other and honor the neighbors we are growing to love.

"The change we have *all* been a part of is represented here. Since the lives of Finnegan and Rosie were taken, an *awakening* has come. Whatever scars Scampy, Marie and myself may carry, we carry them with an awareness of the price for change.

"Those of us who experienced the pain and grief of that traumatic moment are recovering from our wounds. Those who have experienced the grief and weight of oppression of the sex trafficking industry that was once the master of Lawless are recovering from their wounds as well.

"This grand opening represents a grand beginning. It's a new day for Tom and Meadow. It's a new day for Lawless. It's a new day for Little Faith. And it's a new day for you and me."

A round of enthusiastic applause began, but Shamus raised a hand to keep it brief.

"It begins with a new name for a new business. And with the permission of the combined town officials, I have been given the liberty to announce the search for a new name; a united name for a new and united identity. We are no longer lawless. And our faith is no longer little."

Another round of applause arose along with shouts and whistles.

"There's a box inside the bistro where anyone can leave a suggestion. Later, it will be moved to the Post Office for a month where your suggestions can be dropped off. After that, we will announce the three top names. Then . . . we'll have a vote by the community to determine what our new name will be.

"And now I want to invite Tom and Meadow to come and join me."

While the two wove their way from the restaurant through the crowd to the stage, someone in the crowd yelled, "Shamus, you should run for mayor."

The crowd response was immediate. Cheers and applause rose swiftly and then turned to a chant of "mayor, mayor, mayor."

Shamus smiled dryly and raised his hands to quench the momentum. His heart went to MiSeon, then returned to himself. He wanted more than anything to be with her and made eye contact to assure her she was his only ambition.

"Thanks folks, but as you know we don't have a mayor here. We have a council."

"Like you said," someone responded loudly, "this town is changing. You're doing a good job of leading the way."

He needed to change direction before control was wrested from him.

"Let's do this later folks," Shamus said with a stiff smile. "Let's give it up for Tom and Meadow."

Loud applause and hoots accompanied the couple's climb up the steps to the trailer's platform.

"Tom and Meadow," Shamus continued, "it has been an absolute thrill for me to watch you pull your dreams out of the dust and breathe new life into them. And now," Shamus pointed his hand toward the GRAND OPENING banner, "it's become a reality. . . Please share your feelings."

Shamus handed Tom the microphone and stepped back.

"Well first off," said Tom, feeling a wave of emotion, "God breathed new life into me when all my dreams were dead. And it's because of him that I could even hope there was something more to dream of. I want to thank him first before anything else gets done."

He raised his hands, held the mic away and lifted his face to heaven. Although the words weren't loud over the public address system, anyone could clearly hear the "Thank you, God" he yelled.

"Now secondly, it's because of what God did inside of *you*, Shamus, that I saw that he was powerful and loving. That was a huge makeover. If he could do it in you, he could do it in me . . . and Meadow and T and Zetta. We all made that decision at the same time."

Tom turned to the crowd and said with raised volume, "Do y'all understand what I'm saying? God makes all things new. And that's why we are here today. And Finnegan's Rose is symbolic of what God's grace and mercy can do for each one of us."

Over the shouts and laughter one person yelled, "Preach it, Tom!"

"Well, I don't know a thing about preaching, but I am excited about what's going on here with Meadow and me and with all of us as a community. I really look forward to growing old here. I'm looking forward to making friendships with some of the grown up people from Lawless that never got to be kids; the ones that had their childhood stolen from 'em by this devilish sex business. I'm also looking forward to building a business that y'all can be proud of. I want to help you guys prosper, like you helped me. I have never seen or experienced a community like this . . . ever."

"I can hardly wait to see what our town's new name will be, because it will reflect what we're becoming and who we are. Y'all are the most loving and generous people I have ever met. And I just want to thank each one of you for coming out today and being a part of our dream.

"And one last thing. I'm in full agreement with you all that Shamus would make a good mayor. I know we don't have a mayor right now. But when this town gets reorganized, we will need a good one. We wouldn't be enjoying this day today if it weren't for his taking hold of it. He's an encourager and a natural organizer."

The crowd went crazy from the stirring momentum Tom created. They applauded and shouted "Thank you father Tom," while Shamus squirmed with what might become of it. He had no desire to be a public figure.

His eyes wandered over the crowd and rested on MiSeon. She was smiling and applauding along with the crowd. Her affirmation tipped the scales of his uncertainty and his eyes grew wet. He smiled back at her.

When being a loser, he thought, *was the best champion I could ever dream of being, this goes beyond anything I could imagine.*

A trio of doves landed on the sign above the restaurant. Two were grey and one was white. He heard their gentle cooing message above the buzz of the crowd, raising assurance inside. He knew the source of it, yet questioned, *Is this a glimpse of my life's work?* If it was, he knew it could painfully challenge and mold his character. Shamus was tearing up at the amusing timing of the Lord's messages. *Some of God's defining moments are simply hard to grasp,* he thought.

Shamus handed the mic to Meadow to say the closing words. "Everybody is invited for desert on the house. Tom and I have some creations we want you to sample and give us some feedback on. Y'all come!"

VIEW OF THE FUTURE

The morning dawned clamorous. Baby goats bleated for their mother's milk and nanny's responded loudly to their cries. The rooster crowed lordship over his hens and cows bellowed their entitlement of breakfast. The farmland din overruled the contemplative tree breeze, bird song and squirrel chatter he took for granted. *I am so spoiled,* thought Roee.

When grand opening festivities ran into Sunday evening, Del and Kathy hospitably provided an overnight stay. This morning, Roee let mother and child sleep while he set out for a walk. Half the distance of the gravel road to the farmhouse and decently away from the noise, his hope for some quiet started to rise.

"May I tag along?" said the familiar voice from behind.

Roee stopped and thought, *Why now?* Irritated by the intrusion on his quest, he turned slowly to give him time to adjust his attitude.

He sighed, "I was expecting you some time ago, Nara."

"I do ask your pardon, Papa Shepherd," Nara chuckled. "I have been busy starting a family and could not get away."

Roee softened and said, "Really . . . congratulations. Tell me about that."

"We have two very brave and powerful cubs. Their names are Modred and Adar."

"And the wife is doing well?

Nara answered with a grin and a nod.

"When did you meet her?"

"Shortly after our victory above Little Faith, The Hunter introduced us. Kefirah captivated me with her beauty and I captivated her with my charm. The rest is, as you say . . . is now a story. I will bring them to the valley so you can meet them. I'm sure the goats will find them . . . amusing."

The two chuckled. "I think awkward would be a better description, Nara."

"Yes, I'm looking forward to it."

"With that in mind, I'm sure you would like to get back to your family. So, what brings you here?"

"I was told," said Nara, "that *you* would have the plan."

"Well, I'm not precisely clear about it. I'm assuming we are to get up north and take a look at the spiritual condition of Burnus . . . I'm clueless about how we are to do that."

Nara chuckled. "That is strange oh great one, the stories I've heard told are of a man skilled at moving from one place to another without effort. In my experience, time and distance are no consideration once we enter that other realm. Although it should not be complicated, I do not have the words to tell you how it happens. I simply know that I will be there, and it happens."

"My one-time experience has not made me *skilled* in these matters, Nara," Roee responded in protest. "I neither planned it nor practiced ahead of time. It just happened and remains an unsolved mystery."

"Hmmmm, my experience is that I get a running start and just leap into the spirit realm. I can show you how it's done, but I don't believe you will be able to keep up with me."

"Uhhhh, probably not," Roee conceded.

"I think if you are standing next to me when I leap, you will get pulled along."

Nara did a bounding toward the main road, then turned and headed back toward Roee at full speed. Nara left the ground several yards before reaching Roee and gained some altitude. Momentum carried him beyond and he came to the ground without effect.

As he walked back, he looked puzzled.

"I have an idea," Roee injected. "Let's ask Papa how we are supposed to do this."

Nara sat next to Roee and waited. "Okay," he said with a nod.

With eyes open and looking up Roee raised his hands. "Papa, we don't know how to do this . . ."

"What kept you guys?" accompanied the laughter that came next. "Lose your wings?"

They were standing on a white rock ledge similar to Vision Rock's darker colored one in Wonder Valley. Except with a high view above Burnus. Jesus, wore his camo and hunting gear. His face showed eagerness to reveal something important and yet, willing to have some fun.

"First of all, I brought some friends to help us in our adventure."

"Papa Shepherd!"

"Carrrrrie! Oh my goodness," Roee exclaimed as he knelt to hug her neck. "It's so good to see you." As he stood he saw the others.

"You all look so wonderfully perfect and young." Roee said with his hands on his hips. "Heaven has done wonders for you."

They all laughed at Papa Shepherd's humor.

"And Rosie, you're here too." He said rubbing their ears.

"And Finnegan! It's great to see you guys!"

"Since you all are not wearing your armor," Nara observed, "I assume we are not here to fight."

"Not in the tactical sense," Finnegan stated. "But strategically, we are here to engage a fight that is now, but not yet."

Nara's face looked puzzled. He looked at Roee and said, "Yes, of course."

"Please listen," Jesus said. He had removed the bow from his shoulder and an arrow was nocked in the string. The bow had not been drawn to shoot. "There are ninety thousand people in Burnus that belong to me. Very few truly know me and none have seen me as you have. But the city is mine and the people in it are mine. And I have purposed to redeem all of them.

"I have chosen five people who will be the first-fruits of the work I have planned. Roee, you will be meeting them soon. Now watch." He raised the bow, drew back the string and let the first arrow soar. It headed to the north end of the city like a rocket and faded from view. A bright flash indicated it had landed.

"One is in the north, and another in the center." He sent another, then another arrow flying. "There will be one in every district, rich, poor, broken, influential, and dissatisfied. I know who they are and they will know me. These five arrows represent the work I have begun and the grace that will be upon their lives."

He launched the remaining arrows for their respective destinations and returned the bow to his shoulder. His quiver was empty.

"Come and see, children."

From the edge of the rock everything looked far away yet up close. But if they focused to any point of the city, what they saw revealed every detail.

"Remember my friends, that the battle belongs to me and it

is already won. Your own strength will accomplish nothing. I just need your partnership."

"Carrie, Rosie and Finnegan, this will be your station to watch and intercede until the time is right."

Jesus stood at the edge of the rock looking down on the city. He turned to Roee. "I love them dearly, my friend. Will you love them as I do?"

Roee nodded. Jesus reached out with an index finger and touched his chest. Roee felt something flood through him. "You will need more grace for the assignment. Be strong and courageous. Be watchful. The time for this assignment is at hand."

A fire ignited in Roee's chest, impelling him to kneel and pray. When he looked up, he was back in the drive and Nara was nowhere to be seen.

Fire in Town

With their vehicle safely hidden, the black-attired pair sneaked toward the wooden structures by way of the open field to the west of town. Even with a mere quarter moon, there was no mistaking the gas cans they carried. The cans were full to the brim to prevent sloshing noise. They were professionals.

"Oh, I'm gonna love this, Grouch" scoffed one quietly as he moved a tumbleweed with a leather-gloved hand. "These wooden buildings will burn so fast the fire trucks won't get here in time to save 'em. Another job well done, eh Grouch?"

"You talk too much Fingers. Just shut up and let's get outta here before we get seen."

They set a plastic can near the middle of the two story structure. The other can was splashed on the wooden wall. The exposed gas would get the fire started. The second can would melt with the heat and explode.

"If everything goes right, maybe nobody gets hurt. The competition shuts down, and the boss is happy. We get the girls to come to Burnus and work for us and . . . everything is beautiful."

The two were silent as they lit matches, threw them on the spilled gas, and ran as it ignited. Reaching their vehicle, they looked back at the situation before climbing in.

"Damn Fingers, that second can shoulda blowed by now."

There were people running about the building, backlit by streetlights and growing flames. Loud voices shouted something about somebody caught inside the building. The two heard the news as it carried across the field and looked at each other.

"So much for 'nobody gets hurt,' Fingers."

"No worries, Grouch, it comes with the job," Fingers said with uncaring coldness. "Who knows, maybe they're insured." He laughed as they got in the car and drove away with lights off.

Half a block of row housing was charcoal before the volunteer crew got the blaze under control. The old wood was vintage fuel for a fire nearly impossible to stop.

Because of the sex trafficking going on in the buildings, everyone was awake at that hour. It was said, there were only minor injuries and a number of people were now homeless. Yet one person was missing.

As dawn illuminated the damage, relief volunteers took the homeless to the fire station where cots and blankets were waiting to ease the distress of a tense night. Grief hung in the air.

Someone phoned Del to brief him on the situation before the sun rose. Del made calls to appeal for help, and by mid-morning he had a sizeable core of people willing to open their homes. The possibility that somebody died in the fire nagged his thoughts. He called his brother, Jake.

* * * * * * * * * *

Tom looked at the scorched paint on the back side of *Finnegan's Rose*. They were fortunate. Their structure was enough distance across the alley to escape the flames, but not the intense heat. He looked over the blisters on the wall and said to Meadow, "We can fix this . . . We got off light, Meadow." He pointed with both index fingers for emphasis at the scene across the alley and added, "These guys have lost everything."

Tom and Meadow's building was on a corner substantially away from the starting point of the blaze. But the movement of the fire consumed everything directly behind them.

Meadow looked numb. "Tom, I really don't care about the buildings. It bothers me that I don't know where everybody is that lived here. These are my neighbors . . . and Zetta's missing. Somebody said she was trapped inside." Tom stepped up and pulled her into his arms.

As Tom and Meadow stood in the alley, Jake and Del poked their heads around the corner of the building where the side street was.

"We thought we might find you guys back here," Jake said as he stopped next to the couple. "How is it going?" Del kept walking toward the ash heap.

"Our damage is repairable, Jake. But as you can see, the whole block back here is just gone."

"Why would anyone want to burn us out, Jake?" Meadow asked.

"That shouldn't be a hard question to answer. The devil wants to steal, kill and destroy. If he can pull people away from here before they get saved, he can spoil the momentum of what God is doing. And if my understanding is correct, there will be open and eager arms waiting elsewhere to put these girls back to work. That means we have an opportunity in front of us to get them going in a new direction while everything is turned upside down.

"And we're off to a good start. The town has taken in every one of them. But it doesn't end there. We need to support them in their losses, create jobs for them and train them for a new . . ."

"Jake, stop talking," Del declared. "Meadow, do you have a blanket inside?"

"Well of course I do."

"Please go get it."

Jake and Tom walked over to where Del was standing, then

Del stepped into the ashes. Meadow came with the blanket.

"Guys, please don't ask any questions and just listen. If I have to explain it, you wouldn't believe it.

"Jesus said that we would do greater things than he did because he goes to the Father. If God can create a man from dirt, he can create beauty from ashes." Del began to shake like a vibrator was inside him. "Guys, get over here, and bring that blanket!"

"Now pray with me for a miracle . . . We speak to the human ashes in this place and command them to come back to life."

An upward movement rumbled in the ground and raised it where they stood, sending ash and bits of debris into the air. They all lost their balance and stumbled, but they kept praying. Minutes went by. The ash was blinding.

Meadow started laughing as a breeze arrived. "I see them," she yelled. "It's Zetta. She's back!" Meadow stumbled forward and wrapped the blanket around Zetta's naked form.

Like the puff of someone blowing out a candle, a strong but short burst of air cleared the ash cloud. The five of them were left standing in clean air.

Meadow walked Zetta through the debris toward their car. "Tom, I'm going to get her home for some clothes. We can talk later."

The men looked on. Tom had tears in his eyes. Del was still shaking, but smiling. And Jake wagged his head and stated, "With God, all things are possible. With God, *anything* is possible.

"These are the greater works, Del. The works that Jesus said we would do."

"Meadow said, 'I see them.'" Tom interrupted in a daze. "What did she mean by, 'I see *them*? . . . . And did you notice? She didn't have any hair!"

SANDY BEACH

"That's unexpected," Tom said to the condiment bins. The bell at the back door announced a delivery while Tom was making his daily preparations. He pulled off his food handling gloves and headed for the door. When he opened it, a well-groomed man in his late twenties greeted him with a smile and handed him a business card. "My name is Sandy. Are you Tom?"

"That's me." He responded and they shook hands.

"I'm a claims adjuster for your insurance carrier, Bradley Mountain Insurance Services. And I'm here to look at the fire damage and verify the changes you reported to your business."

"Okay," Tom responded while reading the business card. "Sandy Beach, I'll bet there's a story behind that name."

"You have no idea, Tom," he rejoined.

"Give me the short version," Tom said with a warm smile.

"Sandy isn't my real name," he began slowly. "But when I was in school, the kids rarely used my real name. They called me everything they could think of and then some. Rocky Beach, Windy Beach, Stormy Beach and some miscellaneous perversions I won't repeat in good company."

"I tried Rocky for a while, but all the tough guys saw me as Rocky Balboa, back in the day, and wanted to boost their reputation fighting me. As you might imagine, Windy encouraged crude noises and Stormy just wasn't my nature. So I concluded that it was best to get ahead of the game and settle on something I could live with . . . I chose Sandy, and that's been my name ever since."

"Well Sandy, it's a pleasure to meet you. Welcome to *Finnegan's Rose*. What can I do to help you get done and back on the road?"

"You reported a change in your operations. So, I'm going to take some pictures and make a report to the guys who'll jack your rates up for all the improvements you made to make more money."

"Well of course," Tom rejoined. "I have more stuff and more liability. I wanna make sure I'm covered." Tom rolled his eyes and added, "And I can always appreciate the increased cost of operations."

Sandy responded, "Everybody does. It's another one of those fuzzy perks passed down from the guys at the top . . . Now, if you would step out in back, I'd like to go over the heat damage I saw out there. Then you can get back to the important stuff while I wrap things up."

"That sounds good to me, Sandy. I have a lot to do."

"I'll take some pictures and get some close ups, but it looks like your damage is limited to heat. Paint blisters mostly, and some warped boards. You'll need some cosmetic work. No burns or warps on the inside?"

"None to speak of. The fire marshal didn't find anything. He checked it out pretty close."

Sandy took in the fire's devastation across the alley and continued. "The second building from the right was one of ours. That will go down as a total loss. I can't tell where one ends and the other starts. What a wreck."

"Yeah," Tom added. "The guy on the end next to it wasn't insured at all. He asked me if I wanted to buy him out."

"Are you going to do it?"

"If I can find out what the property's worth, I'd think more seriously about it."

"I can get that for you. It should be worth about the same as the building I'm making my report on. I can give you a copy with all the personal information blacked out. In fact, this guy is a non-resident owner. He may just take the insurance money and sell the remains. It wouldn't be worth it to him to come cross-country and rebuild . . . Want me to ask about it?"

"I don't know if I have that much borrowing power . . . But it would be worth a try . . . Yeah . . . yeah, if it ain't too much trouble, I'd appreciate it."

"No more effort than what I'm already doing. What would you do with the property?"

"I'd make a parking lot of it until I could put the new building there. Then, I'd switch things around. I'd tear this old building down and turn the property into the parking lot. After this fire, I don't feel real secure in this old wood structure."

"For what it's worth, you would reduce your insurance costs significantly if you get in a building with a better fire rating," Sandy added.

Tom sighed and said, "Yeah . . . A dream for another day . . . Well hey, you and I need to get back to work. I have to be ready when the doors open."

"No problem," Sandy responded. "I'll be in when I'm done."

Sandy walked across the alley while he read the fire marshal's report and stood with the barricades and crime scene tape. Sandy was taking pictures when a dodgy looking middle-aged man arrived.

"Howdy." the man extended his hand.

"Howdy back to you, sir." Sandy returned, taking his hand. "Are you a resident here?"

The man turned and pointed back the way he came. "I own the next to the last building down on this block. I was lucky. Those volunteers got the fire out before it got to my place. They saved my ass and did a hell of a job putting down the fire. Sure got my respect."

"You're not insured?"

"Nope. Oh, you know how it is, good intentions and all. I just never got around to it."

"Even if you were, arson is a tough claim for getting results. Here's my card if you want to talk to us about a quote. I'm an adjuster, so I don't do sales. But the people in the office can get you going."

The man looked at the card and said, "Sandy Beach, eh? . . . I used to know a Rocky Beach. He was an actor. Changed his name and all that."

Changing the subject, Sandy asked, "Did you see anything the night of the fire?"

"Yes I did. I was the one that told the fire marshal about the two guys that ran into that field back there after they lit off the fire. They wore black like they was pros. My bet is it was mafia guys from Burnus."

"What makes you say that?" Sandy asked.

"It just comes with the territory. They're always trying to drive us out or get us to join 'em. They're ruthless competition. If it weren't for that *miracle*, they would have succeeded."

"What miracle are you talking about?" he asked sincerely.

"The second gas can didn't blow up like they planned. It distorted but didn't melt to the flash point. The firemen called it a miracle. When they found it after the fire, it fell apart when they tried to pick it up. If it had touched off, this whole block might be gone today. Even Tom's place could have fried.

"I saw it all and I think it was a miracle, too. Angels was watching over us that night."

"Are you a religious person?" Sandy asked.

"With all that's been going on around here these last months, I been thinking 'bout it. I got stories and so does Tom; you can ask him. There's the one about this goat shepherd . . ."

"Another time perhaps," Sandy interrupted. "I have to get my work done."

"Well, you know what ya gotta do." The man turned and said over his shoulder as he walked away, "Have a cheery day."

Sandy finished his notes and headed inside. He photographed equipment and wrote down brand names and model numbers, then stood near Tom with his briefcase in hand waiting politely for Tom's attention. Tom looked up at him and smiled like a father would smile at a son. It opened a familiar spot in Sandy's heart. Peace poured over him and he felt like a child coming home after a long absence.

Sandy leaned against the counter and said, "I feel like I just got adopted, Tom. You sure have a way about you."

"It's God's presence, Sandy," Tom replied quietly. "He wants you to know how much he loves you."

Sandy and Tom locked eyes.

"My father loved God, Tom. He wasn't much of a church goer, but he had these experiences. He was sick, you know, and couldn't get about much. But, in the last years of his sickness he was always happy. He told me about times when God would *check in on him*. I thought it was the medications, so I didn't give his visitations serious thought. When I was feeling that presence, as you called it, I missed my Dad and I remembered his experiences . . . I wonder if they might have been something like what I felt."

"You can have that sense of belonging for eternity, Sandy. It's what Jesus died on the cross for, to take away all your sins and make you a son in his family. He found me just a short while back and I've found he's everything I've ever wanted. And he's such a good father.

"Sounds like what your Daddy experienced might be trying to get your attention. Would you like to know the Jesus your Daddy knew? I feel him pullin' at your heart."

"Is it that simple, Tom?"

"It can be if you're ready. Turning to him is simple. Then, you just have to decide to respond to his love with yours. It's like an exchange. You exchange your life for his. The believing part has its moments. But you're starting a whole new life with him as your closest friend, so it'll take a little work while you get to know each other. No Sandy, it ain't complicated."

Sandy stood calmly, considering Tom's words.

"Yeah . . . I think I've believed in some way because of my Dad . . . because I want to be with him. But the love part is probably where I've hesitated. Kind of selfish, I guess. But, with what I'm feeling right now . . . Yeah, I want that love. . . I guess I just don't know how much I can give back to him."

"Jesus receives whatever you give him, Sandy. It makes him happy when you're just with him. . . Like I said, it ain't complicated." Tom raised a finger and added, "I got something for ya."

Tom wiped his hands, then went to his office and returned with a New Testament. Holding it toward him he said, "When you've read that a couple of times we'll get you a better one. Start with the book of John. I know it's a ways to come from Burnus, but maybe you could make your way back here on the weekend and we can talk some more."

"I'd like that, Tom. I'm sure to have some questions. There's some things my Dad said that are making sense . . . Gosh, I hate to leave . . . but we have work to do. I have your number and you got mine. What's a good day?"

"Well, I'm closed on Monday. But if you want to come down and party with us, we have a really fun time around the place on Saturday evenings. You could spend the night with us if you like . . . You married?"

"No I'm not, but I have a girlfriend."

"A handsome guy like you *should* have one. Bring her with ya."

"Alright," Sandy responded. "I'll email you the report I turn in and the sales people will quote your new premium with all the deductibles."

"I'll walk you to the door so I can lock it behind you."

Sandy offered a hand outside. But Tom gave him a fatherly hug instead and prayed for him. His return trip to Burnus was full with thoughts of what he had just experienced. Memories of conversations with his Dad replayed with added meaning. Now he understood some things that he hadn't before.

"I sure miss you, Dad."

Shamus' Choice

"This is compulsive, Shamus . . . Slow down and think about what you're doing!" Jake was aggravated and talking loud. But he wasn't angry.

With the Jeep running and packed with enough for several days, Shamus sat in the driver's seat, hands on the steering wheel.

"Jake, I have to find my parents and make things right before I move forward. They're like sharp little teeth that keep gnawing at my soul. When I deserted them fifteen years ago, I made a huge mistake."

What he said sounded hollow and it wasn't undetected by Jake. What Shamus said was true, but it wasn't the whole story. Shamus kept avoiding eye contact.

"Shamus, you're rushing this and running blind; you don't know where to look . . . What's the real problem? . . . What do you need?" Jake could see that he was trying to find an honest response. A thought came to Jake and his tone softened. "What are you running from, son? Are you afraid this town is going to elect you mayor?"

The question triggered a reaction, and Shamus boiled over.

"I'm being set up to *fail*, Jake. I'm a sentimental favorite for the job. I'm not qualified to run a city."

"God doesn't want or need your talents, Shamus. Some versions of scripture say we are supposed to make talents multiply. Those talents are units of money, not natural gifting. Jesus was talking about resources the master turns over to those who serve him and how diligent we should be to use them well. It looks like Papa is turning over to you a life of politics. All you have to do is say yes and let him strengthen you where you're weak. Sure, your past will cause problems. But watch what he does in spite of it. This is not about living for *your* honor; it's about living for *his*."

Shamus sat back in the seat, looked up and sighed.

"My past will make flaming arrows available for anyone else who has ambitions for the job. And they'll shoot them at me when they need an edge. I can't put MiSeon and all my friends through that kind of fire."

Jake moved to the front of the Jeep and put his hands on the hood to get Shamus's attention.

"Everybody in this small town knows your past, Shamus. Anyone who uses it against you will be branded for the political maneuvering behind it. And you know you will have all the help you need to grow into the job. We want your success more than you do, Shamus. This is not Washington, D.C. with its alligators and snakes . . . There's something else that's eating at you."

Shamus and Jake locked eyes as Shamus searched his heart. The lie he was buying into was hiding behind a half-truth he couldn't see.

"Could it be that you don't feel you're *worth* the love and grace it takes to build a future, Shamus? Your past was forgiven by the greatest act of love humankind will have the opportunity to benefit from. And believe me when I tell you, it'll take courage to possess the inheritance *you've* been handed . . . Sure there will be accusers and liars that will promote themselves at your expense. You faced worse when you were on the streets. So the idea of opposition and bad-mouthin' isn't what's bothering you, is it?"

Shamus considered what he was hearing, and the truth lurking at the edge of darkness, ready to jump into light.

Jake moved back to the driver's side of the Jeep.

"Is it possible that you're afraid the love we have for you will fail when things get messy? Are you afraid when you need us the most we will abandon you like your parents did in their brokenness?

"Sure there's risk involved. Some people will distance themselves when the mud starts flying. Good-intentioned people have fears, too. There are no perfect people, Shamus. But most of us will be tough enough to stand with you while God does what he wants with you. What has happened in these towns is making a difference, and you're a major player along with the rest of us.

"I think you should come down from that Jeep and have the balls to believe God, trust him, trust us, and take your place in our future. Where else are you going to find love like that?"

The lie was exposed. He was afraid and running from a love he felt unworthy of, and commitments that held the prospect of failure. Unworthiness and the accompanying fear made it difficult to love himself. He wasn't good enough to receive love and it was scary to trust people that could leave him standing alone when he needed reinforcements.

Understanding the paradox didn't make the choice easier or take the knot out of his chest. Could he stay and accept his destiny? Did he belong here? Was this his tribe? Could he trust? He could see that out of the ashes of the town and his own past something beautiful could grow . . . But that process would take a braver man. He wasn't that man yet.

With those thoughts Shamus banged the Jeep into gear, strongly wanting to bolt. Jake backed away, letting him make the decision. With one hand on the steering wheel and the other on the gear shift, Shamus looked skyward and yelled, "Damn it all Jake, I wanna run so bad! I'm in *way* over my head."

Instead of popping the clutch, he turned off the key and jumped out of the Jeep. The two hugged heartily. "Help me Papa," Shamus prayed, "I'm scared to death of what lies ahead."

Jake remained silent for awhile.

"Don't take me wrong," Jake said as they stood apart. "I agree that you need to find your parents and put that relationship to rights. If you need any help, I'll be there for ya. In fact, all of us are willing to invest in you without any guarantees.

"But, you weren't being honest with yourself or with me. You would have spent all your time finding yourself instead of your parents."

"Thanks Jake," Shamus said feeling humbled. "You're a true friend."

"Do you have any idea about where to start looking?"

"Reno, Nevada was where I turned my back and walked away from them. I can start there with an internet search and see what I come up with. I know it's probably as easy as you said . . . I just need to do it."

The conversation stalled long enough for Shamus to pull his belongings out of the Jeep.

"I guess I'll settle back in and get to work." He turned and shifted his load, then looked Jake in the eye. "Thanks again, Jake. I love you."

* * * * * * * * *

It was uncertain whether the phone number and address were still current. But Shamus had a place to start for a Steve Breen in Las Vegas. When he called, a man's languid voice answered. Shamus stated his purpose in calling and who he was looking for. An awkward pause followed.

"A couple of years after you left," said a quivering voice, "your mother and I were in a car crash. I was drunk, and she was killed. Shamus, I killed your mom. Are you sure you want to call me your father?"

Shamus was stung; he was too late for his mom. His emotions spun and he couldn't find a response. "Fill my mouth, Lord," he quickly prayed then plowed ahead shakily.

"It hurts me to think I'm too late. But we have to do something, Dad; anything. I don't deserve to be called your son. I ran. I deserted you and I made a ruin of my life and the lives of so many others. I'm no better or any worse than you."

"I don't know if I can agree with you about that. I went to prison for manslaughter after that crash," his father said. "I've been out a while and I'm trying to get my life together. And I'm trying to get my health back. All those years of drinking and drugs took a toll on me. I'm afraid, Shamus. I may not have much time left."

The conversation went back and forth recounting storms and mistakes. Empathetic silence absorbed the shockwaves of brokenness and recovery that each had experienced. The gap between them was shorter.

When talk shifted to Shamus' encounter with Jesus and the new life he was living, an idea came to mind.

"Do you have any way to get here, Dad?" Shamus pleaded. "We can do something about your health if you could just get here."

"I got an old Camry that might make it there."

A ROAD BEGINS

Tom and Meadow were chatting with customers at different tables; their backs against the windowed front of the bistro. Meadow was the first to feel the vibrations in the window. She turned and craned to look out; she was not in position to see anything. The low rumble increased before it arrived and drew attention to the street. A pickup with flashing lights followed by oversized heavy equipment transports pulled onto the gravel of the railroad easement across Main Street. Assorted vehicles pulled in front of the sidewalk. The vehicle insignias displayed Department of Transportation. On the trailers were graders, earth movers, dozers and water trucks.

Tom and Meadow looked at each other as Tom declared, "That's not a sight you see every day."

"Not exactly pothole maintenance," somebody said.

Men and women piled out and milled around. Some headed for the front door while others grabbed sack lunches and sat in the shade of the covered sidewalk.

"Welcome to *Finnegan's Rose*, my name is Tom and this is my wife Meadow. How y'all doing?"

"Fine!" . . . "Great!" . . . "Doin' good," some replied while others remained quiet.

"You want to eat together or at separate tables?" Tom gestured toward the tables with his palm up. "I can pull these together for you if you like."

"Yeah, let's pull 'em together," said one woman.

Tom quickly moved tables while Meadow took orders for sodas and coffee. Two of the men jumped in to help Tom move chairs into place.

"Meadow will get your drinks coming and I'll grab some menus for ya."

Tom and Meadow performed with seasoned efficiency putting table service, drinks, and menus in front of their eager visitors.

Del and Kathy walked in. The sight of workers and equipment stirred their curiosity. It showed on Del's face as Tom walked by. "Del, if you want to find out what their up to, feel free."

"Thanks Tom."

Del struck up a chat with the people at one end of the table while food was being prepared. An energetic woman with Shannon embroidered on a name patch gave the overview of their agenda. Another man filled in some details. When Tom and Meadow started serving, Del excused himself, "I'll let you guys enjoy your food. This is a *fantabulous* place to eat."

"That's what we heard," one of the crew responded, as he reached hungrily for the plate in front of him and pulled it closer. As he held up his sandwich for inspection, he continued, "The surveyors were through here awhile back and they *raved* about this place." He took a small bite, closed his eyes and groaned in delight. . . "They were right . . . They were so right." Then he took a moderate mouthful.

With so many to serve, Tom curtailed personal courtesies until everybody had their food.

"Meadow," Tom hollered from the kitchen, "when we get all the orders on the table, go outside and see if anyone wants a cup of coffee? Tell them it's on the house and use to-go cups."

"That's a great idea, Tom," she responded.

As the workers paid their tab, Tom said their drinks were free this time around.

"And that was some *nice* coffee, Tom," Shannon said. "Did you roast it yourself?"

"Ahhh, thanks Shannon. But the roasting is a well kept secret. Next time you come, I'll make you one of my world famous coffee creations. I *guarantee* you'll love it."

"You're a barista, too!" She turned to the rest of the crew and exclaimed, "I think we found us a gold mine, guys."

"And if you happen to be around here on a Saturday evening," Tom shamelessly plugged, "we have special barbeque entrees and music. Y'all come and have a lot of fun."

After the workers left, Tom and Meadow sat down with Del and Kathy.

"Well, what did you find out?" Meadow asked.

"Tom, you better get serious about buying the land in back for a parking lot. If what they're saying is true, you're going to get busy when they're done. Maybe even before if they spread the word around."

"Done with what?" asked Tom. "What're they here for?"

"They're here to cut a road through the mountains to the other valley where the shepherds came from. I think it's called Grindlay Village. It'll wide enough for utility easements as well. There's some plan to connect us and Burnus to other parts of the state. My guess is there's politics, commerce and real estate involved."

"So," interjected Kathy, "this is not going to be the *end of the road* anymore. This *is* a big deal, isn't it?"

"Yes, Kathy, this is a big deal . . . This is a momentous deal. . . Actually, this may be an enormous deal! We'll have access to markets northwest of here, utility access for mountain land to the west and who knows what else we could dream up . . . Tom, I think starting this project unlocked something."

"And," Tom added with a smile, "there will be travelers not only needing a place to eat, but places to stay. Did they say how long it would take to complete the project?" Tom asked. "I'd like to have an idea of how long we have to get ready."

"Shannon said six months to a year depending on soil types and weather."

"Del," Tom continued, "you got the administrative mind around here. What do you think we should do?"

"Tom, this is favor potential that's bigger than anything this old farmer has ever seen. The first thing I intend to do is pray. We can't move too fast or too slow. Missteps could be costly. Loose talk could put our ideas in the hands of the wrong people. And we need to spread this news around to our neighbors so they can benefit by this, too.

* * * * * * * * *

Tom made phone calls the next morning. His second call was to the main office of the tiny branch bank located next to the post office in Little Faith. They had given him the name of a loan officer to talk to in Burnus. He would find out what his buying power was.

His first call was to Sandy. After preliminary greetings Sandy asked, "What can I do for you?"

"I'm moving toward a serious interest in that property behind us, and I'm calling to see if you might have a market value worked up for the place."

"I'm getting close, Tom. I need to hear back from the owner before I can legally make any information available to you. By the way, I'd like to come down and visit if that offer to stay at your place is still open."

"Of course it is, Sandy."

"Something happened last weekend that I really want to talk about. Friday afternoon, I was telling a client about my experience with you. He said he wanted to have that experience, too. I put my hand on his shoulder to pray for him like my Daddy used to do with me, and he fell down. That was strange . . . and I couldn't explain it."

"I've never heard of that, either. What did your friend experience?"

"I don't have the time right now. I'm arriving at a client's house and need to stay on schedule. Can we talk this weekend?"

"Sure, Sandy. I'll find someone better equipped to answer your questions."

"Great Tom, I'll see you then."

Tom's call to the bank set events in motion. The loan officer, after hearing Tom's story, was eager to come to Lawless and see the site. An appointment was set for when Tom would be normally closed.

Tom made a third call to recruit extra ears and brighter brains for the meeting.

* * * * * * * * * *

Del, Jake and Tom took a table after the lunch rush, leaving Meadow to clear plates and clean.

"You guys have your high-level discussion while I relax with the dishes," Meadow said. "I already know what this is about, and its beyond my pay grade. Tom can answer my questions later."

"Thanks, love, we shouldn't be long," Tom responded with his *I only have eyes for you* look.

She smiled and walked toward the kitchen. Del asked, "So

what's up, Tom?"

"Well, things are happening, and I need more minds to help me walk through it all. Since the *whole town* will be affected, I need input. I'm too naïve to do this alone.

"There's an oxymoron," responded Jake with a smile. "More brains mean a bigger head."

Del shook his head and laughed. "Jake, I think it has something to do with safety in having counselors."

"I know, big brother. Just keeping it light."

"Well you did that."

Tom shared the elements of his calls and his relationship with Sandy Beach.

"Well first off," stated Jake, "we need to get Roee here for the weekend so he can meet with Sandy. I can go get him . . . You know what? We need to get those guys a vehicle."

"I'm not sure they want one, Jake," Del responded. "But it would be easier for *us* if they had one."

"I'll give him a call and see if he could come for the weekend," continued Jake.

"And as far as adding more minds," Del said, "we can tap into the town commissioners. Working with banking minds requires experienced skill. Jason Phipps is a sharp guy to have with you when you meet with bankers. He sees through schemes and reads between the lines better than anyone. He could tell us what they're up to."

"There ya go, I knew you plow chasers could help me see the bigger picture," Tom responded with a chuckle.

"Speaking of bigger picture," Del continued looking at Jake, "let's get moving on the government changes and getting a new mayor elected. Changing our structure can't be that hard can it?"

Jake nodded then stated, "It's time for doing paperwork, and waiting time for responses. Bureaucracy isn't about difficulty; it's about time and political favor. I can do the time on the paperwork and Shamus can do the politics." Jake chuckled. "It looks like Shamus got a gift for that whether he likes it or not."

Del leaned back in his chair and sighed. "Y'know guys, who would have thought that getting people saved would cause God to pour out a blessing on this community that we have to scramble like crazy to keep up with."

BANKERS

"Wow," declared Tom. "I'm not sure what to make of them two. They seemed a bit too hungry if you ask me. What's your thoughts, Jason?"

"A reputable banker," stated Jason Phipps confidently, "isn't going to encourage you to borrow beyond reasonable ability to pay it back like they did . . . And there's only one reason these guys are looking for Shamus. They're looking for a back door for their own agenda . . . Don't trust them, and don't show them your cards. I highly recommend that whatever plans you develop be kept top secret."

"How long would it take us to set up our own bank, Jason?" asked Del.

"The average is more than a year. We need key people, a sizable chunk of money and an air-tight business plan to present to the state for a charter. We can come up with the money, but what we don't have is the time to stay ahead of these guys. My guess is they'll try to move in on this opportunity covertly and immediately. With the new road being public knowledge, opportunists will abound."

"I strongly believe," Del responded, "we should work toward having our own bank or credit union, whether it's for Tom or for anyone else. We need to invest in the future of this community."

"I agree," replied Jason. "We need to get the other commissioners and key players together for a think tank. In the meantime, let's pull in another institution that doesn't have a personal interest in screwing us."

"What about the developers that owns the property up in the

valley?" Del asked.

"Now there's a good idea, Del," Jake rejoined. "Give *them* a call."

"Jake, you've talked with them before. Can you make the contact?"

"I'll get on it as soon as I get back to the store."

Jake made a call to Jackson Kromberg, his contact at Clydesdale Development. A couple minutes of reacquainting, and Jake settled into his purpose for calling.

"Jackson, there's been some changes going on here that directly affect you folks. For one, the state is building a new road with railroad and utility easements that are within reach of Wonder Valley."

"We are aware of that, Jake. We were involved with the state's decision about some of the details. That road will service several properties for us when it's completed. Getting utilities is still a few years away from real impact on Wonder Valley. So your ministry there will have plenty of time remaining. Is that what you're calling about?"

"Not really. But I would like to thank you and your people for letting us use the place free of charge. It's helping us to make a difference."

"We enjoy being an extension of God's hands, too, Jake. We just do it with different resources. And like we've said before, just take good care of the place and we will be happy to keep you there."

"Thanks Jackson. You guys are deeply appreciated."

"What else can I do for you?"

"Should I assume you have looked at our area for investment purposes? You know about the road, so you would be aware of our future potential."

"Jake, I'm going to be direct about this. We see ourselves as God's servants to the land. God is in the land as much as he is involved with the people. When the land is defiled, it is hard to make it prosper. That's a theology we hold that helps us make wise decisions with the money God has given us. One reason we've balked at investing around you is the defilement that has some deep roots in your town.

"There's a large parcel of fallow ground out west of you that we've been offered first consideration on. Anywhere else, we'd jump on it. It'll be up for investor vote next week, but frankly speaking, we're probably going to take a pass on it and the future sale will go public. I'm sorry . . . "

"Jackson," said Jake interrupting. "Something has happened here that would be worth your time to see firsthand. Holy Spirit has turned this town upside down."

"Really," Jackson said. "Tell me about it."

"Many in the believing community are being awakened. Dozens in the sex trafficking business are being saved. Miracles are happening. What was going on in Wonder Valley is spilling out on us."

"Jake, I'd have to come before the vote next week. I'll see if I can get away. If I can't, maybe one of my sons can meet with you. . . That's the best I can offer on short notice."

"I have one more thing to ask, Jackson, and I'll let you go."

"What's on your mind?"

"With the road at hand, potential growth is staring us in the face. And we'd like to do our best to keep it local. It's a *lucrative* issue and the bankers we have here are showing questionable practices. We can come up with local money, but we don't have a store front. Is there anything you can do to help?"

Jackson answered slowly. "We have a credit union that is our public face. I can get some heads talking to see how to do it . . . Somebody will be in touch in a couple days."

"Thanks Jackson. That is good news. I'll be looking for that call."

New Order

The grand beginning at the *Finnegan's Rose* started a momentum for change. It was a prophetic statement that represented the new spiritual atmosphere. The creative minds of the community were stepping up to give it an identity. Three names stood above all others in the suggestion box; Abundance, Paradise and Transformation City. A special ballot would follow.

In the time between, the press to influence the vote thrived in every humorous form short of extortion and bribery. A friendly arm-twist here, a smiling coax there and promises to return the favor to induce friends and neighbors to vote as their point of view would fancy. The favorite was platters of cookies and brownies with a name preference written with icing on top.

At the appointed time, ballots were cast and a meeting called at the Community Center to reveal the results. Jason Phipps stood at the pulpit, gaveled the meeting to order and gave the minute keeper the necessary remarks according to Robert's Rules of Order.

"I call this special meeting of the combined officials and residents of Lawless and Little Faith to order." The gavel hit sounding block. "For the record, we will waive public roll call of the commissioners and the reading of previous minutes. Will the secretary please note all commissioners in attendance.

"This meeting is for the specific purpose of announcing the results of a special ballot that selected a new name of our proposed incorporation that will reunify Lawless and Little Faith after nearly one hundred years of division."

The attending crowd stood applauding, shouting and whistling enthusiastically.

Jason stood waiting appreciatively before rapping his gavel for quiet.

"Before announcing the results, I wish to report, and ask the secretary to write into the minutes, that all the paper work is filed for a new charter as reorganized. It will be established as a de facto government as soon as a newly elected mayor is sworn in. It will become official at the time that the charter is approved by the state.

"All the combined current commissioners shall preside as city council members pro tem until the next state established voting cycle. At that time all who wish to run for office will be encouraged to do so and the number of members will be reduced from eight to five by decree of who received the lesser votes or who did not run in the election. We are proposing two year terms with alternating cycles to prevent the potential for a complete turnover of officers. It will take a few years to sort out cycles of service.

"According to our charter we will have a mayor as chief executive of the city with veto power over city council legislation and a vice mayor who will preside over the city council.

"And with all the boring stuff out of the way I wish to announce that by a modest margin the name of Transformation City has been voted to be our new name."

Whoops and groans mixed together good heartedly with clapping in enthusiastic response.

Jason laughed then continued. "I understand there was strong, impassioned and delicious support for *all* the names involved, but the vote has spoken. Thank you for accepting the outcome.

"With the results of the ballot binding, there is no need for a motion on the issue. The chair announces Lawless and Little Faith will henceforth be called Transformation City." Jason gaveled the announcement into the minutes. Cheers followed.

"Who's running for mayor, Jason?" someone yelled.

"There are two hats in the ring at this time. Myself and Shamus Breen."

There were murmurs and enthusiastic hoots in the room as eyes turned toward Shamus. As he glanced here and there at faces, he saw many approving faces and some disapproving. A knot formed in his chest. *Papa, give me courage. It's so much easier to have a cold heart than to care and be strong. Who in their right mind would choose a life of politics?*

God's inner voice responded. *"I chose you, Shamus."*

"Go for it Shamus!" someone yelled, followed by several slaps on his shoulders. A chant got started, "Shamus, Shamus, Shamus, Shamus."

Jason gaveled the room to order.

"Anyone can run or do a write-in campaign," Jason stated. "Whoever gets the highest votes will be mayor. Second in count will be vice-mayor. It's real simple. And if you want further explanation, you can read the minutes of the last commissioners meeting.

"Is there any further discussion regarding the name change?"

Heads looked about but no one came forward.

Jason stated, "May I please have a motion to adjourn the meeting."

"I move that the meeting be adjourned, Mister Chairman," Del declared.

"I second that motion," Jake added.

"It has been moved and seconded that this special meeting

of the joint commissioners be adjourned," Jason thumped the wood block with his gavel and declared, "It is so done."

From gavel to gavel, the meeting took less than half an hour. But the extent of how far the ripples of change would extend beyond Transformation City; and for how long; would be unfathomable for several generations.

Restored

To the undiscerning eye, the stranger that entered Finnegan's Rose that afternoon merely seemed a thin middle-aged man that walked without limping but needed a responsive cane for the unexpected. His clothes were simple and unpretentious, but not slovenly. Grizzled hair and moustache were well-groomed and his bearing controlled. A more perceptive watcher of people would see the living-in-the-moment grace of those who had wrestled the heavy weight of regret into a soldierly posture of brave dignity.

He was an old hand at big losses, and because of the hard knocks had learned to fight intensely for personal victories. His pallid and pock-marked face along with his careful movements revealed a battle that was not yet won. He wasn't sure he could win this one and had determined to reconcile what he could, while he can.

Meadow led him to a table near the street, introduced herself, and placed a menu in front of him. He requested a cup of coffee with room for cream and reached for the menu. She smiled warmly and told him, "You're in for a treat. I'll be right back with your coffee, and to get your order when you're ready."

He studied the surroundings with interest. The inside décor of the bistro was old west. It was tastefully done to stimulate imagination. He could visualize horses pulling up in front, cowboys dismounting and tying off at a hitching rail outside. The thud and jingle of boots with spurs should have been a natural background noise. A passing automobile honked, changing the daze.

The view outside was largely the high berm of the railway across the street. Young elm trees had been recently planted in the easement; probably to break up the berm's tedious appearance. The street lights that were sprinkled in with the trees looked new but had vintage intentions. And the sidewalk with its overhang was classic architecture. He smiled, it felt right; it felt good. His thoughts returned to his purpose.

Preferring an unannounced visit, he wanted to know the kind of reception he would have before it happened. Plus, he wasn't comfortable with special attention. Before entering town, he sensed peacefulness. And as he sat reflecting, an even greater calm surrounded him. Was this place trying to welcome him?

Meadow returned with his coffee and a plain ceramic creamer. The fragrance of the brew captivated him. Before Meadow could take his order he took the mug with two hands and sipped. He closed his eyes and sipped again, set the mug down with appreciation for its contents, then added cream.

"I'm sorry to keep you waiting, but that was a moment to savor."

"I enjoyed the wait. Your face spoke a thousand words of praise . . . Do you have any questions? Or see anything you'd like to try?" Meadow asked.

"I'll have a French dip with onion rings instead of fries. And if you have it, I'd like some horseradish. Straight, not the saucy stuff."

"Tom makes a special horseradish sauce for the weekend prime rib. I think you'll love it, but I'll bring you both and you can decide for yourself."

"That would be fine," he said. "And please take your time. I'd like to enjoy this coffee for awhile."

"I'll pass that along. Tom will bring your food out."

Meadow entered the kitchen and informed Tom there was a first-timer near the window. Tom perked up and looked at the order she handed him while she explained the special requests. He grabbed two finger bowls and filled one with his special sauce and the other with a rounded teaspoon of hot horseradish from the jar.

Tom put the bowls on the table and extended his hand.

"I'm Tom, the owner of Finnegan's Rose. Glad to have you with us."

"I'm Steve," he replied.

Tom thought Steve's face looked familiar. He couldn't place it and continued, "I make my own breads for my sandwiches, Steve. For your French dip I have a pretzel crust, regular baguette, whole wheat and sour dough. What would you prefer?"

"The bread doesn't matter much to me. I mostly just like the meat and horseradish. Whatever you recommend is fine . . . uh, except the whole wheat. By the way, the coffee is *really* good. It's not the typical café stuff."

"Thanks. I have it roasted to my own preferences and change the source country from time to time just to mix it up. When you come back next time, I'll can do a pour-over of your favorite at no extra charge."

Steve nodded his head. "Well, if I can have a warm-up on this while I'm waiting, I would be grateful."

"Meadow will take care of you while I get working on your order . . . enjoy."

"Thanks, Tom."

On his way to the kitchen, he chose sour dough for the stranger's sandwich. Then the familiarity in Steve's face connected. Once in the kitchen, Tom stopped at the phone.

Steve determined to reverse engineer the flavor of Tom's shaved beef in the French dip. He pondered Tom's choices of spice. *Most cooks,* he thought, *use salt like a crutch to mask their lack of creativity.* Salty was the predominant flavor while Steve was in prison. He determined to discover other things when he got out.

With his taste buds provoked by the good coffee, he took another bite, sat back with his eyes closed and searched for the ingredients. Oregano, garlic, onion, thyme, with a hint of rosemary out in front . . . he expected that. But something unfamiliar lurked in the background. *The secret ingredient,* he reasoned, *cumin or tarragon or coriander . . . maybe a mixture of each. There was just enough of something to evade detection and make the aftertaste unique. Tom's good.*

When he opened his eyes, he caught the movement of someone who had entered the back door. He turned in curiosity. Their eyes connected and something stirred in Steve. Regret, guilt and fear popped to the surface. He pushed them aside, chose courage and stood up.

Shamus walked intentionally toward him as friendly hands reached out along the way. Someone used the title Mister Mayor. Apparently his son had made greater changes than he'd let on. And equally apparent to Steve was that those changes weren't important to Shamus. Respect and hope filled the voids of loss.

Shamus graciously deflected being drawn into a conversation as he waded between tables. When Shamus finally got to Steve, Shamus didn't hesitate to reach for a hug. Steve stepped into those arms with the assurance that everything was going to go well no matter how awkward the honesty would get.

As they sat down, Tom brought a coffee for Shamus and walked away. Shamus thanked him and took a sip as Steve considered how healthy Shamus looked.

"You look like a happy man, Shamus." Steve said pushing the plate with the second half of his sandwich to the side. He smiled and waved for Meadow as she poured refills for nearby customers. He popped the last onion ring in his mouth while Shamus continued.

"Materially speaking, I have nothing. And yet, I am wealthy beyond anything I could ask for."

Steve looked at Shamus quizzically and said, "I don't understand what you mean by that."

Shamus chuckled and responded, "Yeah . . . maybe its nerves. I guess it does sound overly philosophical, but it's what I feel. What I am today is the product of the riches of the love in this community and lavish doses of God's grace. The happiness you see doesn't come from prosperity. It comes from knowing who I am and who God is."

Meadow walked up at that moment, smiled and looked at Steve. "What can I do for you?" she asked.

"Can I have a little box for the rest of my sandwich, please? I'm not in the disposition to eat it all."

"Sure thing," she responded and turned to fetch the box.

"Meadow," Shamus called. She turned to look back at Shamus with a smile.

"May I introduce you to Steve Breen. This . . . is my Dad."

She extended her hand and said enthusiastically, "What an enormous pleasure to meet you, Steve. Welcome to Transformation City. And welcome to our family."

Steve stood slowly and said, "I am glad to be here and pleased to meet Shamus' friends."

"As you probably noticed when Shamus entered the room,"

Meadow continued, "there are more than a few of us who are his friends. I hope you get to meet them all."

"Would you mind if I introduce you while you're standing?" Shamus asked while getting out of his chair.

Steve hesitated and looked at Shamus, who was smiling broadly. Steve submitted and nodded his head. "Sure. That would be good."

Shamus caught the gathering's attention and introduced Steve. Everyone rose and approached Steve to give their names and greet him heartily. Steve's smile relaxed from stiff to natural. His heart was warmly at ease when he and Shamus retook their seats.

To Steve it was obvious his son had faced up to the emotional abandonment of their past. But he was inquisitive. What was it about this loving community that provided his healing? How could Shamus treat their estrangement as if it never happened? Why would these people extend themselves to the one who caused so much destruction in Shamus' life? He was undeserving of what they offered.

Shamus took note of a face that reflected a man who had tackled his demons and prevailed. He stood tall with dignity rather than bowed over in guilt, blame and shame. He wasn't groveling for reconciliation or playing the victim. He saw a man who understood the patience and perseverance of restoration, and hungered for more. That was a foundation they could build on.

His health had obviously suffered from things still unknown to Shamus. Yet he saw no hint of self-pity; he was unafraid if anything. His dad drew respect without demanding it. Shamus chose to give it.

"I think," Steve said with a finger raised, "I just got a taste of the wealth you were talking about." He added slowly and deliberately, "Money doesn't buy second chances that pay off with a new destiny." Then he said confidently, "*That* is a treasure any sensible man would give all his wealth to have."

"Dad, there is so much more. Could you grab some things for an overnight excursion and let me take you someplace special? . . . It'll give us a chance to talk without being interrupted . . . maybe."

Steve packed up his sandwich, plopped down a generous tip and headed for the register. Tom was there with a smile, anxious to have a turn at talking to Shamus' dad.

"How was your meal, Steve?"

"Your creativity with spices is refreshing *and* intriguing." Steve held up his cane below the crook and added, "You've got some secrets." He handed Tom the tab and concluded, "And I would love to drag them out of you."

"So, you like to cook do you? I'll bet you have your own secrets. Maybe we can collaborate when you get a chance."

Tom leaned over the ticket with pen in hand.

"Let's see here . . . first time customer discount, Shamus' dad discount, middle-aged citizen discount and let's not forget the 'I'm glad to meet you' discount and that will be two bucks, please."

Steve laughed freely, handed Tom a five dollar bill and said, "Keep the change, and don't you dare refuse me. It's worth every penny of your normal price . . . You've got a great place, Tom. I will look forward to coming back here and getting to know you . . . Thank you."

Shamus paid for his coffee and headed for the back door. Although Tom would have been more than happy to give Shamus the coffee without charge, Shamus insisted in not doing it in front of people who could see it as favoritism. Outside, Steve stopped and took a deep breath of the clean air. Shamus stopped and looked around again at all that was new in the neighborhood.

"This parking lot used to be my home, Dad. It burned down awhile back and I sold it to Tom for his new expansion."

"Why didn't you rebuild?"

"It was a shadow of my old life, and I had no desire to keep it. And what Tom has in mind is a huge influence on the future of Transformation City."

Shamus took a breath and with a hint of regret on his face, filled his Dad in with some of his story.

"I ran a brothel here. I sold women for pleasure to whoever wanted to buy. I was a ruthless, hard, uncaring human being until a couple of years ago . . . or however long it's been. But, that raises questions that we'll have time on the road to talk about."

Steve grabbed a small travel bag from his car and laid it in the back of Shamus' Jeep. And then he climbed in stiffly.

STEVE'S ENCOUNTER

As they buckled their seat belts, Steve asked, "What's it like being a mayor?"

"Being mayor is like being the servant to everybody. I exist to make things happen and pull the right people together. This community grows by getting things done. But as you could imagine, there's a lot of drama and politics involved, too.

"Sit back and relax, Dad. With the jeep topless, the wind noise makes it hard to talk. We'll pick things up when we get off road." Shamus put it in gear and they hit the road. Asphalt ran a few miles to feed what farms were outside of town. It eventually morphed into dirt. Before the usual turnoff for the valley, there was a Department of Transportation control point. A woman stood at a set of concrete barricades that limited traffic with a hand held stop and slow sign. A larger sign on top of the barricade said *CONSTRUCTION ZONE, YIELD TO HEAVY EQUIPMENT.* Shamus obeyed the smaller sign to stop.

"Hi Shamus," she said as the Jeep pulled next to her. "Heading for the valley?"

"Yes we are! . . . How's your day going?"

"Well, it's my day to direct traffic . . . borrrring. But hey, I got sunshine, fresh air and lots of trees. What more could I ask for? . . . Who's your passenger?"

"Shannon, this is my father, Steve."

"Hey, I can see the resemblance," she said with a strong construction hand extended. "It's a pleasure to meet you. Are you visiting?"

"Yes I am," Steve responded. "Do you live in town?"

"Nope, the road crew is mostly from Burnus. But we spend a lot of time in town during the week. It's a great place and we like hanging out there. Hey, if you get a chance, stop in at Finnegan's Rose. I love the atmosphere. And the food's amazing."

Steve chuckled and raised his take-out container. "I'm on that one, Shannon."

"Cool, Steve. You'll be a fan in no time . . . Hey Shamus, the foreman had a road graded to make it easier for you guys to get back to your valley. What do you think of that? It's not real long, but it should save you some time and keep you off the volcanic stuff. Anyway, it's not marked but there's a huge boulder at the turnoff; you won't miss it."

Shamus turned to her and responded with a sigh, "I'm not ready for easy access, Shannon. Being difficult to find is what makes it so mysteriously special . . . But I guess a little progress will help the developers prepare for the future. So, with that in mind, thanks for sharing that. And give my appreciation to the guys for getting it done."

Shannon's two-way radio squawked.

"Sorry Shamus, progress is what my job's all about . . . Well hey, I'd love to chat," she said firmly, "but there's heavy equipment barreling down on you and they don't want to stop. You'll need to pull over and get out of the way." She stepped away from the Jeep and concluded, "See you guys! Nice meeting you, Steve."

Steve nodded and said, "You too, Shannon." Shamus checked his mirror and quickly pulled forward and to the right. A moment later, a pair of gravel trucks rumbled through the opening in the barricade. They were followed by a dust cloud that billowed over the Jeep. Shamus turned to wave at Shannon, who was waving and laughing.

She yelled, "Next time check the wind direction, Shamus."

Within minutes Shamus spotted the boulder, turned off and slowed the pace. That's when Steve opened up about his wife's death and the weight of regret that still crushed him at times. "But I came face-to-face with myself. And in spite of it, my health still broke while I was in prison and forced me to embrace sobriety; you'd be shocked at what a guy could get inside if he wanted to be an addict. When I got out, I had a plan and a good support group. And so far, so good. But to be honest about it son, talking about your mother's death with you is hard. There's things you need to hear about that I just can't bring myself to share. I can't go there, now . . . but maybe later."

"We have time, Dad. We aren't in a hurry. Maybe I can tell you some of my journey. The first years after leaving home, I got a lot of hard knocks. I learned survival in a street world that was loveless and cruel. Like you, regret takes the wind out of me from time to time." Shamus paused then stopped the Jeep.

"Dad, I can see that you're a changed man. The rage is gone and there's a different person sitting here that wasn't in my life back in those days. I *hated* the man you used to be . . . When I deserted you and mom, I was angry and broken because of the life we had. If I had stayed . . . Well, let me put it this way, I thought about killing you more than once . . ."

Steve raised his hands. "Shamus, however convoluted life was and now is, we've been given another chance. I desperately need your forgiveness for making a wreck of things. You say you've already done it, but I need to hear it. Will you do that for me?"

"Of course I will, Dad. I want to put all of it behind us as much as you do. That doesn't mean we won't talk about it again. But I believe we can get to where we will talk without flinching or hesitating. With that in mind, I forgive you. And, God knows, maybe we will help others who've been where we've been. The world is full of people like us looking for answers and hope."

"Do you have hope, Shamus?"

"Not only hope, Dad. I have faith and love. Love for myself and love for you. Jesus gave me that love and I won't ever let go of it. It's a love that gives me a future worth dreaming about."

"What are your dreams, Shamus?"

Shamus smiled. "My most important dream is to marry the most beautiful woman in the world. Her name is MiSeon. And she's as pretty inside as she is on the outside. I have faith that that day will come, Dad.

"Beyond that, my dreams are happening faster than I can think about them. I'm living a life that's a gift from God . . . What about you?"

"I'm not there yet, Shamus," Steve said stoically. "Because of my health, my future looks rather short. But, I'm okay with it because I know I'm going to end well. In a way, that is hope. Being here with you today has added a lot to my hope. We have something we never had before. For me, *that's* a dream come true."

Shamus smiled and thought *There's always the God factor to consider.* "It ain't over till it's over, Dad."

"Yeah, we'll make the best of it, Shamus. . . Let's go. I can't wait to see this valley you've raved about."

Further on, they made the turn at forest's edge and moved slowly on the last leg of their journey toward the valley. The fragrances, the tranquility, and the beauty were perfect ingredients for slowing the pace down even more and sharing the bonds that should have happened years before.

An outdoorsman wandered out of the forest and into the path of the jeep. Shamus braked as the man waited on the passenger side. He unnocked his arrow and shouldered his bow.

"Hi, Shamus. Top of the day to ya." He smiled softly and looked into Steve's eyes. "And welcome to my world, friend." Jesus said.

"You look like you're out hunting." Steve responded

"I'm forever hunting. I can't help myself."

"Did you find what you're looking for?"

Jesus handed Steve the arrow he was holding and said, "Yes I did."

Steve looked at the arrow quizzically. He noticed a large scar on the extended hand, then looked into his eyes.

"My name is Steve, I'm Shamus' father," he said as he extended his hand.

Jesus took Steve's hand with both of his and responded with affection, "It is my sheer delight to welcome you, Steve. Some people call me The Hunter, and I like greeting newcomers to my valley. I've been doing it for the longest time. Ask Shamus, he knows about my secret places and backwoods adventures. This place is one of my favorites . . . the *why* of which you will shortly discover. And I know you will fall in love with it too.

"As usual Shamus, and to you as well, Steve, make yourselves at home. I will catch up with you later. Enjoy yourselves. And Shamus, don't forget to show your dad our spot on your way back to town. He'll love it."

Speechless, Shamus nodded approval, then put the Jeep in gear. He smiled gratefully at Jesus and drove on.

Steve was puzzled. Given the location, it was unusual, but not at all awkward. And The Hunter's friendliness reminded him of the restaurant. He had been warmly greeted at the front door and shown in. But the arrow was mystifying. He studied it with wonder.

Steve turned stiffly to look back. The Hunter was standing in the road. But what appeared to be a family of mountain lions had joined him. Oddly, the largest cat appeared to be talking while The Hunter laughed and stroked his head. The Hunter waved, and Steve waved back. When a bend in the road removed them from view, he settled into the seat and absently watched the road and surroundings.

A small waterfall appeared ahead. The creek it created went across the trail. Shamus drove through the creek, parked the Jeep and got out. He grabbed a canteen from the back seat and poured out its contents. As he walked toward the falls he said, "This is a great spot to get out and stretch . . . and enjoy some of the planet's finest water."

He filled the canteen and brought it to Steve, who was out of the Jeep and reflectively walking toward the falls. Steve took the outstretched canteen and gulped down a couple swallows. His eyes brightened. "Ahhhhh, that *is* good."

Shamus relished his father's pleasure; it was the response Shamus was looking for. Steve swilled a longer drink and passed the canteen. Shamus topped it off again at the waterfall, drank what he wanted and refilled again.

The serenity of the grove affected a long pause that ticked through a moment of time with no past or future. All was well in the now. Steve parted the veil it created and said, "The Hunter, he was an unusual man . . . an *enjoyable* man. Is he one of those developers you and Shannon were talking about?"

"Dad, where we're going is beautiful beyond anything I have ever experienced. The Hunter . . . had a strong influence in making it what it is."

Steve looked back where he had seen The Hunter with a family of mountain lions and considered the possibility that what he experienced might be just a small tip of a larger iceberg. He looked at Shamus, raised his eyebrows and smiled. "Lead on, Shamus."

As the two piled back in the Jeep, Steve noticed a lesser effort than at the parking lot.

"I think this place is doing me some good already, Shamus."

A lean figure sat in the rocking chair on the veranda. He stood spryly as they approached and leapt off the porch. As the Jeep rolled next to Rigo's pickup, Shamus jumped out of the Jeep and ran for the cabin. The two greeted with a hug.

"Vince! It's so good to see you! What brings you out here?"

"I come here a lot, Shamus. It's just too wonky to tell you about it at the jail when somebody's listening in," Vince said, as he curiously watched the stranger climb out of the Jeep. "I've been meeting with Roee and the goats, and they all have become my good friends. They teach me stuff. And when I wake up in the Burnus jail, I share what I've learned with the other guys. I'm doing pretty good for a guy that is supposed to be locked up."

Shamus asked, "How are you holding up when you're inside?"

"Seriously Shamus," Vince shrugged. "Who else do you know that gets to do what I get to do? It's a weird and adventurous life. I had been here for a couple hours and knew it was getting to be time to go back. I was just sitting here, enjoying the peace and quiet and wondering why I'm still here when you drove up. I think I'm supposed to meet your friend here. Who is he?"

Steve was standing a polite distance away, not wanting to intrude. But he had overheard the conversation. Shamus motioned him forward.

"Vince, I want you to meet Steve . . . my dad."

Vince looked at Steve as though the air had lost its oxygen. Steve saw the reaction and leaned in to respond. He extended his hand, but Vince wanted a hug. Then Vince stepped back and settled his body language to explain.

"Shamus and I found each other after he ran away from home. And like orphans on the street we fought our way through an existence that nearly killed us more than once. We were brothers. We covered each other's backs. When he left, I was alone and scared. When Shamus came back to save me from the bad guys, I showed him my *deep* appreciation for it by trying to kill him." He laughed and continued, "It was a wonky twist of fate that by shooting him, he saved my life.

"To see you standing here, something of this story of ours comes full circle."

"How is that, Vince?" Steve asked. "I don't understand the connection."

"To see you and Shamus together after all these years of hell, I feel hope. You see, I want to see my family experience come to something like that, too."

A comfortable silence allowed Steve to think. "What can I do for you?"

"Could you just be family for me? I could use family . . . I wouldn't really know what else to ask. I have no idea how to find my parents. It's really hard to do that from jail."

"I know, Vince. I'm an ex-con."

Vince looked surprised. And it was Steve's turn to laugh.

"I'll do what I can to help you. But really, I'm not sure where you're from and where you're going. How did you get here if you're in jail?"

"Dad," Shamus interjected with a chuckle. "Welcome to Wonder Valley, where the extraordinary becomes ordinary."

"Guys, I'm going to be leaving in a minute. Steve, whatever

you need to know, Shamus will have to tell you . . . It's been a pleasure to meet you, and I hope to see you again soon. It's hard to say with the life that I live . . . Can we talk sometime? Maybe you come and visit me?

"Steve, can . . . can I call you *Dad*? Shamus and I have been family for long time. We've been through a lot together. And . . . ya know?"

"Yeah, Vince, I understand. Let's do that. I'm not much of a father. But, it's what we got isn't it? We can make something with that. Sure, we all can learn to be family . . . together."

Overwhelmed, Vince responded with tears, "I've gotta go in and say goodbye. I can feel the change coming."

Vince and Steve hugged before Vince climbed the steps. He turned and said, "Thanks Dad," then went inside.

Father and son walked to the Jeep and retrieved their gear. By the time they turned back toward the cabin, Roee had come out and was on the ground.

"Hey, hey, this is a surprise. You usually call, Shamus. What brings this pleasure to our house?"

Before Shamus could answer, Roee extended his hand. "I'm Roee, welcome to my world."

"I'm Steve. And that's the same greeting I got from The Hunter back on the road."

"The Hunter shares his world with me, Steve," Roee said with a laugh. "And I really enjoy the honor of being here."

"Roee," Shamus injected, "this is my dad."

"Yeah, I can see the resemblance." Roee responded with excitement. "Shamus told us you would be showing up. And it's so good to meet you. Would you like a cup of coffee or tea or water?"

"We had coffee at Tom's place before we came and water at the falls," Shamus said.

"In that case," rejoined Roee, "You can come on in or get yourselves settled or look around. What'll it be?"

"I think we'll get set up in case Dad wants to rest for awhile. We'll be in shortly."

"Go for it Shamus, you know your way around."

Shamus and Steve headed toward the other house by way of the meadow. Roee returned to the conversation inside.

"I lived here after I left the streets. It was the most amazing time of my life."

"Why did you leave?" asked Steve.

Shamus laughed. "Because Vince tried to kill me. That's why he's behind bars. And because of that I met this nurse at the hospital who's the most incredible woman on this planet."

"Shamus, how can Vince be locked up and be here too? That's not making sense."

"You're right, it doesn't make sense . . . and I don't have an answer to our question. It's supernatural, and it's amazing. But I can't explain it. If you were in Vince's cell right now, he probably just woke up."

"Your world is freaky, son." Steve responded with a shiver. "Where's the spacecraft?"

Shamus raised his hands, knowing nothing more could be said that would make a difference. As they walked through the meadow, Shamus told the entire story of the dream that led him back to Vince, which led him to MiSeon. As he told the story, Shamus would periodically stop. Goats quietly gathered around them, listening.

Steve watched the goats as Shamus told his story. The goats

looked like little children captivated in story time. When Shamus paused, he commented, "They act like they understand what you're saying."

"Not only do I understand what he's saying," declared Tanny, "I can tell the story better than he can."

Shamus roared in laughter. Steve was shocked . . . mouth open . . . speechless.

"We understand what everybody says," added Sully.

"Don't get me wrong I appreciate listening, too." added Tanny. "I honor you, Shamus. You did a good job."

"Thanks Tanny," said Shamus. "Dad, let me introduce you to God's favorite goat herd. This is . . . "

"I smell sickness," interrupted Scampy. He pushed his way forward and stood in front of Steve. He looked up at him, "Are you sick?"

Steve, overcome, responded. "I . . . uhhh, well. . . "

"They didn't tell you we could talk," stated Willie with a chuckle. "I love it when they do that . . . Scampy, pray for the man before he gets his voice back."

Maria moved around behind Steve knowing he would need the padding. She motioned for Sully and Megan to do the same.

"Here," Scampy ordered Steve, "grab my horns."

Steve timidly took hold of his horns.

"In Jesus name, sickness be gone from this body. You have no place in this valley or in this man's life. There's no sickness in heaven and we won't allow it here. BAM!"

When Scampy yelled BAM! Steve was thrown onto the backs of Maria, Sully and Megan where he lay motionless.

"I feel heat flowing through him," declared Megan.

"Me too," said Sully calmly.

Smiling sheepishly, Shamus looked at his father's face . . . he shrugged in spite of his misgivings. "His color is changing. That's a good sign."

Song broke out in the flock. Praises rang while Shamus gently lifted Steve from the goat's backs and lowered him to the ground. Then he sat cross-legged at his father's head and prayed quietly. Minutes passed before Steve's eyes fluttered. He looked to his right and then his left. Seeing Shamus he asked, "What hit me?"

With a straight face, Shamus responded, "It was a freight train, Dad. Sorry, it came out of nowhere."

Steve squinted his right eye at that and raised his left eyebrow. Then his face softened and he chuckled at all the fuzzy faces smiling back at him.

The absurdity between the funny faces, his silly question and Shamus' illogical answer struck Steve. His chuckle moved slowly to a chortle. He reached a cackle and suddenly stopped . . . He remembered something.

"I saw my *guts* Shamus!" he exclaimed loudly and holding his stomach.

"What do you mean, Dad?"

He chuckled again, "My eyes were inside my body. And I was given a tour of my organs." He laughed. "Somebody was with me and we walked up to my liver. . . oh, what a mess. I mean it was grey and red and brown and yellow." At that, he shuddered. "It was *gross*."

His eyes widened and he continued. "And right in front of me, it changed color and became smooth . . . Then I was taken or walked or floated . . . gosh, I don't know how I got there. But I was at my kidneys and the same thing happened." He got excited, and sat up.

"Then I went to a couple of other places, but I have no idea what they were. Small things. Glands of some kind . . . And they changed too. And then . . . Oh . . my . . gosh, you won't believe this." His eyes brightened and he lifted his brows excitedly. "I was inside my heart leaning against the wall and feeling my heart pump . . . boom-boom, boom-boom. And remember The Hunter we met on the road?"

Shamus smiled and said slowly, "Yeah."

"Well he poked his head through a window in my heart and started *laughing*. Then he asked, 'Can I come in?' So I said, 'Come on in! Did *you* fix all these wrecked organs?' So he said 'Yup' and jumped through the window.

"Boy was it crowded," Steve said still chuckling. "And I told him that. So he says, 'It's time for you to go, I'm staying' . . . And that's when I opened my eyes and saw all of you. My first thoughts were, 'What *planet* are we on? Where have you brought me?'"

"Welcome to Wonder Valley, Dad. Welcome to . . . our world. Where the extraordinary becomes ordinary and the supernatural is normal."

"This'll make a good story," added Tanny.

The familiar noise of praise and celebration captured the curiosity of those inside the cabin. As the others showed up, Steve was being helped to his feet by Shamus and well-meaning goat noses.

"I don't deserve this," Steve mumbled. "After all I've done to my body and my family . . . I don't deserve this."

Roee recognized the familiar response to Papa's goodness and jumped in.

"Papa doesn't reward us for our goodness, Steve. He blesses

us because he's good."

"I don't understand," Steve said.

"The greatest marvel of God is his love. He gives it to everyone freely without having to earn it. He simply wants us to believe that all he does for us is done for love. When he forgives our sins, he simply wants us to believe that he has done so out of love, and that he will eagerly and passionately continue to do so.

"When he heals us, all the reasons why we we're diseased or damaged are nullified, cancelled, forgotten. Believe what he says. It's powerful and it pleases him."

Steve considered the words for a few seconds then said, "That sounds too good to be true."

"That idea comes from our earthly sense of justice," Roee responded. "We feel if we do something wrong, we should be penalized. And in the traditional sense of crime and punishment, that's the way it should be. But it's under that system that we could never find a way to have friendship with God. We would end up dead and separated from him.

"He doesn't use the justice system to build relationship with him. He uses the redemption system. He determines all the guidelines of relationship, and we approve those guidelines by agreement and faith. Through that, he comes in and creates a new life with him in the middle of it all."

Roee let Steve think for a while. Steve's lips began to move and then formed a smile.

"That's why he *laughed* when he looked through the window and asked if he could come in. He really wanted to come in, but I had to let him in."

Roee returned a blank look and said, "I don't understand."

Shamus spoke up. "Tanny, you should tell Papa Shepherd the latest story."

The following morning, Steve, Shamus and Roee were sitting about having coffee on the veranda outside the cabin.

"Great coffee," Steve choked, "desperado stuff. Makes me want to rise up and wrangle some cows. But for some reason, Roee, it doesn't feel out of place."

"That's why I calls it cowboy coffee," Roee responded slipping into redneck speak. "Ya gotta have grit to drink it, you do. If fact, you should otta find a leetle grit in the bottom when ye're done. . . Y'know, it's fixt same way as they did a hunert years ago. I slips egg shells in't pluck the grounds away from the surface. That's the way Granny used to do it, so it gots to be right."

"I accused Roee once," Shamus rejoined, "Of using goat droppings for coffee grounds.

"'Yup," he said brightly. "Tain't much dif'rent. A little goat cream, and Bob's yer uncle. A feller can get by with jes about anythin' out chere."

"Ya know Dad, I don't think Roee's cut out for city life."

Roee sighed. "Shamus, the country river runs deep in me. When the day comes to leave this valley, that river will probably buck hard against it. I'm one with the land and everything else in this valley . . . only heaven is a better place than this."

"This is the closest thing to heaven I've ever seen," Steve said. "In fact, I'd like to ask you if we could stay a couple more days before we head back."

"You can stay until you're satisfied and truly ready to go back, Steve."

"I have to be back tomorrow evening," Shamus injected looking at his dad sadly. "Sorry, but if you want to stay awhile, I can come back to get you."

"If I stay too long," Steve replied, "I won't want to leave . . . Tomorrow will have to be enough for now. But, I will be back."

"You're welcome to come anytime," Roee affirmed, then bantered with a smile, "The goats sure took a likin' to ya."

FAREWELL

It was toward the end of Roee's morning watch and his praise was intercession about the good things Papa had in mind for Steve, Vince and Shamus. He was enjoying the view of the mountains on the other side of the valley from the top of Vision Rock and felt a presence behind him. Tawny faces slowly moved into his peripheral vision on either side. They were poised at the same height and their breathing relaxed.

With one on each side of Roee, they leaned slightly forward, looked at each other and nodded. Roee pounced like a trap-door spider. With a roar, he grabbed the beast to his left in a head and body lock. The one on the right sprang straight up in reaction and came down in a crouch. With one mountain lion wrestled to the ground and the other ready for action, hilarity broke out all around.

As the laughter faded, Nara chimed, "Their mother put them up to it. Kefirah[1] is quite the prankster."

"Well, that didn't work like we planned it," Kefirah added still chuckling. "You're a brave warrior."

"I'm not so brave," Roee stated as he got up. "I just knew it was you guys. Now, who's Adar and who's Modred?"

"You have a good memory, Papa Shepherd," responded Nara.

"I am Modred," responded one twin. "But you can't tell who we are by looks."

"I can tell by their voices," Kefirah added. "Their voices are different."

"Yes, a mother with keen hearing like yours would know that

kind of thing," Roee responded. "But, I might have to come up with something else . . . How about if I cut off one of your ears."

"Not fair," yelled Modred. "I would be ugly with an ear missing!"

"Just kidding Modred. I'll put one of Mama Shepherd's ear rings on you."

The cubs looked at each other, smiled and asked at the same time, "What's an ear ring?"

Roee chuckled and responded, "It's a little dangle-d-bob you poke through your ear. It's really quite a design statement."

"I want one," they both cried.

Papa Shepherd laughed, "We can arrange that. We'll put them in different places."

"Dangle-d-bobs," Nara stated with concern. "Papa Shepherd, I'm raising warriors, not raccoons."

"Hmmmm, yes. There's a good idea, Nara. We could paint dark circles around the eyes of Adar."

Nara rolled his eyes and said, "Sons, he's not serious. Please Roee, tell them you're not serious."

Roee smiled broadly. "So, what brings you guys here? Out for a morning stroll?"

"Yes," Kefirah responded. "Jesus said he didn't want the boys to eat his friends. So, he sent us to meet them. And Nara told us about the story teller. Could we hear some stories? That would be fun. Actually, I'm not sure what we're doing here."

"Kefirah," Roee responded. "Be ready to become one of those stories. Picture it, a mountain lion pride making friends with a flock of goats . . . It's never happened before."

Kefirah chuckled, "I'm game."

The narrow trail from the upper rock through the forest left

Roee wading through cats and paws until the boys spotted the neighborhood squirrels. Modred and Adar sprung into mischievous pursuit, leaving Nara and Roee yelling for restraint, while Kefirah rolled in laughter. The squirrels fled up the nearest oak into the sparse limbs and flew from tree to tree after that.

When peace was restored, Adar bumped Modred's shoulder and stated with a chuckle, "Did you see that? We scared the nuts out of 'em."

Nara growled a warning. Kefirah laughed and said, "They're kids Nara. Nobody got hurt."

"This time," Nara finished.

Roee wondered how *this* story would be told when it was finished.

By the time they reached the cabin complex, the pride was surrounded by goats and people. Chatter grew as introductions were given and affections renewed. The cubs were cheered in friendliness from creatures that would ordinarily be picnic fodder. Kids bounced playfully with new mates that would normally be their predators. The littles sprung briefly to the backs of the four cats in balance games. The commotion attracted the curious deer while smaller critters of the forest watched from safer distances.

Interaction was a groundswell of communal celebration that rolled in and around several forms until a satisfied fullness settled in. Goats wandered back to grazing. Cubs basked in sunlit napping and brief chats with passersby. Assorted clusters gathered in scattered groups.

"Shamus," Steve commented after some time. "What was in the water at the falls? Does this simply vanish in a mist when it's over?"

Shamus smiled and responded, "Actually, we have to leave

before that happens."

"I will not be the same after this."

"Anyone who has tasted of the Kingdom of God will never view the world through the same heart. It's what Jesus calls the abundant life. It's the message we'll take to whoever will listen and the lifestyle we live wherever we go."

Steve nodded and responded, "You know, for the first time in my life, Son, I'm satisfied . . . I have peace . . . And I've managed to acquire a rather large and very strange family."

Steve guffawed then stated, "You can't choose your relatives, Dad."

With a chuckle, Steve added, "Nope, I suppose not."

A reflective and lengthy pause followed. "Well Dad, my stuff is loaded and I'm ready to go back whenever you are."

"Sounds good, let's say good bye."

Farewell sentiments had been extended and they mad their exit. Now Steve and Shamus were at the waterfall refilling a canteen and readjusting perspective to grasp reentry into the township life of Transformation.

Steve was quietly holding the arrow that The Hunter had handed him on his way in and leaning against the side of the Jeep. He understood something of its significance. "He found his target, didn't he?"

"I always do, Steve." The Hunter said from a sitting position on a boulder nearby. Steve looked as Jesus then walked toward him. "How about a hug?"

As they embraced, Steve melted in gratefulness. "Thank you, Jesus. When I came here, my body was broken and my heart was cracked. You've done wonders to put me back together. I've never felt this whole inside."

"This is just the beginning of the destiny I have for you. Walk with me and you will inherit all of it. Seek me as you make the choices that are ahead of you and you will make the best ones of your life. Welcome to my world."

Before the Jeep moved away, Jesus laid a hand on each of them and said, "Enjoy your journey and be blessed with righteousness, peace and joy. I love you . . . more than you can think or imagine."

When Shamus came to the tee in the road, he remembered Jesus' charge to share the Shangri-La retreat with his dad; which was to the left.

"Dad, we're going to take a side trip here. There's something special I want to share with you . . . We can get close, but we'll have to walk the rest of the way . . . You up to it?"

"Shamus, I've got more energy than I've had since . . . I can't remember when I've felt so good."

Shamus smiled realizing the extent of the healing his dad received. "We just might get a few more miles out of you after all, Dad. And more years to get to know each other wouldn't hurt my feelings, either."

Steve's eyes got wet in response and with a deep sigh he responded, "I am so grateful to have a second chance, Shamus.

When they arrived at the last point of access with the Jeep, Shamus turned off the engine and said, "If you'll grab the canteen, we'll head toward that mess of manzanita over there."

They hiked beyond the manzanita grove and into the oak and pine woods. But instead of going to the rocks across from the grotto, Shamus headed to the spring. His dad's face looked seriously mystified. Shamus smiled thinking his dad was curious about hearing the waterfall but not seeing it.

"The first thing I want to show you is the source of the water you're hearing. It simply bubbles up out of the ground." Shamus bent over the water and rinsed out the canteen. He refilled it and handed it to his dad without saying a word.

Steve looked at Shamus suspiciously; he sipped with caution . . . "Ice cold." He sipped again and let the liquid swirl over his tongue then swallowed. " . . . and sweet."

Shamus chuckled and fluttered his hands to urge his dad to drink heartily. Steve trusted and pulled freely, then handed the canteen back to Shamus. He stacked his hands over his chest and stomach. "This isn't ordinary water. It demands a response. . . I'm not sure what to give it."

Shamus drank deeply then shuddered involuntarily when he stopped. "This stuff just does goofy things to my senses . . . But I lived through it the first time . . . I think."

The two stood a few moments absorbing the water's elixir. Shamus broke the tranquil moment and said, "Let me show you where this stream goes."

Shamus took his dad to the top of the grotto to see the pond below surrounded by its rock formations and vegetation. Steve's face was questioning something.

"It's the water, Dad. It had the same effect on me. I was caught in another dimension."

"Shamus . . . I've been here before."

It was Shamus' turn to look befuddled.

"Awhile back, I had a dream. I was time traveling and talked with people from the past. They shared the stories of their lives; what they experienced and how they lived. I don't remember their stories, now . . . I should have wrote them down.

"I found a cabin near here. It didn't have a roof and there was old traps on the wall. . . And there was a sign on the wall that said *Shangri-la.*

"It seemed so *real*, Shamus. And now . . . I'm actually here . . . I woke up when a bear chased me. That thing scared the *be-jeazers* out of me."

Shamus listened in awed silence. *Then my time here really was a father and son outing,* he thought.

Shamus and Steve wandered through the cabin and explored the woods pointing out details; one of his vivid dream, the other of a shift in dimensions. They returned to the Jeep and headed to Transformation City; their bonds drawn closer by the shared adventure of Shangi-La; almost as if time had not passed at all.

As they drove away, Steve asked, "Did you happen to find any arrowheads?"

Endnotes

1   Pronounced Ke-feer-ah

CROSSROADS

MiSeon drove from Burnus to meet with Shamus and Steve at *Finnegan's Rose* the following afternoon. Their conversation at the table was filled with dialogue from MiSeon and Shamus about how they met and their dramatic journey. Steve, on the other hand, had just awakened from a future blackened by sickness. His dreams were now filled with uncontested options.

"I've made up my mind," Steve declared, "to head back home tomorrow. Now that I'm healed, I can redefine my future. And as bleak as it was, those who have been a part of that future have decisions to make. Everything will be different for them, too. If you can imagine, they will no longer be anticipating a funeral for their friend. Whatever plans they had, will have to be cancelled . . . In more ways than one, if you know what I mean."

It felt good to laugh freely.

"And there's a woman in my life. She's not my wife, and I'm not sure my new world will fit into her world. How do talking goats, miraculous healings and Shangri-La experiences compare to a life without them? It's too . . . revolutionary! It will cause a ruckus that rather concerns me. And I'm not sure if the two worlds can be reconciled. But, I have to find out if they can. I can't just fall off the edge of the planet and start over somewhere else. It would not be . . . fair or responsible."

"I understand that, Dad."

"And . . . quite honestly, son . . . oh how good it feels to say that word . . . I need to figure out how *you* fit into my new world . . . This is all so wonderful. And I wish your mother could have been here."

A worm hole of regret opened and Steve felt the sucking whirl pull his emotions. He caught himself, took a deep breath and continued with wet eyes.

"Quite frankly, Shamus, this would be a nice place to live. I will consider living here when all the *ifs* and *wherefores* are answered at home. I can see that you understand what I'm saying."

"Yes I do, Dad."

Steve looked at MiSeon while continuing to talk to Shamus. "Then perhaps when you decide to pop the question to MiSeon," he continued smiling, "I, or we, will return for the wedding if I have not returned by then.

"It warms this heart deeply, MiSeon, to see my son considering a life with a woman who is as beautiful on the inside as she is on the outside. I'm not sure it's quite proper for me to ask," Steve said with a chuckle, "But I would ask you to be my daughter-in-law without any hesitation."

"Dad," Shamus responded laughing, "I will ask her to be my wife without any hesitation when I know I will be everything she needs me to be. I know I won't be perfect, but there are a few important things that need fixing. I want the best for her sake."

"It is perhaps," MiSeon responded smiling, "not as far off as you might think. You're everything I've ever wanted in a man, Shamus. And your father being here has healed something in you; I can see it. I'd say more if I knew it would not embarrass you to say it in front of your father.

"I miss you so much when I go back to Burnus," she said taking his hand. "You make me feel complete. And that's what I want for us, with all my heart."

"You're love for each other is extraordinary," Steve interjected. "And my visit here has been more than extraordinary. My normal will never be the same." He chuckled wickedly. "And I am so looking forward to seeing the shock on my doctor's face."

Steve quieted and added, "I will miss you deeply until I return," he said with a shaky voice. "Until that happens, you and I will stay in touch and you can help me understand what happened to me while I was here. I have a lot to learn.

"And please tell The Hunter I said hello the next time you see him."

"You can tell him that anytime, Dad."

"How's that?"

"Remember the window."

Steve's eyebrows raised . . . then his face jerked and his eyebrows went up again . . . "Ho! That window." He chuckled until it turned to laughter. Then he laughed until he roared. The contagion of his joy filled *Finnegan's Rose* until everyone was infected with the ruction of it.

Town Hall

Jackson Kromberg and members of his family were in Transformation City for first-hand probes into existing and future proposals to capitalize growth around the area. The Krombergs had been creating wealth for generations, but it wasn't just a success story. It was a legacy, and Shamus didn't understand the protocols toward people with money. He was out of place and felt awkward. Jackson recognized the symptoms.

"Let me give you some family history. My great-grandfather was a lot like you. In short, he had a rough life. He worked hard, fought hard and drank hard until the Lord found him. And in the process of his restoration, the Lord taught him the difference between wealth and riches. He was given a vision for financing the Kingdom of God while living frugally. What he learned and made, he passed on to his descendants along with his faith. What I inherited wasn't just money, it was a calling; a calling I will pass on to my children and their children.

"In similar fashion, you're called to political influence. What you don't learn in your lifetime, your children will learn. They will build on the platform you build and each generation will excel beyond the previous one. Eventually, your family will own a legacy of being world changers and mountain movers. I see that in you Shamus. Trust God to make it happen."

"I was not expecting that," Shamus responded meekly. "I will take that to heart and remember it with appreciation . . . Thank you, Mister Kromberg."

"Please relax and call me Jackson, if you will. Now, what's on your agenda?"

"There's a town hall meeting this evening. I'd like for you to be there and share what your plans are for this area."

"I'll be happy to share what I can." Jackson responded. "But I can't tell all, you know."

"I understand. It's a little something like politics, isn't it."

"Precisely. The opposition is looking for what they can use to their advantage. You can trust they will be looking for those things."

The town hall meeting at the Community Center launched on a pleasantly warm and partially cloudy Monday evening as Shamus laid his notes on the podium. Frequent eye contact with attendees around the room hinted at the prevailing mood. Seeing their hungry expectation, he smiled and raised his hands to quiet the chatter. He was looking forward to casting his vision about the future.

"There was little in the form of a map to show us the way to where we are today. So how could we know that we had arrived at our destination without careful and intentional planning of our steps? We didn't have that luxury. Like Lewis and Clark discovered in the exploration for a northwest passage, we leaned into each new challenge and made progress. Yet when we climbed to an elevation where we could see better, we found the picture was bigger than we imagined. And like Lewis and Clark, we had to change to meet the heightened challenges of uncharted territory and courageously continue our mission.

"Papa God is giving us more opportunities than we can apprehend. God keeps moving in spite of us and leaves us choices to grasp them or leave them alone. And, at the risk of sounding ungrateful, I want to bring out that we would do well to find a pace to succeed in furthering these blessings rather than developing everything that's coming our way.

"So, how do we wisely steward the gifts we've been given?

"Unlike Lewis and Clark, we aren't pressured with the onset of a deadly winter. We can take the time to learn important lessons and wait for resource and wisdom to catch up with vision.

"That is why I called this meeting. We all fit together to form a greater family, a more dynamic design and a deeper purpose. And I want to take this evening to inspire and encourage your participation.

"In keeping with what our state representative, Larry Cunningham, once told me, "I can help your community if you will help my state." The fruit of his commitment brought a highway to us that expanded our potential. Jackson Kromberg has opened the treasure chest of Clydesdale Development to help us grow. Those of you from Burnus have co-labored with us to build roads, consult with our businesses and take home the fruit of our awakening. With those exchanges, community takes on expanded meaning. And for all of that effort, Transformation City is deeply, deeply grateful.

"God has worked miracle after miracle to bring healing and life to as many as would receive it. Our community is changed. Our influence has grown. The ripples of what and who we affect is now considered in the decisions we make; simple issues are more complex. And with the great minds of this community and their ideas, our progress will have value and wisdom.

"With that in mind, I call to the front a man who represents business wisdom and resource for the future of Transformation, Jackson Kromberg.

"Jackson, the floor is yours."

Jackson smiled, stood and walked to the front.

"In spite of my passion, I understand that only a few would appreciate the level of finance and investment that I represent.

With that said, I will keep what I have to say to a tolerable minimum."

The crowd chuckled with understanding. He didn't want to bore them with technical details.

"First thing I want to extend to you, is the gratitude of Clydesdale Development for your partnership with us to help turn the world upside down for the gospel with your expression of Jesus in the market place. Our core values are wrapped around building relationships of mutual benefit for that purpose. And our mission is to grow capital holdings that increase our resource potential for that end.

"In regards to that mission concerning this area, Clydesdale Development has purchased land west of here that will house the next generation. What that means for Transformation City is having the wiggle room in the years ahead to grow business and industry with new jobs and create housing for those who come here for those jobs. In twenty years, what is now fallow ground will be sustainable living space.

"Along with growth, we are committed to the cultural development of the community. We will donate acreage for a park, recreation center and amphitheater."

Applause was generous from the crowd.

"We will open a branch office here in the near future; furthering your interactivity with us for a variety of financial services.

"Our group has proven its integrity through support of the Wonder Valley re-entry program, which your involvement has made a success. In time, we will move that program here and fulfill the suburban plans we have there.

"Because of your faithfulness, we are motivated to work with you and God for the long term good of this community and this land. Wherever and whenever it may be needed, we will be available. And it is my sincere comprehension that commitment will endure across generations.

"Thank you, Mayor Breen and my good neighbors."

Jackson sat down at a table where he had been seated with his son and daughter-in-law. Leaning in to make a comment to his son, chatter from across the room grew louder and interrupted him.

Shamus raised his voice over the top of the increased noise. "If you have any questions or comments for Mister Kromberg, please feel free to . . ."

Meadow joyously broke in, "Shamus! Hatch is here. No, I'm sorry Hatch, I mean Vince. Vince is here. He just popped in."

All eyes looked to where Vince had uniquely appeared. The striking burgundy tee shirt he wore stood out with the slogan in white, "*God can do anything!*"

"Yay, Vince," Shamus exclaimed. "Just the man we want to see. Come up here and tell us what's happening with you."

When Shamus said "Come up here," Roee heard a penetrating voice echo the same words. He was yanked from his chair and careened with indiscernible velocity through breaking clouds. Unaware of distance and time, he simply arrived at the platform of a gazebo, situated in a fabulous grove of living plants, animals and the familiar sight of angels. Seated across from him, Jesus said welcome by the pleasure in his eyes.

"It's always exhilarating to have a chat with you Roee," Jesus said tenderly. "This is one of my favorite spots for a one on one with my kids."

"I've never been here before." Roee injected, looking about appreciatively.

"The valley is also a favorite. But you weren't home and I wanted to see you. That's why I've brought you here instead. I have important thoughts for you to understand about Burnus.

"Watchmen were assigned to the gates of the city. And they have done well with what I have given them. The time has come to enlarge the spiritual purpose of the city and new gates must be added. You will be a gatekeeper and watchman for those new gates.

The old gatekeepers were given new wine that flourished in their day and gathered many with its flavor. But society has marginalized the old wine and its influence is dying.

"Therefore, I have determined to create a new wineskin and pour new wine into it. Although the world will not connect the difference, I must also keep providing the old wine for those that can drink no other. But those that like the old wine will persecute the new wine because they won't understand it. As you know Roee, I love all my children even when my children can't see the bigger picture and fail to love each other.

"Your next assignment in Burnus will be difficult. The old leaders will oppose and resist you. But what I build through you, and those I have called to help you, will have greater capacity for a greater harvest for it will be built on a broader foundation.

"The way before you is nothing like the road behind you. The journey will take you away from the familiar. And your only directions will be my word and Holy Spirit. You cannot trust in anything else. We are infinitely creative, Roee. Trust that we will show you ways for reaching this generation.

"Adventure, adaptation, challenges and opportunities await you. Be strong and courageous; this is a defining moment for my people. The disturbance that brought you from village to valley started a revolution in languishing hearts that longed for transformation. Transformed people who love me whole-heartedly will pay any price for the Kingdom of God to advance. And those are the hearts that will bring reformation to Burnus."

"I am commissioning you to represent me as I was commissioned to represent my Father. You and I are one."

Roee closed his eyes, pondered the weight of Jesus words, then kneeled.

"Jesus, unveil your majestic excellence so that by it I will intensify your splendor and glorify you on earth by faithfully doing what you show me to do."

AUTHOR'S THOUGHTS

Our generous God freely gives us every good and perfect gift. These wonderful gifts come down to us from the Father of lights, the unchanging God who shines from the heavens with no hidden shadow or hint of darkness." (James 1:17, The Passion translation)

"Write about your experiences with the goats." It was a statement that could have been dismissed as an uninteresting idea. But it was Christmas morning of 2014, and I had asked Papa for a gift that year.

Have you ever been given a gift that was carefully chosen by someone who knows you well? And when you opened it, you saw the gift, but didn't realize the depth of consideration that went in the choosing of it? That is what happened for me that Christmas. As time passed, the gift revealed more thoughtful cleverness as I used it and unpacked its potential.

The essence of my request that Christmas was that I knew it would be thoughtfully chosen . . . by my heavenly Papa. His simple statement in response was the plain wrapping paper in which the gift would arrive; or should I say, *begin to arrive*. For when I sat down to write, a flood of imaginative invention was released that has continued unabated for more than four years.

Papa's opening statement provoked The Renascence Series trilogy; The Ruction, The Revolution and The Reformation. It's Conceptual Christian Fiction; a projected Christian experience with biblical potential.

My wife, Ann, championed the idea from the beginning and helped bring this work to life. Being the spouse of a writer is often a life of sacrifice. Few people are aware of the mind and world of a someone who spends hours in story realm and those occasions when ideas mysteriously show up at inconvenient times and have to be recorded or forgotten. It can be disruptive and disconnecting. She has encouraged without wavering, and I crown her a valued partner and sounding board. She is a woman of valor in that regard, as well as all others, and deserves my abundant gratitude. This work would not have happened without her insight and support.

Thanks to Dean Braxton (DeanBraxton.com) for his inspiration from the book "Deep Worship in Heaven!" My feeble attempts to describe encounters in heaven and heavenly experiences on earth drew from his experience of being there for one hour and forty-five minutes. That liberty is given with his permission. I encourage all Kingdom seekers to read his books and find him in the internet.

My deep gratefulness extends to Emily LaCroix for her insights and questions that provoked me to look deeper and find better; and in a few cases remove altogether. She is a gift and friend.

Thanks to Bruce Blizard for the savage feedback in the early rewrite. It's the substance of what makes writers better writers; it worked. Bruce writes Christian fiction with an edge for young adults. (BruceBlizard.com)

Any comments and questions can be sent to jimpowell@wanderingstream.org